PRAISE FOR

love, cajun style

★"Like a spicy Cajun stew, this mixes together lots of ingredients, and the result is delicious. . . . Les Becquets creates a wonderful world that not only captures the emotions and dreams of youth but also the longings and regrets of adults. . . . This is romantic, real, and lots of fun."   —*Booklist*, starred review

"Filled with playful vignettes of a fun-loving Cajun lifestyle, here's a novel dealing with sexuality that can appeal to both conservative and liberal readers. . . . Realistic, affecting and enjoyable throughout."
     —*Kirkus Reviews*

"This story is told with humor and warmth and is deliciously full of Cajun metaphors and mouth-watering cooking descriptions—and one particular scene with Tabasco that will provoke squirms and giggling."   —*SLJ*

"A sweet, homey novel."   —*VOYA*

"Les Becquets cooks up a pot of small-town southern life that comes together like a jambalaya—spiced with humor and goodwill, with tasty chunks of occasional conflict and misunderstanding that melt away into a harmonious happy ending."   —*BCCB*

love,
cajun style

love,
cajun style

DIANE LES BECQUETS

BLOOMSBURY

Published by Bloomsbury U.S.A. Children's Books
175 Fifth Avenue, New York, NY 10010
Distributed to the trade by Holtzbrinck Publishers

Grateful acknowledgment is made to Ahab Music Company, Inc.
for permission to reprint lyrics from "The Streak."
Words and music: Ray Stevens
Copyright © 1974 by Ahab Music Company, Inc.
Copyright renewed 2002

The Library of Congress has cataloged the hardcover edition as follows:
Les Becquets, Diane.
Love, Cajun Style / by Diane Les Becquets.—1st U.S. ed.
p.   cm.
Summary: Teenage Lucy learns about life and love with the help of her friends and
saucy Tante Pearl over the course of one hot Louisiana summer before her
senior year of high school.
ISBN-13: 978-1-58234-674-8 • ISBN-10: 1-58234-674-7 (hardcover)
[1. Aunts—Fiction. 2. Family life—Fiction. 3. Friendship—Fiction.
4. Louisiana—Fiction.] I. Title.
PZ7.L56245Lov 2005   [Fic]—dc22   2005011948

ISBN-13: 978-1-59990-030-8 • ISBN-10: 1-59990-030-0 (paperback)

Typeset by Westchester Book Composition
Printed in the U.S.A. by Quebecor World Fairfield
1 3 5 7 9 10 8 6 4 2

All papers used by Bloomsbury U.S.A. are natural, recyclable products made from
wood grown in well-managed forests. The manufacturing processes conform to the
environmental regulations of the country of origin.

For Dad,

and Taylor Littleton,

and, as ever,
for Nate, Seth, and Jake
with love

Table of Contents

Falling in Love

―――――

I was riding my yellow-and-blue Raleigh bicycle out to the beach to meet my friends, the sweet, salty air of early summer on my face, a warm breeze through my hair, the rhythm of my legs carrying a certain melody to my thoughts. Mary Jordan had called that morning to tell me she was falling in love. "Falling from what?" I'd said.

"Lucy, I'm serious."

I knew she was serious. I guess that was the part I feared the most.

I rode past the Cove Creek Subdivision, past the Piggly Wiggly. I thought about stopping at the Dairy Freeze to talk to a couple of kids I knew from school, but instead I waved and kept on riding. Before I knew it I was on the county highway that wound its way like a river through the outskirts of town and into the country.

Why did people say they were *falling* in love? Why didn't they step into love, or slide into it like a baseball player heading for home? Was it the thrill, like jumping off a high dive, or the fear of not knowing how you might land? It wasn't that long ago I was sure I'd fallen in love, but by the time I landed,

I knew I'd had it all wrong. What if Mary Jordan had it all wrong, too?

I passed a handful of vendors alongside the lonesome stretch, mostly Cajuns who sold baskets or crawfish or vegetables or voodoo souvenirs. By now they'd gotten used to me and always waved back. A couple more turns and I was on a backwash road, nothing more than a thin stretch of hard-packed sand that carved its way between sea oats and palmettos to the turnoff for Skinny Neck Beach. About fifty yards ahead of me was the parking area. Mary Jordan was sitting on top of one of the picnic tables at the far end, reading a book.

"Hey," she said.

I leaned my bike against the table and climbed up beside her. It was as hot as a bacon skillet that afternoon, but no one could tell by looking at Mary Jordan. She doesn't sweat. She has blue eyes the color of sapphire and loose brown curls cut just below her ears. Her skin looks like china, and her cheeks are naturally pink. Mama says Mary Jordan won't ever need to wear rouge. God has blessed her with it already.

"What are you reading?" I asked.

"Pablo Neruda."

"What's that?"

"Poetry." She proceeded to read about breasts and hearts and wings flying off somewhere as high as heaven.

"You're either thinking about God or Doug," I said.

Mary Jordan swatted me with the book. "It's a poem about love," she said. She stared off toward the levee. The gulf lay on the other side. From where we sat, we could hear its waves.

"How do you know you're falling in love?" I said.

"Because I've never felt like this before."

She sat like that a couple more minutes, then opened her book and continued reading. I could feel all sorts of things stirring around inside her, but I wasn't sure how to get to them. Maybe that's why she read so much, as if books were the only places where she felt most understood.

I didn't know names like Pablo Neruda, but I read a lot, too. Not at the library, and not at school. At home, or in the grocery store. I'd stand behind the rack of books that spins around. Sometimes I'd read novels by Julie Garwood, or Catherine Coulter, about exciting men who fall in love with beautiful women. Before leaving, I'd mark my place lightly with a pencil, then stick the copy I was reading behind all the others. And sometimes I'd read adventure magazines about climbing mountains, about people surviving avalanches, about tiny towns in faraway places.

"Where's Evie?" I asked.

Mary Jordan tucked a pine needle somewhere in the middle of her book and looked up at me from beneath the curls falling over her eyes. "She had to spend the night at her dad's. Said she'd meet us here."

Evie's dad had walked out almost five years before, when we were in sixth grade. He moved into a cabin a few miles west of town, where he managed a catfish farm and drank beer. That was when Evie's mom started dating every single man in Sweetbay. If she was going to be entertaining some man into the night, she'd send Evie out to her dad's. Evie said all those men were simply salve on a bad wound, only her mom hadn't figured out that the salve didn't work.

Mary Jordan and Evie and I had lived in Sweetbay our whole lives and stuck together like glue ever since third grade, when we started catechism together at St. Marc's Catholic Church. One Sunday after our class, we got the idea to put an egg in Father Ivan's chair right beside the lectern. No sooner had he said, "The Lord be with you," and the congregation responded, "And with thy spirit," than he sat down, getting the strangest look on his face. The catechism class was sitting together in the back row. Evie and Mary Jordan and I started giggling so hard that Evie let out a snort. She does that sometimes. With all the ruckus we were making, Father Ivan had a good idea who was responsible for the egg he'd just hatched. As soon as the service was over, he had us meet him in his study, but not a one of us would confess. "God knows," Father Ivan said, pointing a finger at us. "And His punishment is always just."

About a week later, after Mary Jordan said she was having trouble sleeping, Evie decided we'd write a letter to the priest in the next parish over, confessing our sins. The priest wrote us back telling us to say the rosary ten times and our sins would be forgiven. We did what he said, and sure enough, Mary Jordan started sleeping again.

I was thinking about Evie and her dad and the jumbled up life she had at home when I heard the loud *whoop* she was good at making. She'd just turned into the parking lot and was riding toward us on her Giant with fat tires.

"Damn! That's some ride out here." Her long red hair was soaking wet, and beads of perspiration stuck to her eyelashes. Evie's eyes are as dark as Cajun coffee. Gold freckles span across her face. She has freckles down her arms, too. She climbed off her bike and laid it in the sand.

Mary Jordan reached into her backpack and tossed a can of Off to Evie. "Mosquitoes are going to suck you dry with all that sweat on you."

"I lathered myself in Skin So Soft before I left," she said, tossing the can back to Mary Jordan. Evie smelled more like Coppertone suntan lotion to me. Evie always smells like Coppertone, even in the dead of winter. She says its aroma gives her a desirable disposition.

Evie kicked off her shoes. She grabbed hold of the tail of her damp T-shirt, pulled it over her shoulders, and pitched it onto the handlebars of her bike.

"Let's go for a swim," she said.

Mary Jordan and I exchanged glances, both of us grinning. We peeled off our shoes and tossed them next to Evie's, then pulled off our shirts and shorts and left them on the ground in a heap.

"Race ya!" Evie said. She took off for the levee, wearing nothing more than her black bra and red-white-and-blue panties.

Mary Jordan and I followed. The levee was steep and thick with sand. Trying to run our way over it was about as good a workout as anyone would care to have. The closer we got to the top, the heavier our breathing sounded and the slower our legs moved. Then Evie backfired, and the three of us doubled over laughing, grabbing our sides and gasping for air.

Evie made it to the top first and shouted, "King of the mountain!"—a five-foot-five statue with fists held high. The three of us stripped out of our bras and underwear and ran for the water, squealing like a bunch of five-year-olds.

The water was murky brown and the bottom squishy, sucking at our feet as we tried to leap over the small waves. After making quite a splash, we sailed on our backs, baring our chests to the heavens.

"I just hit a warm current," I said.

Evie laughed. "That was me."

"Evie!"

"I'm just kidding."

"How was it at your dad's?" I asked her.

"You know, it might not be so bad if I had a decent bed. He's got me sleeping on this cot. Every time I roll over, the springs sound like a gopher with its tail stuck under a bulldozer. Makes me wonder how many other people have done their share of rolling over on it, too."

Mary Jordan swooped a wave over Evie. "You're so weird." Evie just paddled herself farther away, kicking water into Mary Jordan's face.

Evie and Mary Jordan and I all lived in old houses. Once, we got to speculating about how many couples had had sex underneath our roofs. Of course Evie said they might as well call her home the Love Palace ever since her parents got divorced.

"I saw my parents do it once," Mary Jordan had confessed.

"No way!" I declared. Mary Jordan's parents were as old as Bunker Hill. Both she and her brother, Billy, had been a surprise to them. Of course, I wasn't quite sure I understood the surprise part. You'd think after Billy surprised them two years before, they'd have been a little more prepared.

"They were in the pantry," Mary Jordan had told us. "I was supposed to already be in bed, but I got hungry and couldn't sleep."

From then on, every time the three of us were at Mary Jordan's looking for something to eat, we'd get to laughing and not a one of us would have to explain why.

I was still floating on my back. Evie floated toward me, bumping my head.

"Hey," I said. She reached for one of my hands as we continued to drift away from the shore. Then Mary Jordan coasted toward us and grabbed hold of our other hands so that the three of us formed a sort of star. We kicked our legs just enough to keep us on the surface, our bodies riding the gentle currents.

"We ought to try out for one of those water ballet teams," Evie said.

"I always wanted to be a ballet dancer," Mary Jordan said.

"Since when did you want to be a ballet dancer?" Evie asked.

"I don't know. Since I was little, I guess. Ballet dancers have great bodies."

I closed my eyes, letting the sun bask down on my skin and the water carry us. "Remember the first time we started coming out here," I said.

"The summer before our freshman year," Evie said. "We finally talked our parents into letting us ride out to the beach by ourselves."

"Remember that day we were out here and we got to talking about sex, and how we said we were going to wait until we were married?" I asked.

"I remember," Mary Jordan said.

"You think that's changed any?" I asked.

"Why would that change?" Evie said. "You got some boyfriend on the side we don't know about?"

"I wish," I laughed.

"It's because of that poem I read, isn't it?" Mary Jordan said.

"What poem?" Evie wanted to know.

"She read some poem by Pablo somebody about breasts and love."

"Pablo Neruda," Mary Jordan corrected me.

"Yeah," I said.

"Speaking of breasts, can nipples sunburn?" Evie said.

Mary Jordan laughed. Evie let go of our hands and paddled herself away, then rolled over onto her stomach.

"Your buns can burn, too," Mary Jordan hollered.

She and I were still holding hands and floating side by side.

"I hope we always come out to the beach like this," I said.

"We will," Mary Jordan said. "Hey, Lucy?"

"Yeah?"

"I know what you were saying, about us still waiting till we're married. But things change."

"I don't want things to change," I said.

"I'm not saying I'm going to have sex before I'm married, but I'm not fourteen anymore, either."

"I know," I said.

Evie had been the first one to declare her celibacy, and I knew her decision had something to do with her mom, something to do with the hurt Evie kept all wound up inside like a tight skein of yarn. I kept wishing one day that skein would unwind itself. But knowing Evie, I was fairly certain it never would. And knowing her decision had something to do with what she was feeling, and not knowing how to wiggle myself into that tight skein and make her pain go away, I joined in. Maybe Mary Jordan had felt the same thing as me, because she joined in, too. Now, several years later, I wondered how strong our declarations would be if reality put them to the test.

"Sharks like barbeque," Evie shouted. She was now a good fifty yards away. "Breast meat especially."

Mary Jordan and I laughed.

"I love her," Mary Jordan said.

"Me, too," I said.

We flipped over and swam toward Evie. As we approached the shore, we remained in the water, making sure no one was around. The closest person we saw was a man about a half mile away fishing.

"Coast is clear," Evie said.

The three of us stood and ran for the levee, crossing our arms over our naked selves.

"I don't believe it!" Evie shrieked once we were at the top. "They were right here!"

Sure enough, Evie's Old Glorys and Mary Jordan's Hanes Her Ways and my Kmart specials were nowhere to be found.

The Streak

We hurried down the levee to where we'd left the rest of our clothes. Mary Jordan just stood there with her mouth hanging open. I had one hand spread out to cover my pelvis, and my other arm crossed over my chest, walking around in a panic, searching.

"Maybe the wind blew them in the grass," Mary Jordan said.

"Yeah, right. The wind just happens to come along and lift three pairs of heavy shoes into oblivion." Evie was as steamed as a hot iron.

The three of us, butt naked, stormed around in circles.

Then we heard a car. Evie quickly ducked behind the picnic table. Mary Jordan and I crouched beside her.

A gray Eclipse whipped into the parking lot, stirring up dust and sand, and stopping no more than ten feet in front of us.

"Hope you don't catch a cold!" It was Doug Hebert with a carload of his friends from the baseball team.

Like us, Doug was going to be a senior in the fall. He and Mary Jordan had been going out ever since he took her to the Valentine's dance last winter. Doug was popular and good-looking, with thick brown hair and hazel eyes. It wasn't because he was popular or good-looking that Mary Jordan liked him, though I'm sure that didn't hurt matters any. She liked him because he was smart. Doug wouldn't stay in Sweetbay. He'd get a scholarship to some fancy college far away. My fear was that Mary Jordan would follow right behind him and we'd never see her again.

Evie sprang up, charging after the car. Doug sped away, kicking dust into her face, all the guys laughing their heads off, a couple of them hanging out the windows, watching her and *whoop*ing it up something fierce. I knew Evie would never live it down, her chasing after that car like a banshee on the run, her breasts bobbing up and down.

Mary Jordan and I were still crouched behind the picnic table. "Give it up!" Mary Jordan yelled to Evie.

We could hear those guys still laughing as the car tore off down the road, its tires screeching.

When Evie turned around, streaks of dirt ran down her face from the dust on her wet body, and her hair stuck out in one frizzy mess. "I thought you and Doug were going out!" she yelled.

"We *were*," Mary Jordan told her.

"Are we missing some information here?" Evie planted her hands on her white hips, her red pubic hair glistening like copper.

I started to laugh.

"What's so funny?" Evie hadn't moved.

"*You* are," Mary Jordan said.

Evie tried not to laugh. She couldn't help herself.

"Now what do we do?" she said.

"Never rode a bike naked before," Mary Jordan said.

I felt my face wince. "That's got to hurt."

"I'm not riding clear through town naked as a jaybird. I have my limits," Evie said.

"It's not all that far to my aunt's place. Let's ride out there and get her to drive us back." Tante Pearl lived a couple miles past the beach in the opposite direction of town.

Mary Jordan and Evie looked at each other, then back at me.

"I'm not spending the night out here," Evie said.

We picked up our bikes and swung our legs over the seats.

"You've got to be kidding!" Evie said.

We eased ourselves onto the road, the three of us riding side by side.

"I want to know why it is Doug swiped our clothes," Evie flat-out stated.

"I guess he was mad or something," Mary Jordan said.

"I was looking for something I didn't already know," Evie said.

I looked at Mary Jordan, who was coasting in the middle. Seemed to me there was a big contrast going on between all that poetry she'd been reading and Doug and his friends laughing their heads off at Evie.

"All right," Mary Jordan said. "Last week Doug had to get a new driver's license. We were at the Dairy Freeze. When he took out his wallet to pay, I grabbed it from him to check out his picture." Mary Jordan paused, taking so long I wondered if she was ever going to finish her story.

"And?" Evie said.

"And when I opened up his wallet, there was a condom inside."

"What did you do?" I asked.

"I threw his wallet at him and stormed off down the road."

"What did he do?" Evie wanted to know.

"He got in his car and followed after me, yelling through his rolled-down window for me to get in."

"Did you?" Evie asked.

"No. I walked the rest of the way home."

"Did he follow you the rest of the way home?" I asked.

"No. He gave up after about four blocks."

"He should have followed you the rest of the way home," Evie said.

We kept riding our bikes at a steady pace, my body so slick with sweat I was sure I was going to slip right off my seat.

"He called," Mary Jordan told us.

"Did you talk to him?" I asked.

"No. Mama answered the phone. I told her to tell him I was in the shower."

"How many times did he call?" Evie asked.

"I don't know. A couple, I guess."

"He should have called more than a couple," Evie said.

I agreed with Evie, and I might have said so if she hadn't yelled, "Car!" just about the same time I heard it, too.

Evie pedaled in front of us and cut over to the shoulder. We followed behind her, me hoping to the heavens I didn't know a living soul in the approaching vehicle. As the white Lincoln slowly passed us, I looked up, not recognizing the car or its two elderly passengers who were shaking their heads.

"To liberation!" Evie yelled in the car's wake. She held her legs straight out to the sides and let out a loud *whoop*. I brought my bike up to a good coasting speed, then lifted my feet to the edge of the seat and slowly stood, mooning the world.

"Go, Lucy!" Evie yelled.

A blue Subaru turned around the bend, heading toward us. As the car sped past, Mary Jordan let go of her handlebars and held her arms out to the sides, flaunting her bare chest. The car honked its horn several times before disappearing behind us. We squealed and laughed, Evie and I both shocked at Mary Jordan's bravado.

As we rode on, I recalled one of Mama's forty-five records Evie and Mary Jordan and I used to play over and over until we had all the words memorized. Riding side by side with my two best friends, I held one fist up to my mouth as if it were a microphone. *"Hello, everybody, this is your action news reporter with all the news that is news across the nation."* I made my voice as low as I could, mimicking Ray Stevens's. *"On the scene at the supermarket there seems to have been some disturbance here."*

Evie and Mary Jordan were laughing so hard they both had tears streaming down their faces.

"Pardon me, sir, did you see what happened?" I held my fist out in front of Evie.

"Yeah, I did. . . ." She leaned into the imaginary microphone. *"I was standing over there by the tomatoes and here he come, running through the pole beans, through the fruits and vegetables, naked as a*

jaybird. And I hollered at Ethel. . . . I said, 'Don't look, Ethel.' It was too late. She'd already been incensed."

Evie pedaled faster. Mary Jordan and I kept up, racing beside her, the three of us singing out as loud as we could, *"He ain't rude, boogie-dy, boogie-dy. He ain't lewd, boogie-dy, boogie-dy. He's just in the mood to run in the nude."*

Snooze Button

Tante Pearl is Daddy's older sister. She lives in a cypress-sided bungalow along Pigeon Bayou, though I don't know why it is they call it that. I've never seen a pigeon in those parts. As Mary Jordan and Evie and I climbed off our bikes, Tante Pearl's dog, Moses, ran to greet us, his bushy tail bounding back and forth. Moses and Tante Pearl have lived together for almost fifteen years, and as far as I know, he's the only male she's ever shared her living quarters with. She says he's a collie. He looks more like a mix between a German shepherd and a bulldog to me.

Tante Pearl's car wasn't in the driveway.

"Now what do we do?" Evie said.

"Find something to put on," I said, knowing Tante Pearl always left her house open.

"If I fit into your aunt's clothes, I'll kill myself," Evie said.

My aunt was probably the largest woman I'd ever known.

We laid our bikes in the grass alongside the house and ran inside. Mary Jordan and Evie waited in the kitchen while I padded my way back to the laundry room. On the shelf above the washer and dryer was a stack of beach towels. I reached up and took three down. Just as I turned to leave, I noticed Tante Pearl's fishing pole leaning in the corner next to the back door. Next to her fishing pole was another fishing pole, their lines tangled up together. The only person I'd ever known my Tante Pearl to fish with was me. My fishing pole was at home in the garage, somewhere behind the lawn mower and the Weed Eater and some tools for Daddy's motorcycle. At least that's where I thought it was.

I couldn't remember the first time my Tante Pearl took me fishing. It just seemed like something we'd always done together. But then I realized, if someone were to ask me when was the *last* time my Tante Pearl and I went fishing, I couldn't recall that, either.

I don't know that Mama has ever been fishing. And if my daddy ever went, it was before I was born. They both smell real nice and their clothes are always clean. Tante Pearl isn't like Mama or Daddy. Sometimes she smells like the ocean, like saltwater and fish and sweat. And sometimes she smells like the earth, like pole beans and cabbage and muddy dirt. She has long, shiny brown hair she braids down her back, and wears men's army fatigues and blouses with no sleeves.

When I was little and Mama and Daddy would go out, Tante Pearl would take me to her house to spend the night. She'd pack up sandwiches for dinner in a five-gallon pail and drive us to the beach with our fishing poles. We'd watch the sunset and tell each other stories. When we'd get back to her house she'd pay me a quarter to brush out her hair, which I was more than willing to do so that I could stay up.

I didn't brush out Tante Pearl's hair anymore. I didn't fish anymore with her, either. And seeing those poles up next to the door made me wish I did. It hadn't dawned on me before that my Tante Pearl would go fishing without me.

When I brought the towels into the kitchen, Mary Jordan and Evie were standing at the counter eating from a bag of wedding cookies, their fingers and mouths covered in powdered sugar. The sight of my two best friends standing in my aunt's kitchen butt naked got me to laughing so hard, tears stung my face.

"What'd you do? Fly to Mexico and back?" Evie said.

I tossed them the towels, still laughing. We wrapped the terry cloth snugly around ourselves. Then I took tumblers down from the kitchen cabinet and filled them with iced tea from a pitcher in the fridge.

We settled in around the table and drank our tea. Evie gulped hers down in a hurry and started chewing on the ice. I could tell she was thinking. "Who do you think he was planning to use that condom with?" she asked, getting right to the point.

Mary Jordan shifted slightly in her chair, unsticking the backs of her legs from the green vinyl. "I think that's what's bothering me so much. If I knew exactly why I was mad, I'd be better at acting mad. It's like there's different degrees to being mad, and I'm not sure which degree I'm at."

Evie helped out, holding up a finger in the air. "One, he's already having sex with someone or else he's *planning* on having sex with someone other than you. Or two," she said, extending a second finger, "he's hoping to have sex with you, and he wants to be prepared."

Mary Jordan nodded her head real slowly. "Right," she said.

"Which do you think it is?" I asked.

"I keep thinking if he was having sex with someone else, I would know. All someone has to do is yawn funny in this town, and everybody hears about it."

"There's one more scenario," I offered. "Maybe he just wanted to have it in there for the other guys to see."

"Maybe," Mary Jordan said.

"I had a dream a couple of nights ago," she went on to tell us. "Usually I don't remember my dreams. But this one was different. Like I wasn't really sure whether I was dreaming it or it was actually happening." Mary Jordan tucked her hands underneath her legs. She wasn't looking at me or Evie. She was just staring off at nothing. "I was dreaming that I was sleeping," she told us. "And I just wanted to keep sleeping, it felt so good. But then the alarm clock started buzzing, not really buzzing, more like cawing, like a bunch of crows. And I knew I could either turn it off and get up for school, or hit the snooze button."

"Which did you do?" I asked.

"I woke up before I could find out," Mary Jordan said.

"To an alarm?" Evie asked.

"No. I just woke up."

Mary Jordan shrugged her shoulders and looked down at the table. "What would you have done?" she said.

"I would have hit the snooze button," Evie said. "I always hit the snooze button."

I knew Mary Jordan never hit the snooze button on her alarm. Her clock radio was plugged in on top of her dresser on the other side of her room so that she had to get up to turn it off.

"What do you think the dream's telling you?" I asked.

"Maybe that condom was like the alarm, something to get my attention, like a warning, and I've got to decide what I'm going to do."

"Don't turn the alarm off, then," Evie said.

"Evie's right," I said. "If you hit the snooze button and ignore the alarm, you could end up in a situation you might later regret." I thought of my own situation the summer before and knew how my body had played with my mind. "Remember Tommy?" I said.

"I remember." Mary Jordan laughed. "But sometimes it feels so good just to be held. To feel like someone really loves you."

"We love you," Evie said defensively.

"Do you think Doug really loves you?" I asked.

"I think he does," Mary Jordan said. "He tells me he does. A lot."

I scooted sideways in my chair so that I was facing Mary Jordan. "Does he tell you when he's kissing you and you all are making out? Or does he tell you sometimes when he's just watching you study, the way you turn a pencil over in your fingers the way you do, or the way you tuck your hair behind your ears and swoop those big eyes of yours up at the world?"

Mary Jordan looked at me curiously, but didn't say anything. Evie didn't say anything, either.

I got to thinking about Tommy. He'd told me he loved me, too, and for a while I was certain I loved him back. Tommy wasn't athletic like Doug. He wasn't as smart as Doug, either, though I thought he was smart enough. I liked Tommy because of his voice. Tommy sang with the chorus in a Christmas program one evening at school during our sophomore year. After the chorus performed a couple of songs together, Tommy stepped in front of the microphone, his black hair swooping over his dark eyes, and crooned about chestnuts roasting on an open fire. Jack Frost wasn't nipping at my nose, but something like love was nipping at my heart. I decided right then and there I was going to make him fall in love with me. So, on Christmas Eve, Evie and I snuck into his car, a ten-year-old Honda Civic, which was parked in the driveway in front of his family's garage. It wasn't locked. We crept up to it from the hedges in front of the house and left a small package on the driver's seat. The package was a chocolate Kiss wrapped in a small box. On the little strip of paper coming out of the chocolate Kiss, Evie had written my name and telephone number. Lo and behold, a couple of days later he called. He wasn't sure who I was. After I told him my last name, he looked up my picture in the yearbook and decided we could meet at the Dairy Freeze.

We ended up going together for almost three months. I liked the way he looked. I loved the way he sang. And kissing him felt better than anything I'd ever known. From my limited experience and understanding, I thought I had all the ingredients as far as love was concerned. Then Tommy's dad got a job in Houston with an oil refinery. I got caught up in the whole emotion of him moving away, and thought my heart would shatter into a thousand pieces.

Tommy and I went driving around the night before he left.

He was playing a Nirvana CD that he liked real well, and singing along with it. After a while he pulled off to the side of the road and the two of us hiked down the wooded hill to a sandy spot along Rummy River. Mama says nights in Sweetbay are as sultry as John Coltrane on saxophone. It's easy for bodies to stick together. Mama's right, because that night I was with Tommy Pierre, I'm sure our bodies were stuck together a lot closer than my mama would have liked. The moon was close to being full, and we were kissing each other good. Then he said it, those three words I'd been waiting for. Just as I was fixing to say, "I love you, too," we heard a bunch of car doors slamming at the top of the hill. Before we knew what was happening, the entire Trudeau High baseball team came storming toward us. As soon as they saw us, one of them kindly asked us if we'd leave, saying something about them initiating the freshmen players. Tommy wanted to find out what the freshmen were going to have to do, so we made up the hill like we were leaving, but then we snuck back down and hid behind a big cypress. All four of those rookies took every stitch of clothing off. The only naked boys I'd ever seen before were the ones in the magazines Evie kept under her bed. Seeing them in the flesh was a whole lot different. They're kind of like breasts; not a one of them looks the same.

A couple of the older players on the team pulled out a stack of inner tubes they'd stashed behind some trees. Sure enough, each one of the freshmen had to float their bare bottoms down that river. Rummy River isn't like one of the bayous. Its current will carry you a good five miles through town before slowing down enough for you to paddle your way to the shore.

"I just hope they don't hit any rocks," Tommy said.

"Or meet up with any gators," I added.

Most of the players I didn't know very well, but two of them were in my geometry class. I knew I'd never be able to look at them the same again. I was right. Funny how that works. No matter how hard I tried, I couldn't meet their eyes, and yet it wasn't their eyes that were giving me the problem.

Tommy said he would call, but he never did, which made me think he never really loved me, either. Mama says boys tell you they love you sometimes, because their bodies get confused. Maybe my body had gotten confused, too. My heart didn't break into a thousand pieces after he left. Instead, I realized all the things he didn't do. He didn't want to hear my stories. He didn't ask me questions. He didn't smile when I was talking to him. He didn't hug me out of the blue just to make me feel good. His hugs were always a preamble to something else. And after he was gone, I wondered if he ever knew me at all.

All this reverie shifted my thoughts right back to Mary Jordan. I hoped Doug loved her. I hoped he loved her with all his heart. I also hoped with all my heart he could see the things about her that she overlooked in herself. Everyone knew Mary Jordan was smart. But she was more than just smart. She had something gentle inside her. Maybe it was the way she could catch a lightning bug, hold it up to her ear as if she could hear it talk, then ever so slowly open up her fingers and let it fly away. Evie and I would never let ours fly away. We'd trap them inside jars that we'd set on our nightstands. No matter how many holes we'd poke in the lids with a ballpoint pen, the bugs would always be dead by morning. Or maybe it was the way Mary Jordan had cried when Evie's dad walked out. Evie never cried. In some ways, I think Mary Jordan cried all the tears Evie never could.

I finished my tea, my head still deep in thought, when Mary Jordan said, "So what do we do about our clothes?"

"We have to get Doug back," Evie said.

"How?" Mary Jordan asked.

Evie said, "I'm not sure."

As we sat thinking about what we could do, Tante Pearl pulled up. Her car door slammed, and within seconds she walked into the house, carrying two grocery bags.

"Hi, Tante Pearl," I said.

She set the bags of groceries on the counter and turned to us with an inquisitive look on her face. "Why is it you girls are wearing my linen closet?"

"'Cause Doug Hebert swiped our clothes," Evie told her.

"We were swimming," I explained.

"We didn't have our swimsuits," Mary Jordan added.

Tante Pearl said, "So I gathered."

She began unpacking the bags of groceries, setting sausage and spinach and beans on the counter. "What are you going to do about it?" she asked us.

"That's what we're trying to figure out," I told her.

Tante Pearl reached into her grocery sack and took out a bag of flour and a bag of suger and a bottle of Tabasco sauce.

Evie got to looking at that Tabasco sauce, and her eyes started grinning.

I said, "What?"

"Trudeau Tigers are playing the Leeville Lakers Friday night. Home game." Evie had one of those smirks on her face she gets when she's thought up something good.

"So?" Mary Jordan said.

"Could be a hot night in Sweetbay," Evie went on. "Could be a mighty hot night."

"What are you saying?" Mary Jordan wanted to know.

"Players bring their uniforms to the locker room."

"Go on," Mary Jordan said.

"Coach has them run a couple of laps on the field to warm up before they dress out," Evie explained.

"Mm-hmm." Tante Pearl was now leaning her backside against the counter, just as curious as the rest of us.

"So what if we get ourselves in that locker room while they're running their laps. Don't you know Doug plays catcher, and you know a catcher always wears himself one of those plastic thingamajigs over his southern parts."

Tante Pearl had her arms folded over her bosom and got to laughing, kind of slow and easy at first, but then her whole body was shaking. She took that bottle of Tabasco sauce and planted it on the table in front of Evie.

Evie and I got to laughing, too. Mary Jordan didn't get it.

"You've been thinking how Doug might want you to light his fire," Evie told her. "Well, now's your chance."

It didn't take but one hair-split second for all four of us to laugh our ribs crooked. Then Evie snorted, and we got to laughing even harder.

The game was five nights away.

"What time does it start?" Tante Pearl wanted to know.

"Seven," Evie said.

"This is one game I don't want to miss," she said.

Then the four of us got to laughing some more.

Cayenne Peppers

Lily Dawn. That's my mom. She always thought her name sounded like a brand of laundry detergent, until Daddy walked into her life. She and Daddy met at a crawfish fest over in Beaufort her senior year in high school. The next week he drove to Sweetbay to take her out, showing up at her door with a bouquet of lilies and yellow roses. She says her name has suited her just fine ever since.

Mama is beautiful, with shoulder-length black hair as straight and shiny as fine silk. She parts it on the side and tucks it behind her ears, making her look both young and smart. Since I'm the only child she or Daddy ever had, she managed to keep her small waist, and over the years added just a pound or two to her hips. I get my long legs from Mama, and my long neck, only I'm a lot taller than she is. By the time I hit eighth grade, the kids at school couldn't decide whether to call me a beanstalk or the Jolly Green Giant.

Depending upon her mood, Mama can sing like Linda Ronstadt or Patsy Cline. She still has her record player from when she was a young. Still has her forty-fives and albums, too. I've listened to Linda Ronstadt and Patsy Cline, and others like Crystal Gayle and Barbara Mandrell, since I was born. When I was a baby, Mama set her record player up next to my crib, thinking all those ladies' talents might make me musically inclined. They didn't.

Mama is the music teacher over at the elementary school. In the afternoons and throughout the summer, she teaches piano lessons out of our house. When I walked into the living room after Tante Pearl dropped me off, Mama was sitting at the piano playing a duet of "Alloutté" with one of her students, Amy Dupris.

Still dressed in a towel, I snuck past them and headed upstairs to take a shower. But when I stepped out of the bathroom, my long black hair combed back from my face, and my body wrapped in my pink terry-cloth robe, it wasn't Amy whom I heard playing the piano anymore. I wasn't sure it was Mama, either. I walked quietly down the staircase and across the entry hall to the living room. Mama wasn't sitting at the piano. She was standing with her shoulders pressed against the wall, her eyes closed, while her hips swayed from side to side. Sitting on the piano bench with his back to me was a boy who looked about my age, with a head full of thick blond curls.

He just kept on playing, and Mama just kept on standing there with her eyes closed and her hips swaying like the tire swing behind our house.

Mama says there are people who play music and people who *make* music, just like love, and from what I could tell, this boy was making some mighty fine sounds. I turned and climbed the stairs, the boy's music following me like a hot flame running down my spine. Mama had never had anyone that good before. Most of her pupils were students of hers from school who were still trying to play "Jingle Bells," even though it was summer, or else women from the church who hadn't yet mastered "Salve Regina."

I lay on my bed and listened. After he finished, Mama and he started talking, but I couldn't make out what they were saying. A couple of minutes later, I heard their footsteps in the entrance hall. I scrambled off the bed and hurried over to the window in the dormer. Below me, the door opened and shut. The boy walked down our brick path between Mama's turquoise irises. Mama is the only person in the entire state of Louisiana to grow turquoise irises. *Southern Living* magazine said so. They did a full-page article on Mama's flowers in their July issue two years back.

On account of the giant oak tree in front of my window, I couldn't see his face. Just the top of his thick hair. From my vantage point, he didn't look very tall, but I decided that was just because of my being up so high.

I dressed in a pair of cutoff shorts and a T-shirt, tied my wet hair up in a knot, and joined Mama downstairs in the kitchen. I wanted to ask her about her new student, but I wasn't sure I should. Knowing Mama, she'd take it upon herself to set me up with him. She used to tell me not to worry when the boys didn't call. She said I was a late bloomer. I didn't think I was such a late bloomer. I just thought I'd bloomed way too tall, like a giant sunflower. Last time Mama planted sunflowers in her garden, come fall she'd had to cut down their tall stalks with a handsaw. But the older I got, the more convinced I was that Mama thought she was Saint Valentine reincarnated.

Not long after Tommy moved, Mama tried to set me up with Ms. Pitre's grandson, who had come down to visit from Birmingham, Alabama. His name was Justin. Mama had the notion in her head that he would bring some culture to my life, seeing how he was from a big city. So one day, she took it upon herself to write Justin a letter:

Dear Justin,

There is a girl living in Sweetbay named Lucy Beauregard. She has long, flowing black hair and walks with the grace of a gazelle. You are to seek her out. Her telephone number is 933-3195.

Sincerely,

God

Mama believed in divine intervention. But she said sometimes God needed a little help. I guess the fear of the Lord hadn't come to Justin yet, because not only did he never call, his grandmother showed the letter to everyone she knew, which in a small town like ours was no different than hiring the Goodyear Blimp.

No, I was fairly certain I shouldn't bring up the topic of Mama's new student. I'd let Mama introduce the topic herself. She was standing at the counter frying crabcakes Lisette and singing along to Billie Holiday on the stereo. Mama liked to cook. She said cooking was like life. With the right ingredients, it could be quite an affair. She said eating was like life, too. You could wash it down in a hurry, or you could savor every bite.

"How was the beach?" Mama asked when she saw me.

"Okay," I said. I wasn't about to tell her about Evie and Mary Jordan's and my naked ride to Tante Pearl's. She'd have me in church the very next day confessing indecent exposure.

I started taking down dishes from the cupboards to set the table.

"A new family moved to town," Mama told me. "Mm-hmm. He's an artist," she went on to say.

"Who?"

"Moved here from Detroit."

I closed the cupboard and turned around, my back against the counter. "Who moved here from Detroit?"

"He's a widower. His name's Victor Savoi. Moved down here with his son. Says he's opening up an art gallery in town. Going to offer lessons, too."

Mama turned the patties over in the skillet with one hand as she layered paper towels onto a plate with the other. "I told him I taught school."

Tante Pearl once said that listening to Mama tell a story was like milking a cow with a bad teat. By the time she finished, you weren't sure whether to cry or get drunk.

I leaned over the stove and turned off the burner. Then I grabbed Mama by the wrist and pulled her over to one of the upholstered chairs in the corner of the room. I sat in the one caddy-cornered to her. Grandma Sissy called them our oven chairs. Said every woman needed a comfortable chair in her kitchen to take the weight off her feet once her dish was in the oven. As long as I could remember, Mama had had two oven chairs in the kitchen on account of there being two women in the house. I didn't like to cook. But Mama said that didn't matter. She didn't like to be alone, so the two chairs worked out just fine.

"Dewey came by this afternoon," she went on to say. She lifted her eyes to the ceiling as if she was going to recite a prayer. "Lucy," she said, letting out a sigh long and deep. "The Lord smiled upon me today." She held her palms flat across her chest as if she were about to swoon. Mama was always acting dramatic to emphasize whatever point she was wanting to make. The Lord smiled upon her a lot, too. At least she seemed to think he did.

About that time, Daddy walked through the back door, having just gotten home from work. "Lily," he said the minute he stepped into the kitchen, "have you seen my golf shoes? I left them right by the door."

Daddy wears Levis and white starched shirts. He has black, wavy hair he styles straight back from his face, and blue eyes, and drives a BMW motorcycle the five blocks to and from work.

"Yes, you left them by the door," Mama told him. "Where I stepped on them and almost broke my neck."

"So where are they?" Daddy wanted to know.

Mama hesitated before speaking. "Well, I couldn't decide whether to put them in the trash can or upstairs in your closet. But in the end, God gave me a benevolent heart."

"I'll be sure to thank Him," Daddy said. He walked through the kitchen, noticing me for the first time.

"How was the beach?" he asked.

"Okay," I said.

Then he continued on his way to the stairs.

Two things my daddy seemed to care for more than anything in the world were his golf clubs and his motorcycle, and I suppose that afternoon, his golf shoes, as well. When he wasn't working down at his flower and gift shop, he was soaking up the sun on the greens of Sweetbay's public golf course, or else taking his motorcycle for a spin along Louisiana's country roads.

He hadn't always been that way. There seemed to be a time not too far back in my memory when Mama played just as big a part in his life as his other two interests. They'd watch TV together or go for walks. Sometimes he'd even help her in the kitchen. I would never forget the night when I'd come upon the two of them on the porch. I wasn't more than ten years old. Evie and I'd been sleeping over at Mary Jordan's. After Mary Jordan threw up half the pecan brittle we'd eaten, Evie and I decided to go back to our own houses. No sooner had I turned the corner to our yard than I'd seen Mama and Daddy lying together in the chaise lounge, the light of the full moon falling over their naked bodies like gossamer. I ducked behind the hedges and crept around to the front of the house, my heart flip-flopping in my chest and my skin as hot as a waffle iron.

"What about supper?" Mama hollered at him as soon as he came back through the kitchen with his golf shoes in his hands.

"I'll warm up a plate when I get home," he said, his last word leaving with him as he shut the door.

Daddy was always warming up his supper plate. I thought by now, Mama would have gotten used to it.

"So," I said, wanting to bring her back to her earlier story. "Who's Dewey?"

"Didn't I tell you?"

I shook my head.

"Oh," she said. "Well, I was in the grocery store, and this man I'd never seen before was standing in the produce aisle for the longest time. I wasn't sure if he was confused or was just trying to cool himself off. You know, sometimes people will do that when it's hot outside. Stand in the produce section or the freezer aisle to refresh themselves on a summer day."

I sat back in the chair, dangling my legs over one of the arms, then nudged Mama in the side with my foot. "Back to the story, Mama."

"Well, since I wasn't sure whether he was confused or just trying to refresh himself, I decided the Christian thing to do would be to see if he needed any help. So, I said, 'Excuse me, sir, are you just hot, or do you need some assistance?'"

"What did he say?"

"He said he was trying to make some Creole vegetable soup and couldn't seem to find the cayenne peppers. I told him any kind of pepper other than a bell pepper was in the Heat Wave section a couple of aisles over. He said he was new to town and would I be so kind as to show him where that might be."

"And being the Christian woman that you are...," I prompted her.

"Well, of course. So I led him to the cayenne peppers, and as we got to talking, he told me he had just moved to town from Detroit with his son, Dewey. While he was trying to decide which pepper to buy, I asked him if he liked to cook, and he said, 'I guess I'm going to have to now that my wife has passed on.'"

"That's terrible," I said.

"Mm-hmm, I thought so, too. He went on to tell me about his son playing music. I told him I taught piano lessons. He told me about the new gallery he was opening in town. He said he was going to be offering art classes. Well, you know how I've always been interested in art."

"Since when?"

Mama swatted her hand in the air. "Well, I have, I just might have forgotten to mention it. Mr. Savoi and I got to talking, and I started thinking that maybe I could teach him how to make a few dishes, seeing as how food's always been a passion of mine. You know they all go together. Kind of like the four food groups. A meal just isn't complete if you leave one of them out."

"What all goes together?" I asked.

"Well, you know, the four big ones: music, art, food, and sex. They're all part of the same pie, and a woman should make sure each piece is the same size. That is, a *grown* woman, of course," she said, giving me one of her direct looks. "Someone who is married."

I got the point.

"Well, I got to thinking," Mama continued; "my pie's kind of lopsided. I have about as much art in my life as Father Ivan has sex."

I tried hard to ignore her last comment. "What about the son?" I reminded her.

"Dewey?"

"Mm-hmm."

Mama got that same dreamy look I'd seen on her face when I came home from the beach. "He came here wanting lessons. No sooner did I hear him play than I knew I was in the hands of a genuine prodigy. Oh, Lucy, the hands on that boy, and the passion." She clutched her fist over her bosom. "That boy doesn't need help from the likes of me. He played Brahms and Beethoven and Bach. Then he moved into opera as if it was his native tongue. *The Marriage of Figaro, Tristan and Isolde, Madame Butterfly.* I've never had to turn a student down before, but that's just what I did. I told him he should start playing for folks around town, share his gift with the world. Yes, Lucy, the good Lord smiled on me indeed."

My mama had just delivered herself one of her finest tributes. I'd never seen her so taken with a person my age. His playing had absolutely swooned her into a rapturous silence. And although I had never shared as passionate an appreciation for music as my mama, he'd caught my attention, as well, not to mention, this boy wasn't from Sweetbay. He was from somewhere far away.

The Big, Bad Wolf

For the past twenty years, Daddy's owned Straight from the Heart, a floral and gift shop smack dab in the center of town on Main Street. A couple of years ago, he brought in Ethel Lee Mabree as his partner, and nothing's been the same since. Ethel Lee moved to Sweetbay from New Orleans, looking for a simpler way of life. She's a little woman with big breasts, high heels, and short hair the color of cranberries. First thing she did when she joined Daddy was give the place a facelift. She painted the walls fluorescent pink, added a green-and-white awning off the storefront window, and planted all kinds of bright petunias in a cow trough she'd situated along the sidewalk. Instead of ceramic pots and get-well cards, Ethel Lee filled the shelves with potpourri and bath salts and romantic CDs. She sold candles with names like Eros Vine and Summer Sensation and Tender Lavender. Before long, she'd devoted half of the shop to her passionate notions.

"It's a Love Affair," she called the new line. With the influx of customers, Daddy didn't seem to mind. In fact, he started getting rather original himself. He stopped tuning into 107.6 Jubilation on the shop stereo and began playing all kinds of classical music by people like Vivaldi and Chopin and Schubert. In the mornings he offered his customers chicory cappuccino, and in the afternoons he poured glasses of Chablis.

At first Mama wasn't too surprised by Daddy's new way of thinking. She said everybody needs a little salt in their shaker from time to time to keep the sediment out. But when Daddy and Ethel Lee started selling fancy underwear and sexy negligees, Mama felt sure he'd had himself a midlife crisis.

Daddy and Ethel Lee didn't stop there. No sooner did they start selling lingerie than Ethel Lee began giving free makeover consultations, offering customers her own line of Amour Cosmetics, including a mélange of gourmet lip glosses. Women would get their faces made over. Then they'd sip their coffee or Chablis and watch Daddy arrange some pretty bouquet of flowers. It seemed like every woman from the age of sixteen to eighty-five was visiting their premises on a regular basis.

In the summers, Daddy hired me to make deliveries and do whatever else needed getting done. I'd ride my bicycle the five blocks to town, then lock it to an old fence post between the shop and Bessie Faye's Creole in the Mornin' Diner. Bessie Faye always left her back door open, and there wasn't anything better than starting off my day with a whiff of her chaurice sausage and creole coffee and shrimp beignets. Mama often said folks don't know the meaning of living until they've experienced one of Bessie Faye's shrimp beignets.

It was a Tuesday morning. A couple of days had passed since Doug swiped Evie's and Mary Jordan's and my clothes and I'd found my mama being swooned to kingdom come.

"The help has arrived," Ethel Lee whooped as I let in a gust of warm air through the back door.

Ethel Lee was standing by the cosmetic counter consulting with Ms. Pitre, who'd already had her face made over half a dozen times. She'd bought everything from the Fountain of Youth Facial Serum to a tube of Luscious Lip Exfoliator. Ever since her husband had died two years back while fooling around with another woman, she'd joined the singles' group at the church and was *coming out*. That meant doing her nails up and adding a swagger to her walk. She traded in her Buick Riviera for a bright red Mustang convertible. Ms. Pitre changed her attire, too. She no longer wore sweaters with bright orange pumpkins appliquéd on them at Halloween, or red sweaters with jingle bells at Christmastime. Instead she looked more like the women in the New Orleans' Junior League who came to our town each Easter to raise money for the underprivileged. They wore silk pantsuits and big leather belts, and gold and diamond jewelry. Ms. Pitre didn't belong to the New Orleans Junior League. She just looked like she did.

"I want to make sure I look my best for the tryouts," I heard Ms. Pitre say.

Daddy brought Ms. Pitre a cup of his special blended coffee. "Alberta, when have you not looked your best? Not a day goes by you don't make some man's head turn," he said.

Daddy had a way of making all those women at the shop feel good about themselves. I didn't see why he couldn't work his charm on Mama at home.

"J.C., if you aren't the kindest man to ever walk this earth," Ms. Pitre said.

"That's why his mama named him J.C., after the good Lord himself," Ethel Lee chimed in.

Daddy's name is Jonathan Calvin. Growing up, everyone just called him J.C.

Just as I was about to head out the front door to water the petunias in the cow trough, Ima Jean Balfa bellowed her way into the store. Every week Miss Balfa had her hair set by Noel at Sweetbay Hair Benders a couple of blocks over, then stopped in the shop for a cup of coffee. She was wearing baggy khakis rolled up to just below her knees, and a bright yellow tank top that hung below her hips. Her fingernails were painted the color of okra. A Kurex seashell hung from each of her earlobes. Miss Balfa liked big earrings. She liked them so much, the holes in her ears had been stretched to at least half an inch long. Usually Miss Balfa wore rubber flip-flops, the kind the Piggly Wiggly stocked each summer by the checkout counter, but that morning Miss Balfa had on white Keds sneakers with holes at the end, exposing her toes, which were also painted green.

Ms. Pitre said, "I see Noel did a fine job on your hair. You look just the same as you did last week."

"I've looked the same for twenty years. If I had any intention of changing, I would have done so already," Miss Balfa said right back.

Noel moved to Sweetbay a couple of years before Ethel Lee. Noel was somewhere in his late twenties. He had long blond hair he tied back in a ponytail, and wore Calvin Klein cologne. Miss Balfa said, now with Noel in town, getting her hair done and her annual appointment with her gynecologist were the only times she could get a man's hands on her.

Personally, I thought Miss Balfa was crazy in the head. I'd had my first appointment with Doc Fredericks a few years before, after I'd turned fourteen. Mama had explained it was one of those coming-of-age sort of things, like getting your period, and she and I would celebrate by going to lunch once it was all over. Having Noel fix my hair was one thing, but sprawling my legs out like a Butterball turkey about to get stuffed had to be the most unpleasant of experiences I could think of. Not to mention Doc Fredericks was as old as the Parthenon.

I began unpacking a box of scented pillowcases that had arrived the day before, while Miss Balfa and Ms. Pitre carried on. Ms. Pitre was trying out some of Ethel Lee's new lip color. Daddy was now at the back of the store, putting together an arrangement for me to deliver to the Walbridge Wing. The Walbridge Wing is Sweetbay's home for the elderly.

"What do you need new makeup for? You've already bought out half the store," Miss Balfa said.

Miss Balfa and Ms. Pitre had been friends for as long as I'd known them, which was all my life. We'd all gotten used to their teasing each other. It was their way of showing affection.

"Because I want to look my finest at the tryouts, don't you know."

"What tryouts?" Miss Balfa asked.

"Haven't you heard?"

"If I'd heard, I wouldn't be asking," Miss Balfa told her.

"The play tryouts," Ethel Lee filled in. Ethel Lee handed Ms. Pitre a tissue to dab her lips.

"What play tryouts?" Miss Balfa asked.

"The high school hired a new drama teacher. He's starting a community theater," Ethel Lee said.

"He's going to be directing *A Midsummer Madness,* a play about four lovers," Ms. Pitre declared.

"It's a spoof on Shakespeare's *A Midsummer Night's Dream,*" Ethel Lee said, turning to me. "Lucy, what about you? You and Evie and Mary Jordan should try out."

This was the first I'd heard about the play and had no intention whatsoever of participating. The last time I'd set foot on a stage was in the eighth grade when I received my middle school diploma. Mama later told me my neck had turned as red as a fire engine. Standing on a stage in front of people wasn't something I cared to repeat.

"I don't think so," I said.

"Have you met the new teacher?" Ms. Pitre asked me.

"He must have been hired after school was out," I told her.

Miss Balfa said, "Forget it, Alberta. He's too young for you. Besides, he's married."

"How do you know he's married?" Ms. Pitre asked.

"It's a small town. I hear things."

"You didn't hear about the tryouts," Ms. Pitre reminded her.

"I only hear things I'm interested in, and I'm not interested in any theater."

"I don't know why not," Ms. Pitre said. She looked at me and then at Ethel Lee. "I'll have you know when we were in fourth grade, Ima Jean was the star of the show."

"What show was that?" Ethel Lee asked.

"Little Red Riding Hood."

Looking at Miss Balfa, Ethel Lee got a big grin on her face. "You played Little Red Riding Hood?"

Miss Balfa finished her coffee and made to leave.

Ms. Pitre answered for her. "No, she played the big bad wolf."

By then everyone except Miss Balfa was having themselves a laugh. Sometimes watching Ms. Pitre and Miss Balfa carry on reminded me of Mary Jordan and Evie and me, and I'd wonder where the three of us would be forty years down the road. Of course I hoped none of us would end up a widow like Ms. Pitre, or a bachelorette all our life like Miss Balfa, but I also hoped we'd face the world together like these two had.

The Shuffle

Daddy had put together an arrangement of pink mist scabiosa and parrot tulips in a large vase. They were addressed to Mrs. Forez, a widow at the Walbridge Wing. I strapped the vase into the basket Daddy had rigged for me on the front of my bike. The Walbridge Wing was on the north side of town, three blocks up from the square. It was almost ten-thirty. Usually by that time of morning, the residents would have long finished breakfast and be back in their rooms. But as I rode up to the lobby windows, I saw a whole group gathered together in the commons area, their white heads bobbing and rocking back and forth. One of the men was waving his arms in the air. No sooner did I open the door than I heard someone playing "You Make Me Feel So Young" on the piano. Mary Jordan's grandfather, Pappy Jacques, was sitting in a wheelchair at the back of the room and singing his heart out as if he were Frank Sinatra.

I spotted Mrs. Forez on the far side of the room. I wove my way between wheelchairs and walkers and set the arrangement of flowers on a table beside her. I'd known Mrs. Forez my whole life. She used to throw all kinds of Tupperware parties clear up till she had her stroke two years back. She took my hand in hers when I kissed her and squeezed it with her frail fingers. She couldn't talk so well since her stroke. Her fingers didn't work so well either, so I opened the card for her.

"'Dearest Anita, Happy Birthday. Love, Clyde,'" I read aloud. "I didn't know it was your birthday," I told her.

She smiled, and her gray-blue eyes got a tad bit watery. I kissed her cheek. "Happy Birthday," I said. I wondered who Clyde was. Maybe a brother. Maybe a friend. I wondered if anyone at the Walbridge Wing had sung to her yet.

I walked toward the piano, thinking I'd ask the pianist to play "Happy Birthday." Just as I stepped past a row of metal folding chairs and oxygen tanks, I saw the boy, whom the good Lord had smiled through on Mama. He wasn't even looking at the keys while he played. Didn't even have sheet music in front of him. He caught me watching him and smiled. That's when I noticed his nose and decided it was entirely too big for his face. I smiled back, though all the while I was wishing his nose wasn't so big. His face was smooth and tan and his eyes were a deep marble blue. He ran his fingers up the length of the keys real fast and started right in on "I Got Rhythm." I didn't know how he could play the piano without looking at the keys, much less know all those old songs.

Hands around the room began clapping, though hardly a one of them was on beat. I found myself laughing for the sheer fun of it all. Dewey inclined his head to the audience, steering my eyes toward Mrs. Forez. A tall, thin man with a head full of white hair was asking her to dance. He bowed and held out his hand toward her. She took his fingers in hers and slowly stood from her chair. As Dewey continued to play, their feet shuffled together the tiniest bit. Their faces were all lit up, both of them smiling and twinkling their blue eyes at each other.

"It's her birthday," I said to Dewey, moving my body a little closer to the piano so he could hear me.

With that he did another one of those fancy moves with his fingers and began playing the jazziest rendition of "Happy Birthday" I'd ever heard. I stood beside the piano and started singing while others joined in. I don't have a great voice, but neither did anyone else in that room. As we finished singing, the man dancing with Mrs. Forez clapped his hands and gave her a kiss smack-dab on the lips. All those frail voices around the room cheered and hooted. "Way to go, Clyde!" I heard someone say.

Clyde helped Mrs. Forez back to her seat, then pulled up his chair beside her and held her hand. Both of them just kept right on smiling, and as they did, Dewey played "Love Is a Many-Splendored Thing." People started singing, about as off-tune as they were offbeat.

Dewey was amazing. I loved watching his hands move so deftly across the piano keys, and I loved listening to all those old people sing. I was standing just behind Dewey's left shoulder. "This is wonderful," I said.

He looked back at me, a beautiful, wide grin on his face. I was sorry I had to get back to the shop. "I gotta go," I said. "Thanks for playing."

Dewey nodded his head in acknowledgment and kept right on with his accompaniment, smiling the whole time. He looked like he was having just as much fun as everyone else in the room. I was glad Mama had suggested he share his talent with the world, and I felt my own appreciation for music make a bountiful leap. I slipped out the back door, savoring all that music trailing behind me.

Gone with the Wind

The next day after I finished working at the shop, I rode my bike out to Tante Pearl's place to give her a pedicure, like I always did on Wednesdays. She'd pay me five bucks for the effort, and another five bucks for giving Moses a good shampooing and brushing. I didn't help her out for the money. I did it because it gave me a chance to spend time with her, like a girls' day out.

I laid my bike in the grass beside the porch and started up the steps.

Tante Pearl met me at the door. "We're not doing the pedicure today," she said. "Not giving Moses a bath, either."

"What is it we're going to do, then?" I asked, following her into the house.

We walked back to the kitchen, where she reached inside her large straw purse on the table and pulled out a quart jug. "Gator milk," she said.

"Un-huh. Gator milk." I gave her one of those drop-jaw looks of disbelief. "Tante Pearl, alligators don't have boobs."

Tante Pearl laughed, her bosom heaving up and down.

"They just call it gator milk," she said. She started unbuttoning her blouse.

"Tante Pearl, what are you doing?"

"I had to go to Doc Fredericks the other week, and while I was sitting in that waiting room I got to reading this magazine he had out on the table. In the back was an advertisement for gator milk. You're supposed to rub it all over your skin."

"What for?"

"So it'll soak clear through to the fat cells. Supposed to work like vinegar on baking soda. They call it a chemical re-action. Guaranteed to change fat cells into gas."

"And what happens to all that gas?" I asked, looking her over.

"Well, I'm not sure."

"You know that's just some hoax."

By now she'd taken off her blouse and dungarees and was standing in her underwear and sneakers with the jug of gator milk on the floor beside her.

"Lucy Marie, are you going to help me or not?"

"What is it you want me to do?"

"You know I can't reach my backside."

I'd never known Tante Pearl to take such an interest in her physical self. "Since when did you become so concerned about your size?" I asked. As a little girl, I'd always enjoyed the cushion of my aunt's abundance and had never entertained the idea of her preferring to be thinner.

"Since Doc Fredericks told me I was becoming a health hazard to myself."

I looked my aunt over, thinking Doc's words harsh and un-kind. "What about one of those spas in New Orleans," I said.

"They give full-body massages. You could take this jug to one of them."

Tante Pearl picked her clothes up from the chair where she'd dropped them and strode off down the hall. She slammed her bedroom door. I followed after her and rapped as softly as I could. "Tante Pearl?" I said.

She didn't answer, so I rapped a little more loudly.

"They ain't kin!" she finally hollered at me.

"Tante Pearl, open up. I still think it's a hoax, but if you want me to help you, I will."

I waited a minute before she finally opened the door, holding the jug out in front of her and wearing a blanket wrapped over her shoulders.

I got a smile on my face and started to laugh. Before I knew it, Tante Pearl was laughing, too.

When I'd finished at Tante Pearl's house, I rode out to the beach. I liked my friends, but I also liked to disappear into the quiet of my head and think about things, like what I was going to do with my life after I graduated. I knew I'd be going to college, and probably like everyone else I'd go up to LSU in Baton Rouge. But sometimes I didn't want to be like everyone else. Sometimes I'd think about saving my money and buying a car and driving to a place I'd only read about, like Maine or California or Washington State. No one from Sweetbay ever went to college that far away, as if the South was as much country as our little town would ever need.

Evie didn't want to go to college. She said she was going to get a job right after school. Mary Jordan would probably go somewhere elaborate with a full-ride scholarship. The three of us had never liked to talk about what would happen to us after we graduated. Once in church, Father Ivan read from the Bible that a cord of three strands is not easily broken. I'm sure that had something to do with God, but all I could think about was Mary Jordan and Evie and me. Now that Mary Jordan was getting so serious with Doug, I worried that our cord might be losing a bit of its strength.

That late afternoon, the sky was fretted with clouds. I sat on the beach, the wind whipping my hair across my face, the kind of moist wind that's native to these parts. I'd brought my backpack, as I usually did. Inside was my journal, some magazines, my headphones, my CD player. But that day I didn't feel like listening to music. I didn't feel like looking at magazines, either. Instead I listened to the wind and watched the tiny whitecaps over the water. Again I got to thinking about Tante Pearl. Something had changed. Then I remembered the two fishing poles and it hit me. Of course she'd always cared about her weight. She'd just never had anyone to notice her before. Tante Pearl had been alone so long, I'd never imagined her preferring it any other way.

Tante Pearl deserved to have someone care about her, someone other than a seventeen-year-old who was too busy with her friends these days. I hoped I deserved to have someone care about me, too, someone other than Mary Jordan and Evie, or a boy like Tommy Pierre, who had never really cared about me at all. Tante Pearl once told me that when she was little, her family had a wishing well in their backyard. She said she would write her wishes down, wrap them around a rock, and toss the rock into the well. I stared out at the ocean, thinking I had about as big a wishing well as anyone could care to have right in front of me. I took out a pencil from my backpack and tore out one of the pages from my journal. I closed my eyes, trying to imagine someone tall and dark and wonderful. I thought about what he would be like, and as I did, I wrote down the words that came to mind: *Kind. Funny. Someone who will want to know what I'm thinking. Someone who will hold my hand and dance with me on the beach underneath a starlit sky. Someone who will love me like a first kiss, and keep on loving me again and again.*

With the list in my hand, I walked toward the shoreline, the clouds lowering upon me with each breath of wind. The water washed warm currents over my feet. I strolled along the beach, kicking the water up in front of me, splashing my legs. It was then that a gust swept up from behind, snatching the paper from my hand and tossing it into the sky. I watched my wish sail to and fro, dipping and dancing through the air, till it was finally out of sight somewhere over the water. I stood there for some time, feeling the wind against my skin and listening to the Gulf roll in. And for a moment I got a strange flutter in my heart, like a whisper, that an angel had been with me that afternoon, and maybe it was an angel who had carried my wish away.

One Big, Beautiful Pearl

━━━━━━━━━

At long last, Friday night arrived. Tante Pearl volunteered to drive us girls to the school. As we pulled up, the baseball team had just run onto the field for their warm-up laps. Tante Pearl stayed outside while Mary Jordan and Evie and I snuck into the school building. The locker room was full of open cubby-holes, with each player's number marked in black electrical tape on top. Doug was number eleven.

"Well, lookey here," Evie said as she rummaged through his duffel bag. She started tossing our clothes out in a heap on the floor. Then she took out the little helmet that was supposed to protect Doug's personal parts.

"Probably shouldn't take our clothes with us," Mary Jordan said. "When he comes back to get dressed, he'll know we were here."

We shoved our clothes back into the bag, except for our underwear. We tucked our bras and our panties into Mary Jordan's backpack, hoping Doug wouldn't notice.

Evie opened up the bottle of Tabasco sauce.

"Let *me*," Mary Jordan said.

Mary Jordan dabbed some onto the stretchy fabric covering

Doug's plastic armor and smeared it all around with her fingers. The three of us started blowing on it to make it dry faster.

"You can barely tell," I said.

"You sure it's going to work?" Mary Jordan said.

"It'll work," Evie said. "Just as soon as he starts working up a sweat."

She placed Doug's belonging back in his duffel bag; then the three of us hurried outside, where we met up with Tante Pearl in front of the school.

"I can't remember ever having been so eager for a baseball game to begin," Tante Pearl said.

We started walking around the school to the baseball field. I'd been so caught up in our locker room mission that I hadn't paid any attention to my aunt's attire until that very minute. She wasn't wearing her camouflage dungarees or a blouse with cutoff sleeves. She had on a blue-and-yellow-print skirt and a white knit top.

"Tante Pearl, you're wearing a skirt," I said.

No sooner did I stop to stare at her than Mary Jordan and Evie stopped to stare at her, too.

"Been born again," Tante Pearl said. She kept walking. We followed behind her.

Mary Jordan said, "You been going to church?"

All my life I hadn't seen my aunt so much as set her big toe in a church.

"Lord knows I'm no Pentacostal," Tante Pearl said. "But yes, ma'am, I've been born again."

"Well if it isn't the Holy Spirit, just what is it you've been born again in?" Evie said.

Tante Pearl stopped walking to catch her breath and wipe the perspiration from underneath her big brown eyes. "When I was a little girl, I used to swing with my meemaw on her front porch. One night she asked me if I knew what God was. I said, 'Why, Meemaw, he's big and he's got eyes all over his head.' I said that on account of my mama always telling me God could see everything I was doing. Meemaw got to chuckling. 'Well, he's big all right,' she said. But she felt pretty sure I didn't have it all right. 'God is love,' she told me. 'Soon as all those church folks and evangelists get their notions about Him straightened out, the world just might get straightened out, too.' She said when you're feeling loved or you're giving love away, you might as well be looking God in the face, 'cause He's all around you."

Mary Jordan said, "I never thought about it like that before."

Evie said, "I never thought about it like that before, either."

Lately I was learning a lot of new things about my aunt. I'd never known Tante Pearl to have a religious bone in her body. I'd never known her to have an opinion on love, either.

She rubbed her fingers down the sides of her yellow-and-blue skirt and rolled up the sleeves on her shirt to cool off her arms. "Yes, indeed, I do believe I've been feeling the good Lord these days," she went on to say.

"Who is it you've been feeling the good Lord with?" I asked.

Tante Pearl smiled. She turned away from me and started walking toward the baseball field as if she had no intention whatsoever of answering my question.

"Tante Pearl!" I said.

"I guess you could say I'm being a little careful." She kept right on walking.

"Careful of what?" Mary Jordan asked.

Tante Pearl slowed as we approached the field. "My life has always felt like a coarse little piece of sand," she said. "Now it feels like a pearl. I guess I don't want anyone making me feel like a piece of sand again."

I was still just as curious as ever about the new love in my aunt's life, but I had a feeling I shouldn't press the matter anymore. Though my aunt seemed about as happy as I'd ever seen her, I felt sad that she hadn't felt like a pearl all along. I also knew she had just spoken a wealth of wisdom about love. My relationship with Tommy had been the closest thing to love I'd ever come, but he'd never made me feel beautiful inside. Whoever it was in my aunt's life, I was glad that he had found her. It was high time she felt like a pearl, one big, beautiful Pearl.

Tabasco Sauce

The Trudeau Tigers' baseball field sits back about a hundred yards from the school building, with aluminum bleachers behind the batter's box. By the time we reached the field, the players had already finished their laps and were heading back to the locker room via a shortcut off of left field.

"I don't know why it is they put these bleachers behind a fence," Tante Pearl said.

"That's for our protection," Evie told her. "So we don't get hit by a ball."

We climbed up to the back row and took our seats. Mary Jordan said, "You know, Miss Balfa got hit by a ball once. Knocked her clear upside the head."

"No, she didn't," I said.

"Yes, she did. Billy told me so."

Mary Jordan's brother, Billy, used to play for the Trudeau Tigers. He would probably know.

"What was she doing at a baseball field?" Tante Pearl asked.

"Miss Balfa goes to all the games," I said.

The visiting team was on the field warming up. It wasn't

too long before the Tigers appeared, stashing their gear in the home-team dugout. The game was about to begin.

"Which one's Doug?" Tante Pearl asked.

Mary Jordan said, "Catcher. Number eleven."

The Trudeau Tigers took to the field. All four of us squinted our eyes toward Doug as he squatted behind home plate. It didn't look like that Tabasco sauce was having a bit of effect.

The first batter for the Lakers struck out. As he was walking back to the dugout, Miss Balfa strolled up to the bleachers in the brightest pair of pants I'd ever seen.

"What's she trying to be, a jack-o'-lantern?" Tante Pearl said.

Miss Balfa's slacks were fluorescent orange, and her shirt looked like a tourist souvenir from Hawaii. She had a large straw purse hooked over her arm. When she saw the four of us on the top row of the bleachers, she decided she'd join us.

"Don't usually have someone to sit with," she said as she sat down beside me.

She pulled out a tube of zinc oxide, dabbed some underneath her eyes and over the entire surface of her nose, then passed the tube to me. "Lucy, I swear your nose has a hint of red to it."

"Miss Balfa, it's after seven at night. I don't need any sunscreen protection." I handed the tube back to her.

The second batter hit a high fly out to left field, giving the Tigers another easy out.

"You sure we put enough sauce on his thing?" Mary Jordan said.

"We used up more than half the bottle," Evie declared.

"Used up more than half the bottle of what?" Miss Balfa wanted to know.

Tante Pearl took it upon herself to inform our guest. "Mary Jordan thought she just might light her boyfriend's fire."

"Light his fire with what?" Miss Balfa asked.

Evie pulled out the bottle of Tabasco sauce from her shorts' pocket.

"Oh, I do declare, there's hope for this generation yet," Miss Balfa said, laughing.

The third batter hit a fly foul after a ball and two strikes. The left fielder caught that one, too.

Our eyes were glued to Doug as the teams changed positions.

"He's grabbing himself," Evie said.

Mary Jordan said, "No, he isn't."

"He is, too," Evie said.

Sure enough, I thought he was adjusting himself a little.

The first batter for the Tigers hit a single, stirring up a rowdy applause from the bleachers. The second batter got walked. Again fans made a raucous fuss. Doug strode up to the batter's box. He was one of the Tigers' strongest hitters. The first pitch was outside. Doug stepped out of the box and adjusted himself a little more, then stepped back up to the plate. The second pitch was a curveball. The ump called a strike. Again Doug grabbed at himself. Evie began to laugh. Miss Balfa got to her feet. The rest of us did the same.

"This is it," Miss Balfa said. "I can feel it."

Sure enough, a fastball was pitched, Doug's favorite, and he took an even swing with all his might, sending that ball soaring up in the air out past center field. All the Tiger fans and players hooted and hollered while Doug took off for the bases. No sooner had he rounded first base than he grabbed hold of his southern region like he wasn't sure what to do with himself, and his two feet started running faster than I'd ever seen them run.

Evie started singing "Light My Fire," by the Doors. Mary Jordan and I joined in, all three of us belting out the chorus. Doug had hit a home run, which sent up more cheers. We continued singing our hearts out as he rounded third base and was heading home. By now he had both hands over himself. The team tried to high-five him, but he barreled right through their little rally, off the field, past the dugout, and over to the school.

We got to laughing so hard, Evie let out a snort, Tante Pearl backfired, and I felt sure Miss Balfa was going to have herself a cardiac arrest.

The Birds and the Bees

━━━━━━━━

Mama once said the heart is like a vessel carrying all sorts of important cargo, the kind that no one knows about, the kind that can sometimes make you cry, and the kind that can determine the type of person you are. I thought about her words the day after the ball game, when a young woman I'd never seen before walked into Daddy's shop. She had long straight hair that was probably blonde at one point but now resembled the color of dirty sand. She was wearing jeans and a white baggy T-shirt that looked like the ones at the bottom of Daddy's laundry basket. Her skin was smooth and washed out, just like her hair and jeans. She had a way about her that let me know she'd never been in the store before, pausing at every item and acting a bit shy. I could hear my mama in my head saying that girl needed some renovation. Maybe that's why she'd come into Daddy's store. She picked up the tester bottles of perfume, holding their tips to her nose, but not going so far as to spray any on her skin. Then she walked over to Ethel Lee's Amour Cosmetics' counter.

Ms. Pitre and Miss Balfa were sitting at a large table trying to arrange dried flowers. By the way they'd gotten quiet all of a sudden, I knew they were watching the woman, too. I wished Ethel Lee was there, but she was taking her day off, and Daddy was in the back of the store preparing flowers for a funeral, which meant I'd have to help the woman. I was hardly a makeup connoisseur. This woman wasn't wearing any. But as I walked past Miss Balfa to return an item to one of the shelves, she nudged me in the hip, then jerked her head toward the customer. Ms. Pitre cleared her throat and did the same. Of course, as soon as she cleared her throat the woman looked our way.

"Let me know if you need any help," I said, then felt something inside me cringe, because the word "help" was written all over this woman's face.

"I want a new look," she said, her voice sounding all tied up in her throat.

I'd never helped someone find a new look before. All I'd ever done was stock shelves and help Daddy with the flowers.

"What kind of look?" I asked her.

The woman took in a deep breath. "Well," she said, exhaling the air slowly. "Something to catch my husband's attention, I suppose. Things haven't been the same since our daughter was born."

Miss Balfa said, "Haven't you heard of cyanide? Add a few drops to his coffee in the morning. Works every time."

At that, the woman smiled, and I was feeling very thankful for Miss Balfa's and Ms. Pitre's presence, as I didn't have a clue how to help some woman capture a man's attention. Like I knew how myself.

I think Ms. Pitre read my mind. "Let me help you," she

said, scooting her chair out from the table. She walked right up to that woman and, placing her hand on the back of the woman's elbow, steered her toward a stool at Ethel Lee's makeup counter.

"Consider the Garden of Eden," Ms. Pitre said. "It's no wonder Adam and Eve found themselves in the midst of sin when you consider how colorful it was."

This woman wasn't slow. She caught on to Ms. Pitre just fine, and was even laughing a little.

Miss Balfa cleared her throat mighty loudly. "There's underage listeners in our presence, mind you."

I joined Miss Balfa at the table, deciding I'd just watch Ms. Pitre in action.

"What's your name?" Ms. Pitre asked the customer.

"Savannah."

"That's a lovely name," Ms. Pitre said.

"Savannah what?" Miss Balfa wanted to know.

"Savannah Banks."

"Isn't your husband the new drama teacher?" Miss Balfa asked.

"You know, I just love to act," Ms. Pitre said.

And so they took that woman right into their friendly circle. Ms. Pitre brought out the makeup and made over the young mother's face. By the time she was finished, she'd sold Savannah a hundred dollars' worth of Ethel Lee's cosmetic goods. Then she got to talking to her about adding color to her wardrobe and showing off her legs.

"You know, a man always appreciates a good set of legs on a woman," Ms. Pitre said.

I got to thinking about my own legs, wishing I could take them down a few sizes. I was as tall or taller than most of the boys in my class. I hadn't dated a whole lot, and I was certain it was because of my height. Mama once told me that height can sometimes intimidate a man. She said I'd need to find me somebody big in character, which might take me a while, because a lot of boys didn't arrive at their character till much later in life.

I looked over at Miss Balfa. She'd been a bachelorette all her life, and as I considered her in her fluorescent purple attire, I got to wondering why she'd never married, and because I was wondering, I asked her. "Miss Balfa, did you ever think about getting married?"

Ms. Pitre answered for her. "It's like feeding chickens," she said. "If you scatter the feed too fast, they all run away."

It wasn't Miss Balfa's nature ever to be quiet. She jumped right in. "Well, now, if you're going to go taking your sweet liberty to compare me to some animal, I'd just as soon have you compare me to a deer, long and graceful. I'd like to see some man try and catch a deer without a rifle in his hand."

Ms. Pitre said, "You know, Paul Harvey once got to talking on his radio broadcast how everybody's got some animal that best suits their individuality."

"That's like people and their dogs," Miss Balfa said. "You ever see how some man with jowls always has himself a bulldog?"

Savannah laughed. She wasn't looking so helpless anymore, and I got to wondering what kind of dog I looked like. Probably a Great Dane.

Ms. Pitre stood back to take a look at Savannah. "Sweet child, you are a beautiful young woman."

The ladies in our town were always using words like *sweet child* and *honey child,* and I wondered if I'd be doing the same thing when I got to be their age.

"I think she needs to see Noel. Have him do something with her hair," said Miss Balfa, who never was one to hold back an opinion.

Next thing I knew, I was on the phone with Sweetbay Hair Benders, making an appointment for our new customer. When I got off the phone, Ms. Pitre and Miss Balfa had not only taken it upon themselves to rearrange Savannah's appearance but her evening hours as well.

"What they need is some time alone without the baby," Miss Balfa said.

"Mm-hmm," Ms. Pitre said.

I hung up the phone, only to find all three of them looking straight at me.

"Lucy's a fine babysitter," Ms. Pitre said.

"Aside from my husband, I haven't left Mattie alone with anyone," Savannah said.

"Well, honey, it's about time," Miss Balfa said. "Don't you know bringing a baby into this world leaves you with two children to attend to, an infant and a man, both as helpless as the other?"

"I'll babysit," I offered.

And so it was agreed that I would stay with Mattie, the Bankses' five-month-old daughter, while Savannah surprised her husband with a date out.

Savannah said they lived about a mile away on the edge of town. "Do you need a ride?" she asked me.

"No. I can ride my bike."

Savannah stopped at the front of the shop before leaving. She ran her hands over the lingerie.

"You might want a little nightcap after your evening out," Ms. Pitre said. "Did you see the white negligee hanging in the window?"

"I thought you said the Garden of Eden had color," Miss Balfa said. "I'd go with something red."

Or orange or purple or okra green, I thought. Miss Balfa had the most colorful wardrobe of anyone I knew.

"Red certainly captures a man's attention," Ms. Pitre said.

"Hummingbirds like red," I said, not knowing from where the words came, and the way those three women looked at me, I could tell they didn't know from where those words had come, either. But then the bright light of an idea lit up on Ms. Pitre's face.

"Perfume!" she exclaimed. "Every woman needs a little nectar."

I thought of sitting through Miss Trapman's health class in junior high, Sex Education 101. Listening to Ms. Pitre and Miss Balfa carry on served up a much more entertaining education.

Billy

The Bankses lived in a small bungalow on Hill's Orchard, a quiet street on the edge of town. Tanny Hill, one of the earlier natives of Sweetbay, now long passed on, had once farmed a persimmon orchard on that land. After he died, the town expanded into his estate, uprooting trees and building houses, though most every yard still had persimmon trees that bore fruit.

I rode up to the Bankses' a little before six and leaned my bike against the side of the house. About fifteen yards in front of me was a man on a ladder, pruning one of the old trees that looked about fifty feet tall. I watched the man snip a few branches, then take the blade on the end of the pruner and start sawing away at a thicker limb. I knew the wood on persimmon trees was as dense as rock, and its bark the consistency of alligator hide. Whenever the trees died or were cut down to make room for a house, the wood was harvested and sold for anything from golf clubs to baseball bats. Needless to say the man on the ladder had mustered up a lot of willpower to saw off that limb he was going at.

The man was wearing sunglasses and a cap, so I didn't get

a good look at his face, but through his T-shirt, I could tell the muscles on his back bore some mighty fine definition.

"Hi," I said.

He stopped sawing and pivoted his torso around. "Hi," he said back. "Are you the babysitter?"

I stood there with my hands in the pockets of my jean shorts and nodded. "I'm Lucy," I said.

"Tell Savannah I'll be another minute. I'm just going to finish up."

He turned back around with the pruner blade.

I walked to the front of the house and knocked on the door.

When Savannah met me, she didn't look like the Savannah I'd seen at the shop earlier that day. She was wearing a short denim skirt and a pair of platform shoes, making her almost as tall as me. In her arms was a plump, round-faced baby with a head full of blonde hair. The baby smiled when she saw me, giving me one of those toothless grins.

"This is Mattie," Savannah said, gesturing for me to come in. "She can barely sit up, so you have to be careful with her. And she likes to put things in her mouth."

I reached for the baby and started talking all kinds of silly talk to her, to which she responded with more grins and coos and giggles.

"She likes you," Savannah said.

We walked into the living room. Big floral slipcovers were draped over a sofa and chair situated around a TV, and black-and-white photos—mostly ones of Mattie, others of a man with dark hair and dark eyes, whom I recognized as the man on the ladder—were arranged on top of the furniture.

Savannah showed me the kitchen. On the walls were more photos, and a corkboard by the telephone, thumbtacked with all kinds of snapshots.

"I usually feed Mattie around seven, then change her and put her down. Make sure you lay her on her back," Savannah said.

She opened the refrigerator. On the top shelf was a strawberry pie, some cans of beer, Coca-Cola, juice, and a couple of baby bottles.

"You'll need to warm the bottles up in the microwave," she said, "about forty seconds, until the milk is lukewarm. Test the temperature by putting a couple of drops on your arm before you feed her," she explained.

Before we left the kitchen, I looked at the pictures on the walls more closely.

"That's Ted," Savannah said, pointing to one of the pictures of the man.

No sooner had she said his name than the back door off the kitchen opened.

Mr. Banks walked in, removing the cap from his head and running his hand through his sweaty hair.

"Give me five," he told Savannah. "I'm just going to get a quick shower."

Savannah went on talking about this and that about the baby. While she talked I kept thinking about how different she looked from earlier in the day.

By the time Mr. Banks was out of the shower, Savannah and I had moved into the living room with Mattie. Savannah was showing me how to work a battery-operated swing.

"You ready?" Mr. Banks said, joining us in the living room.

I couldn't help but notice him. His hair was thick and wet and his face freshly shaven. He was wearing jeans with a navy blue short-sleeved collar shirt, and the cologne he'd lathered on his skin smelled wonderful.

"We're going to dinner and a movie over in Beaufort," Savannah told me. "Our cell number is on the refrigerator."

"We'll be fine," I assured her.

After the Bankses left, I moseyed around the house with Mattie in my arms, talking to her and looking at all the photos. Pretty soon she started squirming and getting fussy. I warmed up one of the bottles and sat with her on the sofa in the living room. Mattie smacked her lips a couple of times. Her breathing slowed and her crying simmered down. I continued feeding her until all the milk was gone, pulling the bottle away from her intermittently to burp her.

Savannah had told me there was a stroller in their bedroom and I could take Mattie for a walk if I wanted. I found the stroller folded up behind their bedroom door. With Mattie in one arm and the stroller in the other, I carried both outside. I strapped Mattie in and started for the driveway, but then stopped to look back at the tree. The branches were still strewn around the trunk. I wheeled Mattie toward the yard, deciding I'd gather up the limbs and haul them out to the street.

Just a few feet from the trunk of the tree, so close I almost stepped on them, were two broken robin eggs. They reminded me of the colored Christmas bulbs I'd dropped when Daddy and I were stringing lights around the house. Poking out of the broken shells were the tiny, lifeless bodies of baby birds—

heads and bulging eyes and wings and white tufts of down growing along their little spines. And next to the two broken eggs were the bodies of two more baby birds that had already hatched. A sound erupted from clear down to my heart. I looked up at the tree. The nest was still in place. I realized those little ones had literally been shaken from their home. I thought I would cry seeing those birds, and knew I couldn't just leave them there.

I went inside the garage and found a small trowel, then dug a hole underneath the trunk of the tree. All the while Mattie just watched me. One by one I scooped up the shells and each of the dead birds and laid them in the divot I had made. I re-filled the hole and etched a cross into the soft soil with my finger.

"It's okay, Mattie," I said, feeling like I had to console someone.

Later that night after I put Mattie down, Billy, Mary Jordan's big brother, pulled up to the house in his Bronco, with Evie and Mary Jordan in tow. I hadn't seen Billy since March, when he'd come home from college for his spring break. Billy was a sophomore at Louisiana State University in Baton Rouge.

"How's my glamorous Tower of Pisa?" he said, lifting me off the ground in a bear hug before I could answer. Billy had cracked tall jokes on me for as long as I could remember.

Billy looked about as good as I'd ever seen him. He was wearing a pair of faded blue jeans and a short-sleeved shirt. He had straight brown hair the color of dark chocolate that always looked like the wind had just played with it, even if the sky was raining cats and dogs. Unlike Mary Jordan, who was as fair-skinned as a porcelain doll, Mama would tell her, Billy's skin was a deep olive, like his dad's, and his eyes just as blue and clear as a swimming pool.

"I thought you weren't getting back for another week?" I said.

"He ditched finals," Mary Jordan told me.

I grabbed him by the arm and pulled him inside. "You can't do that. What were you thinking?"

"Wait till Mom and Dad find out," Mary Jordan said.

"They don't know?" I couldn't believe it.

"I just got in about an hour ago. They're out playing bridge or something." Billy walked into the living room and fell back into the armchair, letting out a big sigh. "It's not for me," he said.

"What's not for you?" I asked.

"College. Classes. It all feels like such bullshit. I'm just not cut out for it."

Mary Jordan and Evie sat on the sofa. I joined them.

"What are you going to do?" I asked.

"Get a job. Maybe start my own business. Stick around here."

Mary Jordan said, "You want to spend the rest of your life in Sweetbay?"

Billy laughed a little. "Don't knock it, sis. This place isn't so bad."

"You won't see me hanging around," Mary Jordan said.

"Maybe not," Billy said. "But I wasn't meant to keep my head in a book. I got to be doing something. College isn't for everyone."

Billy Jacques hung the moon as far as Evie and I were

concerned. We both swore that he was our first love. He'd called Mary Jordan and Evie and me the three Princesses of Avalon for as long as we could remember. We didn't even know what Avalon was. He said it was paradise. I knew Billy wasn't like most big brothers. Maybe it was because his and Mary Jordan's parents were so old. Instead of fighting with his little sister, he looked after her, and because Evie and I were friends with Mary Jordan, he looked after us, too.

The summer Evie's dad walked out, Billy was playing catcher for Trudeau's junior high team. At the end of the season, he gave Evie his catcher's mitt. "To catch you when you fall," he told her.

He'd played quarterback for the Trudeau Tigers his last two years of high school. We'd wait for him outside the locker room after the games. He'd give each of us high fives if the team won and swing us in his arms. He always smelled of Dial soap and Stetson cologne. If the team lost, he'd give us low fives, and say, "We'll get 'em next time."

Since Billy had been away at college, we hadn't seen him much anymore. He'd stayed in Baton Rouge the summer before, picking up a couple of credits and working at a restaurant. Though I was surprised about his dropping out of college, I was also glad he was home.

I told Billy and Mary Jordan and Evie about the baby birds. Told them how I had buried them.

Billy stood up.

"Where are you going?" Evie asked.

"Thought I'd check out the nest. See if there are any eggs left."

The monitor in Mattie's room was on. Taking the portable with me, I followed Billy outside.

He retrieved a pair of binoculars from his Bronco, then stood on the hood of his truck and hoisted himself onto the garage roof. He walked up to the highest point and, holding the binoculars to his eyes, looked out at the tree.

"Can you see anything?" Mary Jordan asked.

"Mama robin's back," Billy said.

From where I stood I could spot her, too.

"I think there's one egg left," he told us. "Yeah, I'm pretty sure."

I don't know why I'd gotten so caught up in this whole bird thing. It was as if I'd been the one who'd knocked those babies from their home.

"Come take a look," Billy said.

I thought of my babysitting responsibilities, and glanced back at the house.

"I'll check on Mattie," Mary Jordan said.

And so Evie and I climbed on the edge of the Bronco's hood and hoisted ourselves onto the garage roof.

Billy handed me the binoculars. Mama robin was still in the nest. Sure enough as she shifted herself around, I spotted a light blue egg. Strange, but my stomach got butterflies. I felt elated. And I knew I was going to pull for that little bird to make it.

Billy nudged me in the arm. "How 'bout that."

I smiled. "I'm glad you're home," I said.

Statue of Liberty

———

The Bankses didn't get back from Beaufort until a little before midnight. I'd thought their night out was supposed to do them some good. Either they were especially tired, or things hadn't gone so well.

"Sorry to keep you up so late," Savannah said when they walked into the house. "How did everything go?"

I was sitting on the sofa watching TV.

"Mattie was great," I told her.

Mr. Banks had passed by me, not saying a word, and was now in the kitchen.

"Did he like your new look?" I asked her.

She rolled her eyes. "I don't know. But I did," she said. "I guess that should count for something."

"I think you look nice," I said.

Savannah smiled. "Thanks. Would you be willing to babysit again sometime?"

"Sure." I thought about telling her about the birds, but decided she didn't need any bad news.

After Savannah paid me, I left out the front door, not seeing Mr. Banks again that night.

*   *   *

The next morning I went to mass with Mama. On our way home we stopped by the Piggly Wiggly. While Mama shopped, I walked over to the paperback section and picked up a romance suspense book I'd been reading. I found my place, lightly marked in pencil two-thirds of the way through, and sat down on the edge of one of the display shelves stocked with shampoo. Sometimes it took Mama an hour to shop, as she liked to socialize down each aisle.

I was reading about a tall, dark, handsome man who adored a young female artist. She was visiting her aunt in a small coastal town in Oregon. The book got me thinking about myself. I wasn't an artist, or a musician like my mother. I liked my friends and I liked to go to the beach, but other than my height, I couldn't think of anything that set me apart.

I must have read more than fifty pages before Mama showed up at one of the checkout aisles. A person could hear my mom a mile away.

I put the book away and met her just as she finished paying. "Lucy, I have discovered a wonderful opportunity for you."

Next to her was a cart stacked to the hilt with paper bags full of groceries. I took the cart from her and pushed it out to the parking lot to her blue minivan with its JESUS IS THE WAY! and LET ME COOK YOUR CAJUN PEPPERS bumper stickers. "What opportunity is that, Mama?" I asked, completely unconvinced.

"On my way past the dairy department I stopped to look at the postings on the bulletin board. I always check out the postings. You never know what you might come across. Well

I'll have you know there is a play starting up right here in our little town."

"I'm not interested in a play," I said.

Mama ignored my statement. "And I thought to myself, What a remarkable opportunity for Lucy."

I loaded the bags of groceries into Mama's van while she went right on talking.

"The new drama teacher at the high school is organizing the whole thing. There's going to be a meeting Tuesday night. I just love it when young people have ideas. It's so healthy for the community."

"Mama, I'm not trying out for the play," I told her.

"I don't see why not. You and Evie and Mary Jordan all ought to try out."

I closed up the van and wheeled the cart over to the pickup rack.

"You always were a dramatic child," Mama said when I returned.

"*I'm* dramatic?"

"What about that time in fifth grade when you played the Grinch and you got stuck in the chimney? You started hollering to kingdom come till the teacher came onstage and pulled you out."

"They should have known I was claustrophobic," I said.

"Or what about the time in fourth grade when you got hit in the chest with a basketball. You asked the nurse in the infirmary to send you home, certain in your head you had yourself some deadly hematoma."

That was the day the nurse informed me that I didn't have a hematoma at all, but rather my right flower had already started to blossom. I didn't see why my left flower couldn't blossom at the same time.

"Then there was the time you got your first cramps from your monthly visitor and you thought you were dying of stomach cancer," she went on to recall.

"I swear, Mama, you've got a memory like an almanac. Don't you think there are a few things you could selectively try and forget?"

"I just think you ought to go to that meeting. I'd love to see you onstage."

"I'll think about it," I said, seeing no other way to diffuse the matter.

Back at the house, I helped Mama put the groceries away. "What time are Papa and Sissy coming for dinner," I asked.

Papa Walter and Grandma Sissy were Mama's parents. They came for dinner every Sunday.

"They're supposed to drive over once he finishes putting in a transmission in that old car of his."

Papa had been driving a gold Impala since before Mama and Daddy were married. He said good cars were like good women. "Just 'cause they start fallin' apart ain't no reason to trade them in."

Mama had picked up a pound of shrimp at the grocery store and a couple dozen oysters in jars with liquor, which I knew meant we were having oysters Iberville for supper, one of Papa's favorites. After we finished putting all the food away, I went upstairs to my room.

Then Evie called.

"Guess what I just saw?" she said.

"What?"

"That guy you were babysitting for is starting a play. This morning Mary Jordan and I were riding back to town from my dad's. We saw a poster about it in the diner's front window."

"I know."

"He's having a meeting Tuesday night."

"That's what I hear."

"I think we should go."

"Why would we want to do that?"

"I think it would be fun. Maybe we ought to try out."

"I haven't been in a play since fifth grade," I told her.

"So?"

Both of us got quiet for about a whole minute.

"We could at least see who shows up," Evie suggested.

"I'll think about it."

"That means yes."

"It does not."

She laughed. "I'll talk to you tomorrow."

Before long, I smelled Mama's seafood consommé and bourbon pecan pie. I headed downstairs, hunger gnawing at my stomach.

"Want any help?" I asked.

She gave me a head of green leaf lettuce and a cup of chopped fruit to toss together.

I made the salad and went to set it on the table in the dining room. Mama brought in a bottle of white wine she'd just opened and put a Fats Waller jazz CD in the stereo.

The front door opened. "Fee, Fie, Foe, Fum," Papa's voiced boomed through the whole house.

Papa walked into the kitchen, his hands held over his big stomach. "Mmm, mmm. Lily Dawn, you do know how to satisfy a man's appetite."

Papa and Sissy followed Mama and me into the kitchen and sat in the two oven chairs while Mama made Papa a gin fizz. Papa liked his before-dinner drinks. Said they whet his appetite up good. Sissy said his appetite was plenty whet enough as it was.

Papa slapped his thigh for me to come sit on his lap.

"Papa, when are you going to realize I'm too big for your lap?"

"Nonsense."

He grabbed my arm and pulled me over to him, making me fall into his arms, at which time he let out a deep groan.

"Lily Dawn, what are you feeding this child?" Papa teased.

"Told you," I said, trying to get up, but he just wrapped his arms around me that much tighter.

"You're like the Statue of Liberty," he said. "You ever seen the Statue of Liberty, Lucy?"

"Not in person," I said.

"The Statue of Liberty is the most beautiful lady in the world. She's a beacon of light to men near and far."

Mama brought Papa his drink. I stood to help her with the rest of dinner.

It was another thirty minutes before Daddy finally got home.

"'Bout time you showed up. If we don't eat this casserole soon, it's not going to be a bit of good," Mama told him.

"Just let me wash up, and I'll tell you why it is I'm straggling behind."

Daddy was laughing to himself as he walked to the half bath off the kitchen, letting us know he had something good up his sleeve.

Sissy and Papa and I helped Mama bring the food to the table. We sat down and put our napkins in our laps, except for Papa. He tucked a corner of the white linen into his shirt collar as if he thought he was going to spill food all over his front side. Papa always tucked his napkin into his shirt. Mama told him he was unrefined. He said the day he wanted to be a refinery, he'd let her know, the same old joke they'd exchanged for years.

Daddy walked in and poured all the grown-ups a glass of wine. I poured myself some water from the pitcher beside me. Then all of us held hands as Mama bowed her head and began to say grace.

"Bless us, dear Lord, we pray, and this food laid out before us. Thank you for all our rich blessings. Bless the dear souls around this table. Bless this food to our dear bodies. Bless us to thy service. Help us to be more mindful of others in need. Bless us with thy grace and kindness. Thank you for all you've given us. . . ."

I watched Papa roll his eyes. He couldn't stand it any longer. "For God's sake, Lily Dawn, the Lord heard you already."

"Amen," Mama finally said.

"Amen," we all responded.

Papa started scooping the oyster and shrimp casserole onto his plate. The rest of us looked at Daddy.

"Well?" Mama said.

"Well, what?" Daddy said, reaching for the salad bowl.

"Well, why is it you were straggling behind?" Mama wanted to know.

Daddy served himself some salad. He picked up his glass of wine and took a long, slow swallow.

"J.C., you're as slow as Christmas. Get on with it, will ya," Sissy said.

He set his glass down. "Just as I was fixing to close shop, guess who came in?"

"Who?" Mama said.

He took a bite of his salad before speaking, chewing it as if he were performing some kind of digestive exercise. At last he said, "Pearl."

Mama and Sissy looked straight at each other. "Pearl?" they said together.

I don't know that Tante Pearl had ever walked into Daddy's shop before. She grew her own flowers and didn't wear a speck of makeup.

"Came in to buy herself some lingerie," Daddy went on to say.

"Lingerie?" Mama and Sissy said.

Then Mama dropped her fork onto her plate, making an extra-loud clinking sound. "What kind of lingerie did she buy?"

Daddy raised his eyes to the ceiling like he was trying to remember. "Hmm. I think it was black." He shook his head. "No, it was red."

"Red?" Mama declared.

"Mm-hmm. Bought herself some perfume, too."

"Perfume?" Sissy said.

I'd already eaten a good way through my dinner during all their banter. "I don't know why everyone's getting so worked up. Tante Pearl's got as much right to buy perfume and lingerie as anyone else."

"Honey, the only time a woman buys perfume and lingerie is when she's got a man on her agenda," Mama said.

"Maybe she does," I said. "And then maybe she doesn't. I think you should be happy for her."

"Honey, we *are*," Mama said, dropping her chin a lot lower than was becoming on her. "But . . ."

"But what?" I said.

"Being as we are Pearl's closest of kin, I think we have a natural right to know what's going on in her life," Mama said.

"Lucy's probably right," Daddy said. "We shouldn't be drawing so much attention to Pearl's affairs."

Papa had already helped himself to seconds. Holding his wineglass up in front of him, he said, "You know, cars are kind of funny. Sometimes all they need is a little engine lubrication. Take that Impala of mine. She was making quite a ruckus with all that high-pitched rapping of hers. I added some Quaker State—Slick 50 to her motor. She's got less engine friction and is getting better gas mileage and horsepower, too."

"Why, Papa, that's just beautiful," Sissy said, looking like she'd just fallen in love with him for the kazillionth time.

Papa held a forkful of food out in front of him. "What?"

"Mm-hmm, Papa, it sure is." Mama nodded her head thoughtfully and served herself some salad.

Papa looked at Daddy. "What'd I say?"

Daddy smiled. "Well, Walter, I do believe you've just given us a fine analogy on love."

Daytona 500

Mama spent most of Tuesday afternoon baking all kinds of delights for the drama club meeting. She believed preparing food was her charitable calling in this world. She'd made pecan yam muffins, turtle shell cookies, buttermilk pie. She'd even mixed up some hurricane punch, virgin-style, filling old gallon milk jugs with it. I knew her charitable service on that particular day was also her way of getting me to show up at the meeting.

"*Somebody* has to take all this food over to the school," she said. "I've got my weekly prayer vigil at the church."

Mama had told me I could take her car, saying one of the ladies from the altar guild was going to be picking her up.

Though I agreed to deliver the food and give Mary Jordan and Evie a ride, I still had no intention of participating in the play.

"This will be fun," Mary Jordan said on the way over.

"You better not take off," Evie told me. "I'm not walking home."

It seemed to me my friends and my mama were in cahoots with each other. I didn't say anything.

When we pulled up to the school, there were already ten cars in the parking lot. We loaded our arms with Mama's benevolence and headed up the steps toward the commons area. Standing just outside the building, smoking a cigarette, was Mr. La Roche, the senior history teacher, who was the spitting image of Ichabod Crane. He'd been married once, or so we'd heard. His wife asphyxiated herself in the garage about twenty years back. He never remarried. Some of the kids at the high school liked to talk up stories about what really happened, saying it wasn't suicide at all, but that Mr. La Roche had locked his wife in the car, then went on in the house to go to sleep. I'd asked Mama about it once. She declared that that was pure nonsense, saying they didn't even manufacture cars with automatic door locks back then. She said Mr. La Roche would have had to hit his wife upside the head or else tied her up to have kept her in the car against her will, which stirred up Evie's and Mary Jordan's and my imaginations even more.

When Mr. La Roche saw us, he put his cigarette out on the bottom of his shoe and tucked the butt in the pocket of his navy blue blazer. I didn't know why he was wearing a jacket with the night being as hot as it was. I supposed men always wore their sport coats the way old women always wore pantyhose, even in the middle of summer.

Mr. La Roche held the door open for us. "Would you like me to take some of that burden off your hands?" he asked.

We said, "No, thank you."

About twenty people were scattered around the auditorium.

Standing in front of them was Mr. Banks. He saw us and smiled.

"My mom likes to cook," I said as we approached him.

We set the food on the stage.

"You're going to stay, aren't you?" he asked us.

Mary Jordan and Evie each took hold of one of my arms. "We're staying," they said. I knew there was no way they were going to let me out of there.

We sat about a third of the way back.

"He's hot," Evie said.

"And you didn't want to come tonight?" Mary Jordan said.

Before I had a chance to offer an opinion on the matter, Dewey walked up.

"Hey," he said.

"Hey," I said back, drawing the word out with surprise. I was sitting between Evie and Mary Jordan. Dewey was standing just at the end of our row.

"We didn't get a chance to really meet the other day. I'm Dewey," he said.

"I'm Lucy." I shook his hand over Evie. Then I introduced him to my friends.

We moved down a seat so he could join us.

"Why haven't I ever seen you before?" Evie asked.

"I just moved to town with my dad a couple of weeks ago," Dewey said.

"From Detroit, Michigan," I said.

Dewey bent forward with his arms on his knees and a big question written all over his face. "How did you know?"

"My mom's Lily Beauregard. I heard you play at the house the other day."

"You were there?"

Evie interrupted. "Should Lucy and I trade seats? I'm feeling a little out of the loop."

I filled my friends in.

Then Dewey said, "Clyde proposed."

I looked confused.

"Clyde. Over at the Walbridge Wing. He proposed to Anita. I was up there this afternoon."

"You're kidding." I started to laugh.

"He gave her a ring and everything."

"What did she say?" I asked.

"She said, 'Yes.' "

"Who said, 'Yes'?" Evie wanted to know.

"Mrs. Forez, over at the Wing," I told her. "Dewey played the piano up there the other day. She and this old man were dancing."

"I know Mrs. Forez," Mary Jordan said. "That is so sweet."

Mr. Banks began talking. "I'm going to need you all to move in closer so I don't have to yell."

Everyone got up and moved, taking seats within the first three rows. Ms. Pitre and a couple of the women she went bowling with sat in the center of the first row, looking about as eager as a couple of gators in a duck pond. I was now sitting next to Dewey, with Evie on my other side.

"I'm Ted Banks."

Evie whistled.

I slunk down in my seat. "I don't know you," I said.

Dewey laughed.

"How many of you have acted before?" Mr. Banks asked.

Ms. Pitre raised her hand. Mr. La Roche did, too. Mary Jordan reached for my hand and held it in the air.

Mr. Banks caught my eye. "Lucy," he said. "Come on up here."

"I wasn't even supposed to be here," I mumbled to Mary Jordan.

I squeezed my long legs between the seats in front of us and Dewey's knees, and made my way toward Mr. Banks.

He laid his arm across my back, cupping his fingers over my bare shoulder. If anyone else had done that, I wouldn't have even taken notice. But here he was, probably the best-looking man I'd ever seen, and all of a sudden I felt like a shot of pure adrenaline had just coursed through me. My neck gets splotchy when I get nervous, and I was certain it was getting splotchy then.

"What part did you play?" he asked.

I cleared my throat. "I was the Grinch."

Evie whistled again. Mary Jordan laughed.

"Okay, good." Mr. Banks didn't laugh, and his hand didn't leave my shoulder. "We're going to do a little exercise," he went on. "Henry, I saw your hand go up."

Mr. La Roche was sitting behind Mary Jordan, next to Noel La Plume, from Sweetbay Hair Benders. Mr. Banks motioned Mr. La Roche down.

"Now, I want you two to face each other," Mr. Banks said. He laid both his hands over my shoulders and gently turned me toward Mr. La Roche. "Lucy, you're going to mirror everything

Mr. La Roche does. Henry, move slowly so that Lucy can stay right with you. Like this," Mr. Banks said, holding up Mr. La Roche's right hand. "Now, Lucy, you hold up your right hand, and try to move at just the same moment Henry does."

I did as he said. As Mr. La Roche slowly moved his hand to the right, I did the same. As he turned his body to the side, so did I. He raised his eyebrows. I raised mine. A couple of people laughed. Then Mr. La Roche really loosened up. He slid to the right. He slid to the left. I kept right with him. He kicked his heel out in front of him. He kicked his heel behind him. He moved his jaw to the side. He turned his head. He leaned his face toward mine. I leaned my face toward his. I swear our noses were no more than a couple of centimeters apart. I felt that nervous giggle inside me start to erupt. He scrunched his nose. I scrunched up mine. With that, everyone was laughing, and that nervous giggle of mine did a full-blown explosion, snowballing into both a raspberry and a snort, which embarrassed me to no end. I wheeled around, turning my back to the audience.

Mr. Banks laid his arm over my shoulders. With his face next to mine, he said, "Nice job. You were great."

His mouth was so close to my cheek, I was certain I felt his warm breath on my skin, which sent the blood in my body racing like a stock car at the Daytona 500.

Before I turned back around, everybody started clapping, even Mr. La Roche. I still thought he looked like Ichabod Crane, but for that split second, began to fancy that maybe he hadn't asphyxiated his wife after all.

Kite Strings

━━━━━━━━━

After Mr. La Roche's and my demonstration onstage, Mr. Banks talked about the play and announced that tryouts would be two nights away. He passed out scripts so that we could become familiar with the parts.

"I'll be asking the ladies to read Hermia's lines from Act I, Scene I, and the men to read Lysander's part from the same scene," he told us.

Everything had happened so fast that before I knew it, I'd been swept up in the whole affair. When Evie and Mary Jordan and Dewey all agreed to try out, I agreed, too.

The next day I rode my bike to Tante Pearl's. She'd asked me to help her tear off the trim around her windows so that she could replace it with new wood. It was late afternoon. I was on top of a ladder, prying off one of the strips with a crowbar, when a blue Karman Gia convertible pulled into the driveway. In the passenger seat was Evie. Tucked in the back was Mary Jordan. And driving was Dewey. Evie leaned in front of Dewey and pressed on the horn several times.

I had no idea how the three of them had gotten together.

"What are you doing?" I yelled, still standing on the ladder with the crowbar.

"We saw this really cool car driving around town, so I stood in the middle of the road and made the driver pick us up," Evie said.

"What do you think?" Mary Jordan said.

"It's my dad's," Dewey added.

"Out of my good citizenly duty, I told him he had to take us to the beach. It's called welcoming the new resident. Want to come?" Evie asked.

The window trim could wait. I knew Tante Pearl wouldn't care. She and I would probably be at this project for weeks. Maybe we'd finish it sometime next year. That's how Tante Pearl was. She had unfinished projects all over the house—walls half painted, cabinet faces removed, a garage with no door.

Tante Pearl was around back working in her garden. "Let me tell my aunt." I climbed down the ladder, then, looking at the car, said, "Are we all going to fit?"

"We'll fit," Evie said.

Evie climbed in the back with Mary Jordan, saying my legs were longer than hers.

"The radio's broken," Dewey told us.

"That means we'll have to sing," Evie said. It didn't take her long to start singing "I'm a Redneck Woman." Mary Jordan started right in with her. I joined in, too. Dewey did one of those pretend embarrassment things, rubbing his hand down his face as if trying to hide, though grinning the whole time.

"What? You don't like country?" I teased.

He blushed. "No. I guess I never cared for it." He was still smiling.

"Try it. You might like it," Evie said, then kept right on singing.

"Or get the radio fixed," Mary Jordan said.

When we got to the beach, the mosquitoes were having a heyday. Mary Jordan hadn't brought any repellent this time, so we decided to build a fire to deter them, despite the saturating heat. We scouted the area for wood. Dewey went back to the car for matches he said his dad kept in the glove compartment.

It wasn't long before we had a fire roaring. We sat back from it a ways to buffer ourselves from the heat.

"So what's a Detroit boy who doesn't like country music doing all the way down here?" Evie asked.

Dewey had his shoes off and was digging his toes in the sand, as were the rest of us. He stared down at his feet, not answering right away. "I don't know. I guess we just needed a change. Dad used to have family down here. That was a long time ago."

His mood had turned somber, and I didn't think it was just because of the fire.

"Do you like it here?" Mary Jordan asked.

"It's okay."

"Do you ever get homesick?" Evie asked.

"I'm not homesick. . . ." We waited for the rest of his thought, but it never came.

I almost asked him about his mom. Now I'm glad I had enough good mind not to.

"What does your dad do?" Mary Jordan asked.

"He's a painter." Dewey looked up, seeming relieved for the change in subject. "He's getting ready to open a gallery in town."

"That's your dad?" Evie said. "I heard about a gallery going in."

"What kinds of pictures does he paint?" Mary Jordan asked.

Dewey picked up one of the sticks we had gathered and began drawing curves in the sand. "A cross between impressionism and abstract, I guess. Right now he's painting women."

"With their clothes on or off?" Evie asked.

Dewey smiled, still drawing in the sand. "Off."

"Seriously?" Evie couldn't believe it.

"Where's he getting the models?" I asked.

"Around."

"Who?" Evie said, her voice on the brink of laughter. She was now on all fours with her hands dug into the sand as if she might douse him with fists of it should he not give up any names.

Now Dewey was laughing. "I don't know. He doesn't tell me. It's not like I'm sitting there watching or anything."

Evie gave up and sat back in the sand. "We should've brought dinner."

"Hot dogs," Mary Jordan said.

"S'mores," I said. I was scooping up handfuls of the brown sand and letting it run between my fingers. "Do you believe God knows how many grains of sand are on this beach?"

"Where did that come from?" Evie asked.

"I was just wondering."

"You wonder about strange things," Evie said.

"That's one thing really different about Detroit and here," Dewey said. He tossed the stick into the fire. I looked at his drawing, resembling giant waves.

"What's that?" I asked.

"There are all kinds of beaches on Lake Huron, but the sand is finer. If you took an hourglass in Detroit and one from here, the sand from Detroit would move a lot faster. Time moves more slowly down here. Like at the bank the other day. The teller was having a conversation with the woman in front of me about the advantages of using dishwashing detergent on laundry stains. I must have stood there and listened to them a good ten minutes."

"Dewey, you're weird, but I like you," Evie said.

I don't know how long we sat there talking, but before we knew it, the blue sky had softened to a delicate smear of pink and violet, and the tide was pulling out. We left the fire and waded in the water, walking west along the beach. That's when Dewey found the kite, a little battered, but still in one piece, though the string was a tangled mess, and so was the tail. He broke the string off and carried the kite with him.

"A lot of people fly kites along the lakes in Michigan," Dewey told us. "They'll spend hundreds of dollars building all kinds of frames and designs."

"Did you and your dad do that?" I asked.

"No, but I always wanted to."

"I flew a kite with my dad once," I said. "We got it up really high. Then the wind snapped the string and the kite took off till we couldn't see it anymore. That was five or six years ago. I've always remembered something he said."

"What's that?" Mary Jordan asked.

"He told me that a kite string was like people's lives. In one way you could look at the string as holding a person back, but he said you could also say it kept the person grounded, like family, or having a place where you belong, or friends. That without it, a person can get lost.

"I like that," Dewey said.

"As long as the string's not all tangled up," Mary Jordan said.

"You guys are getting too deep for me." Evie turned and started back toward the fire.

Evie's family had been a tangled-up mess for years, and I knew that's what she was thinking. Evie was tough on the outside. And though part of her was tough on the inside, too, there was also a part of her that was sad. She just didn't like to show it.

"Hey, Evie, wait up," I said. The rest of us turned around and walked with her back to the fire.

Naked Ladies

The next day after our evening at the beach, Mary Jordan and Evie and I decided to check out the new gallery Dewey's dad was opening. Mr. Savoi had rented an old building right on the square. Though the door was unlocked, when we walked inside, we didn't see another soul around. Lighted fans were suspended from the ceiling, which was as high as a church. The walls were horsehair plaster and painted stark white. Different displays by regional artists had already been arranged along the walls. The floors were a light hardwood, and all around the room were white pedestals that looked like Roman columns cut into three-foot sections. Classical music was playing from somewhere toward the back of the building.

Not a one of us said a word. It was as if we were standing in a cathedral. We just wandered around looking at all the paintings.

Toward the back of the room was a display by Dewey's dad. Each piece was of a naked woman holding some sort of flower.

"They're beautiful," Evie said.

I stared at those paintings, from one to the other, letting

my eyes travel over each brush stroke, the contour of each woman's body. At that moment, something happened to me, and for the life of me I don't have the words to describe it. Maybe it was something spiritual, maybe it was physical. Maybe it was both. My lips tingled, gooseflesh settled upon my skin, and a yearning came upon me that left me weak in the knees and stomach. I had no idea what that yearning was for, but I knew I'd never wanted something as much.

I looked at Mary Jordan. She held a hand to her breast, her thumb stroking her collarbone back and forth against the neckline of her shirt. I looked at Evie, her mahogany eyes transfixed on the rich oil painting of a heavyset woman with long brown hair, holding a rose against her face, her body backlit by a warm orange glow. As sure as I was standing there, I knew I would never be the same again, and in the silence that hovered between my friends and me, I knew they were experiencing the same thing.

We might have stood there like that for a couple of decades if a sound from somewhere at the back of the building hadn't gotten our attention. It was a woman laughing. Not the kind of laughter that explodes out of people when they're watching a funny movie or when someone tells a joke. The laughter I heard reminded me of when Tommy Pierre picked me up for a spring formal back in April, before he moved to Texas and I never heard from him again. I was wearing a pink dress with spaghetti straps. He'd brought me a corsage from Daddy's shop, made of three baby white roses, only he couldn't decide where it was he was suppose to pin it. As he stood there looking down at my breasts, I felt the perspiration under my arms and let out a giggle. That's when Mama told him she'd get some elastic and I could wear the corsage on my wrist.

Or the little laugh I heard from Mama the night I walked up on her and Daddy in the chaise lounge on the back porch, wearing only their birthday attire.

"Oh my heavens," I said.

"What?" Evie whispered.

I walked to the back of the building as quietly as I could. Evie and Mary Jordan stayed right behind me. There was a door cracked open just a smidgen. I held my breath and peeked through the crack. Lo and behold, there in front of me was my own mama, her bare bottom so close I could have touched it if I'd had a ten-foot pole. I couldn't see the man in front of her. He had a canvas set up on an easel. I wheeled my body around and pinned my back against the wall. Then I realized I was still holding my breath. Evie and Mary Jordan had already taken off to the front of the store, walking on their toes just as fast as they could. They were out the building before I decided to breathe again.

By the time I joined them, I felt like my heart was riding the fastest merry-go-round on this side of the planet, and my voice had taken leave to Tibet. Mary Jordan took my hand and led me down the alley alongside the building. The three of us crouched to the ground with our backs pressed against the warm brick. We just sat like that, not a one of us saying a word. Then Evie reached for a strand of my hair and tucked it behind my ear.

"Dewey told us his dad paints naked women," Mary Jordan finally said.

I still couldn't find my voice, so I just nodded.

"We've never had an artist like that in town before," Evie said. "It's kind of like somebody giving us a pair of ice skates and telling us to go play hockey."

Mary Jordan was sitting on the other side of me. "Evie Thibodeaux, I swear you don't make a bit of sense."

"I make as much sense as Lucy's mom standing butt naked in there."

I finally managed to talk. "What are you saying?"

"I'm saying we don't know a thing about art or people who go and call themselves artists," Evie said. "Just 'cause your mom didn't have a stitch of clothing on doesn't mean she was doing anything wrong. Look at all those paintings in there. It didn't seem to me like there was anything wrong with them."

"They were beautiful," I said.

Mary Jordan said, "I think your mama's beautiful."

"So that's it." I'd been holding my knees up tight against my chest. I stretched my legs out in front of me. "They weren't doing anything wrong. He wasn't touching her or anything."

"He wasn't close enough to touch her," Evie assured me.

"He's just making her into one of those works of art we saw on the wall," Mary Jordan said.

I said, "Oh no."

Evie and Mary Jordan said, "What?"

"He's gonna put Mama up on the wall. Everybody's going to see her naked body. Everyone will know who she is."

Evie said, "How will they know who she is?"

"People aren't blind!" I declared. "Who else looks like Mama in this town? Who else has her black hair and black eyes?"

Evie laid her hand on my shoulder and her face lit up, letting me know she'd gotten one of her bright ideas. "We could steal it," she said.

"You think he keeps the door locked?" I asked.

"It wasn't locked when we walked in," Evie said.

"Even if it was locked, Dewey could get a key." Mary Jordan gave me a smile, coy and subtle.

"All you have to do is put your hand on his leg and look into his eyes," Evie said.

I said, "Maybe I will."

Queen of Sheba

As the afternoon wore on a heat wave settled in. Tryouts for the play were that night and it was a hot one, the kind where a person's greatest fear in the whole wide world is that the air conditioner will break.

When we walked into the auditorium, Mr. Banks was sitting on the stage in a pair of cutoff shorts.

Evie said, "Why can't any of the boys around here look like that?"

We sat a couple of rows back from Ms. Pitre and some of the other ladies from town.

Evie had worn a purple silk scarf over her head and around her neck, saying the attire would complement her performance.

"Aren't you suffocating?" I asked her. The air was so hot in that auditorium, I felt like I couldn't breathe. The school had air-conditioning, but it was kept somewhere above eighty degrees to save on money.

Evie loosened the scarf a little from her neck. "It's all in one's state of mind," she said.

Then Dewey walked in and took a seat beside me.

"Flown any kites lately?" Evie asked him.

"No, but I'm working on it."

"Working on what?" Mary Jordan said.

"The kite," he told her.

As I was listening to Dewey, all I could think of was Mama's white buttocks staring back at me, and I knew there wasn't any way I could let the town see her in the nude. "How's your dad's gallery going?" I asked him.

"Good. He's got an exhibit planned for his open house on Monday."

"What kind of exhibit?" I asked.

"Some of his own work."

"What kind of work?" I asked.

"The kind that had all of you so curious last night." Dewey smiled, kind of bashful, and with his face so close to mine, I noticed how nice his teeth were, and no sooner did I notice his nice teeth than the strangest feeling came over me. All of a sudden I wanted to run my tongue over his pretty smile. I wasn't even sure I liked Dewey, not in that kind of way, at least. I pulled my shoulder away from his, all the heat in that auditorium driving me crazy. Not to mention the seats in front of me were suddenly feeling entirely too close to my knees. I stood up and edged my way around Dewey. Once in the aisle, I sat down and stretched out my legs, the floor cool beneath me and the dust particles sticking to my damp skin.

"You okay?" Dewey asked me.

"Yeah. Just feeling cramped."

Mr. Banks started talking, thanking everybody for coming. "I'm going to have two people try out at the same time," he said. "As I mentioned the other night, I've chosen the dialogue between Hermia and Lysander in Act I, Scene I, beginning with line 128."

He asked for volunteers. Evie raised her hand. Dewey offered to come up with her.

Once on the stage, Dewey held out his hand for Evie, escorting her up the steps. Dewey bowed to Evie before they began. Mr. Banks had taken a seat in the front row next to Ms. Pitre. He nodded at Dewey to begin.

" 'How now, my love? Why is your cheek so pale? How chance the roses there do fade so fast?' "

Dewey was a natural. Every person in the room was riveted by his voice. He moved with such ease, stepping toward Evie, brushing the fingertips of his outside hand against her cheek.

Evie raised her face toward him, her eyes pained. " 'Belike for want of rain, which I could well between them from the tempest of my eyes.' "

" 'Ay me! For aught that I could ever read, could ever hear by tale or history, the course of true love never did run smooth. . . .' "

We all clapped boisterously when they had finished. Mr. La Roche whistled from the back row. That got Mr. Banks's attention. He paired Mr. La Roche with Ms. Pitre next.

"Nice job," I said to Evie and Dewey.

Dewey sat on the floor beside me, pulling his knees up in front of him.

"Did you act in Michigan?" I asked him.

"Yeah. I never was very good at sports."

Just as we were talking, a man walked up and laid his hand over Dewey's head.

"Hey, Dad," Dewey said.

His dad was smiling. "Good job," he said.

Mr. Savoi's voice was rich and deep and eloquent. His face was somewhat thin; he had a distinctive jaw line, and a nose like Miss Balfa's—dignified. His hair receded from his low forehead, and his eyes were as gray as his hair. I'd never seen gray eyes before. There was a weight to his lids, and deep wrinkles etched into the surface of his cheeks and toward his temples like the rays a child makes when drawing a sun.

Dewey proceeded to introduce us. His dad shook each of our hands.

"Do you want to stay?" Dewey asked him.

He was now kneeling next to his son. "I can't. I've got someone stopping by the house." He then looked at the rest of us. "It was nice meeting you."

"It was nice meeting you, too," Evie said.

And then Dewey put his arm around his dad's shoulder and hugged him casually, as if it was the most natural thing in the world. I'd never seen a teenage boy hug his father like that before. "Thanks for coming," Dewey told him.

Mr. Savoi stood to go, walked up the aisle, and closed the door quietly behind him.

"He seems nice," Evie said.

Dewey didn't shrug off her words the way other boys might. Instead he smiled and nodded. "He is."

Suddenly, I wanted to know Dewey's story. I wanted to know what made his dad and him so close. I wanted to be Dewey's friend.

He started to chuckle.

"What?" I said.

He inclined his head toward the stage. "Ms. Pitre's nervous."

Dewey was right. Her face and neck looked like a tie-dyed shirt for the Crimson Tide. Her voice quivered so much she might as well have been a woodpecker trying to sing while perched on a tree trunk and pecking a hole. My heart ached.

"I can't do this," I said.

"Come on. Sure you can."

"I should have worn a turtleneck."

"It's a hundred degrees outside," Dewey said.

"Ninety-seven point eight, but I still should have worn a turtleneck." I pressed my fingers against the hot skin rising from my collarbone to my chin.

"You'll be great," he said.

"I'm already getting splotchy. I can feel it."

Dewey reached for one of my hands and pulled it away to take a look. Then he stood up and removed Evie's scarf from her shoulders. "I need to borrow this," he told her.

He wrapped the scarf around my neck, tying the ends together underneath my long hair. "There. Now you look like the Queen of Sheba."

I felt my neck blush even more.

Mary Jordan was called next. Lo and behold, out of nowhere, Doug Hebert appeared on the stage. Mary Jordan looked as if she would die on the spot. Her face turned as white as chalk.

"This could be bad," I said.

"What's going on?" Dewey asked.

Evie got out of her seat and crouched behind me. "What's he doing here?"

I just shook my head.

"He's up to something," Evie said. "Mr. Banks had to know about him coming out on the stage."

Doug held his pages out in front of him and began reciting his lines. I couldn't help but be impressed.

"I didn't know he could act," Evie said.

"Me, either," I told her.

"Who is he?" Dewey asked.

"Mary Jordan's ex-boyfriend."

The deeper they progressed into the scene, the more Mary Jordan's chalky complexion began to color.

As Doug finished his last line, " 'There will I stay for thee,' " he stepped toward Mary Jordan and pressed his lips to hers.

The scattered audience cheered.

Evie said, "That wasn't written in the scene."

Mary Jordan pulled back, her cheeks now a ripe red, and held her hand to her mouth. Doug grinned big and took a bow toward her.

Then Mary Jordan started laughing. She laughed so hard she doubled over, all the while rubbing her fingers against her lips. Doug started to laugh right with her, and as sure as I was sitting there, he slid his arms around her waist and hugged her to him like there was no tomorrow. Everyone in the audience was still clapping, and some were hooting and hollering, except for me and Evie.

Mary Jordan waltzed off the stage, holding Doug's hand, and what was worse, kept running her tongue back and forth over her lips, as if still savoring his kiss.

She and Doug walked down the aisle and took Dewey's and Evie's original seats, since the three of us were still sitting on the floor.

No sooner had they sat down than Doug wrapped his arm around Mary Jordan, and in a voice loud enough for all of us to hear, said, "Truce?"

"Truce," Mary Jordan said, and no sooner did she say "truce" than she reached her left hand up around his neck and planted her lips on him big. The two of them got to laughing some more.

"Are we missing something here?" Evie said.

Doug reached in his pocket and pulled out a bottle of Tabasco sauce no bigger than the palm of his hand. "Bet you've never had a kiss that hot," he said with a grin.

Mary Jordan smiled right back. "No, sir, Doug Hebert. Can't say that I have."

Everyone had tried out except me. I was still sitting on the floor next to Dewey and Evie.

Mr. Banks stood up, scanning the faces in the auditorium. He held out a clipboard and, looking straight at me, said, "Lucy, you're next."

Dewey gently patted me on the back as I stood. Mr. Banks followed me onto the stage. "I'll read with you," he said.

He set his clipboard on the floor. "You ready?" he asked.

I felt my knees lock up on me. I guess my nervous condition was apparent, because Mr. Banks put his hand on my shoulder just like he'd done the other night, this time his fingers giving me a gentle squeeze, leaned his face in next to mine, and said, "You'll be fine. Just relax."

He took a couple of steps away from me and began reciting Lysander's part.

I cleared my throat, unlocked my knees, and began to read. As soon as my voice came out of my mouth, my nerves seemed to experience some sort of anesthetization. Hermia's lines flowed out of me as if they were smooth honey. Mr. Banks smiled. I looked at him and smiled back. I even made a few poetic gestures with my free arm, which surprised me to no end.

When I'd spoken my last line, Mr. Banks clapped, as did everyone else. Someone cheered. I thought it was Dewey.

I stepped down from the stage and walked back to my seat on the floor. Dewey said, "You did great."

"Way to go, Hermia," Evie said.

I took off the scarf and handed it back to her.

Dewey leaned forward and looked at my neck. "You're not splotchy anymore."

I gave his shoulder a playful shove.

Mr. Banks told us he'd post the results at Daddy's shop the next day.

Mary Jordan took off with Doug. He said he'd put her bike in the back of his car. I walked out of the auditorium with Evie and Dewey. Mr. Banks was walking behind us. He tapped me on the head with the back of his clipboard.

"Nice job," he said as I turned to him.

He was staring so damn intently at me I felt I'd just been paid the greatest compliment in the world.

Once outside, Dewey straddled a royal blue bicycle. The three of us took off. The night smelled of barbeque grills and mowed lawns. I loved summer, and for a moment I wished we could ride out to the beach and sleep under the stars, but I knew Evie's dad was picking her up early the next morning, and I was scheduled to work.

We rode with Dewey about five blocks to his house, a yellow stucco with white trim, green shutters, and a purple door. As we followed Dewey onto the driveway that wrapped around the side of the house, my breath literally caught in my throat like it wasn't ever going to come out. Parked right in plain view, next to his dad's Karman Gia, was my mother's blue minivan.

"Dewey?" Evie said.

He turned around.

"What's her mom doing here?"

Antennae and Étouffée

"She's been teaching Dad how to cook," Dewey said. He led us in through the back door to the kitchen.

Sure enough, standing at the stove was my mama, and standing entirely too close to her was Dewey's dad.

The kitchen smelled of garlic and basil and Mama's Jean Naté perfume, and the same musky cologne I'd smelled on Mr. Savoi back at the auditorium. Daddy didn't wear cologne.

"How did tryouts go?" Mama asked, just as casually as could be.

"Good," Dewey said. He strode right in. Evie and I were still standing by the door.

"Your mother's a wonderful cook," Mr. Savoi went on to say.

Mama was stirring something on the stove. Looking at her, I said, "I thought you had a prayer vigil at the church."

"I *did*," she said. "We just finished up."

I couldn't help but wonder how all that food got made if she had just finished up at the church.

Then I got to considering Mama. She was wearing a pair of khaki capris, which looked brand-new, and a white T-shirt that scooped down in the front. Little beads of perspiration dotted her collarbone like a floating necklace, and her feet were bare, revealing her pedicured toenails painted fluorescent pink.

"Where's Dad?" I asked.

Mama looked at Mr. Savoi. Mr. Savoi looked at Mama. I didn't know why they were looking at each other.

"He's down at the shop working on some flowers for Anita and Clyde's wedding. They're getting married this Saturday," Mama said. "The whole town's been invited."

"That's the thing about getting older," Mr. Savoi said. "When you're living on borrowed time, you spend it while you can. You never know when the bank might repossess."

At first I thought he might be talking about his wife, since Mama had said he was a widower, but then something inside me began to feel a little uneasy, as if he might be referring to himself and my mom. Less than two hours earlier, I'd thought he had about the most soulful eyes I'd ever seen, but him steering those soulful eyes toward my mama was a whole other story.

"What are you cooking?" Dewey asked. "I'm starving." He was looking over Mama's shoulder into the pot she was stirring, as if there wasn't a thing in the world wrong with our parents' interactions.

Mama said, "Looo-Zee-Annah étouffée."

I loved Mama's étouffée. She'd made up her own recipe, using crawfish and shrimp and a little crab, but under the present conditions of the evening, I knew I wouldn't have loved it very much that night.

"We should let you two eat," Mama said, tapping the spoon against the side of the pot.

"Stay." Mr. Savoi's face looked just a bit too pained.

"No, really, we should be going," Mama told him.

I looked over at Evie, who hadn't said a word, which was highly unlike her.

"It's late," Mama went on, as if trying to convince herself to leave. She disappeared into the room off the kitchen, and reappeared with a pair of leather sandals on her feet and a straw purse slung over her shoulder. I couldn't help but wonder why it was her shoes were in the other room.

"Do you girls have your bikes?" she asked.

Mama knew we had our bikes, and I gave her the kind of stern look that said so.

"Well then, I'll see you at the house," she told us. "Goodbye, Victor." She was out the door before he responded.

Evie finally spoke. "See ya, Dewey."

"See ya," he said.

I didn't say anything.

By the time Evie and I were on our bikes, Mama had already backed out of the driveway in her van and driven out of sight.

"How long's she been giving him cooking lessons?" Evie asked me as we pedaled into the street.

"I don't know," I said.

"She looked awfully pretty."

I said, "Mm-hmm."

"Your dad know she's giving him cooking lessons?" Evie asked.

"You sure do ask a lot of questions," I said.

"Did you see your mama's shirt?"

"What about her shirt?"

"I was just wondering if you saw it, that's all."

"I saw her shirt."

Evie said, "Did you notice anything funny?"

I said, "What do you mean by 'funny'?"

"I was just wondering if you saw anything that didn't look right."

"No, I didn't see anything that didn't look right."

"Un-huh."

"Evie Thibodeaux, I swear you can crawl under a person's skin like a june bug. If you've got something to say, then just say it sometime before I get age spots and wrinkles."

"There was a lot of steam in that kitchen," Evie said.

"They were cooking," I said.

"Then why was it your mama's nipples were sticking out like a couple of antennae?"

All that night's sultry air seemed to get stuck somewhere in my throat. I stopped my bike. Evie stopped hers beside me.

"I don't know that I like you talking about my mama's nipples."

"I just thought it was kind of out of the ordinary, that's all. Only two times a woman's nipples stick out like that. When she's got the shivers or when she's got the quivers. And there ain't no way a woman's gonna get the shivers standing by a hot stove cooking étouffée."

The air was so ripe and muggy that night, I thought my eyelashes would stick together every time I blinked. I knew Evie was right.

"What should I do?" I asked.

"There's nothing you can do."

"Should I tell my dad?"

"What would you tell him? It's not like they were doing anything."

I thought about Mama standing naked in front of Mr. Savoi at his gallery. I thought of her standing too close to Mr. Savoi in his kitchen. I thought about her talking about the great pie of life and how a woman needed her pie cut in equal slices. And I hoped with all my heart when it came to the slice of love, she and Daddy shared a mighty big piece.

Helium Hearts

The next morning while I was working at Daddy's shop, Evie and Mary Jordan strolled in wearing long dresses that looked a couple of centuries old.

Evie extended her arm in front of her and swooned her eyes toward the ceiling. "'I know not by what power I am made bold, nor how it may concern my modesty, in such a presence here to plead my thoughts. . . .'"

Mary Jordan stepped in front of her, "'But I beseech your grace, that I may know the words that may befall me in this case . . .'"

It didn't take a single second for Ms. Pitre to chirp in, "'If I refuse to wed Demetrius.'"

Daddy yelled, "Bravo!"

Ethel Lee hooted and hollered, "Oooh, this is going to be good."

"Where'd you get the dresses?" I asked.

Mary Jordan said, "At the Salvation Army. We thought they'd make good costumes for the play."

Evie said, "Do you want us to get you one?"

I said, "No, thanks."

Once all the commotion settled down, Daddy asked me to help him put together a bouquet of helium balloons. He told me they were for Clyde, the man Mrs. Forez was marrying. I was to take the balloons over to the church where the soon-to-be newlyweds were rehearsing for the wedding the next day. All the while Daddy was talking, I kept thinking about the cooking lessons Mama had given Mr. Savoi the night before. I knew Daddy didn't always pay Mama special attention, but looking at him that day I felt sad for him. I came to the conclusion that it wasn't his intention not to pay her special attention. It was just that he forgot.

Evie and Mary Jordan and I left the shop, the two of them strutting proudly in their new costumes. I tied the balloons to the basket on the front of my bike.

"Read the card," Evie prompted.

"I'm not going to read the card," I said. "That's trespassing."

"Who made you Mother Teresa? Read the card," Evie said.

"Why do you want to know what it says?" I asked.

"Two old people falling in love and getting married. That is so cool." Evie reached for the card that was tied to one of the ribbon strands. She smiled as she read it, then lifted her eyes to the sky and clutched the card to her chest.

"I want to see," Mary Jordan said. She read the words out loud: " 'Your love keeps lifting me higher than I've ever been lifted before. Love, Anita.' "

"I think that's a song," I said.

"Of course it's a song," Evie said, and proceeded to sing it so off-key, none of us could recognize it, and all three of us got to laughing.

"Love is so magical," Mary Jordan said. "It's like this spell that makes you all dizzy in the head."

"You're thinking about Doug," Evie said.

Mary Jordan gave us a goofy smile, dreamy and coy all at the same time.

"Seems to me it wasn't all that long ago you were talking about alarms going off," Evie told her.

Mary Jordan was looking down at the ground, but still smiling a little.

"Did you all ever talk things out?" I asked.

"We talked," Mary Jordan said.

"And?" Evie asked.

"He said he'd just wanted to be prepared, that was all. He's not pressuring me or anything."

"That's good," Evie said.

"Do you feel pressured?" I asked.

Mary Jordan looked up. "No. I think by talking about it, we got closer. I don't feel pressured," she said.

I wasn't exactly sure what she was telling me, but I also knew Mary Jordan well enough to know she wasn't going to tell me any more. Mary Jordan liked to try and work a subject out in her mind first before sharing it with Evie or me. It was when she couldn't find an answer on her own that she sought our compatriot thoughts.

"I've got to deliver the balloons," I told them. "I'll catch up with you two later."

When I got to the Catholic church, Savannah was outside taking pictures of Anita and Clyde. I remembered the photos I'd seen at her house, but I hadn't realized she was a professional photographer.

She waved when she saw me. I propped my bike up against a tree and untied the balloons, then brought them to Clyde. As he took the helium bouquet from me, I had this fleeting image of them carrying him away, lifting his frail body to the heavens. He read the card and smiled, then took Anita in his arms and kissed her tenderly on the cheek. "Thank you, love," he said.

I felt like I was watching a movie right before my very eyes. Clyde adored Mrs. Forez. He adored her in the kind of way that said to the world, "I'm proud of her. I cherish her." They were dizzy in love, and I wanted to be dizzy, too.

I was about to leave when Savannah stopped me.

"Hey, Lucy, I was wondering if you might be able to babysit tonight? Ted and I were thinking about going out for dinner. I'm sorry for the short notice."

"What time?" I asked.

"Could you be at the house around seven?"

I said, "Okay," wondering all the while how successful Savannah's attempts had been at rekindling their relationship.

I climbed on my bike and rode away, not wanting to go back to the shop just yet. All I wanted to do was ride and feel the warm air through my hair. I meandered along the back streets through town, up and down the sidewalks, taking my time.

Maybe thirty minutes passed, maybe forty. Before I realized it, I was coming up on Dewey's house. Perhaps in that subconscious part of my mind I'd wanted to run into him, like some element of fate. Then I saw my mama's van parked in the driveway, and this horrible slap hit me, literally zapping the air right out of my lungs. I screeched on my breaks, planted my feet on the ground, my legs stiff. I felt like my heels were digging holes clear through the concrete. I just stood there, staring at her car, unable to move. I couldn't imagine Mr. Savoi needing cooking lessons again so soon. Mama had cooked up enough étouffée to last him a week. Then it dawned on me as clear as glass. My own mama had lied. The night before she'd told me she was going to a prayer vigil at the church, when she knew all along she was going to Mr. Savoi's. Now, here she was at his house again. Part of me wanted to storm my way into Dewey's home, walk right in without one single knock, and confront them. The other part of me wanted to get as far away as I could, and I guess that part of me was bigger than the first, because that's exactly what I did. I slammed my foot on the pedal and rode away, sweat thickening on my skin and running into my eyes. I rode till my legs ached as much as my heart, and the heat and all my confusion seeped completely into each other till I could no longer tell one from the other.

Up ahead on my right was St. Vincent's Park. Over the years, whenever Mary Jordan or Evie or I had a rift in our hearts, we'd meet at St. Vincent's playground, scoot ourselves into the swings, and talk over our blues. Just hearing the squeaking pendulums overhead and feeling the sand between our toes had a soothing effect on the worst of bad days.

I laid my bike in the grass and walked over to the swing set, oblivious to anything or anyone else around me, until someone called my name. I looked up, completely startled to see Mr. Banks sitting on a bench with Mattie's stroller in front of him. He tilted his head to the side and stared at me straight on, as if trying to figure me out, as if seeing all the confusion that was muddling my mind. Then he smiled and motioned me over to him.

I sauntered his way like a pouty child.

"Hi," he said.

"Hi," I said back, sitting beside him.

I smiled at Mattie, put my foot on the front of the stroller, and pushed it back and forth.

"A penny for your thoughts," he said.

I forced a laugh. "They'd cost you a lot more than a penny."

He reached into his back pocket and pulled out a five-dollar bill. "It's the best I can do."

I looked away, staring down the street.

"No takers?" he said.

I didn't answer.

"You did really well at tryouts," he told me.

I felt myself grin, kind of small and embarrassed.

"Really well," he said.

"Thanks."

He held the five-dollar bill in front of me. "I can't interest you?"

"I'm okay," I said.

He took the bill, rolled it up, then reached his arm behind the bench and tucked the bill into my shorts pocket. "What happened to the bright-eyed Thespian I saw last night?"

I startled at first and thought about giving his money back to him, but shrugged my shoulders instead. "I don't know."

"Where are your friends?"

"Off somewhere. I saw them earlier. I'm supposed to be working."

"You work for your dad?"

"Yeah. I was out making a delivery."

"Taking a breather?"

"Guess so."

"I'm a good listener." His arm was still over the back of the bench, but it didn't feel weird. It felt nice, and I thought maybe he *was* a good listener, that maybe he cared a little bit about how I was feeling, only I wasn't sure what I was feeling, other than confused.

"I'll tell you what. I have to get Mattie home. I'll be up at the high school this afternoon getting some things ready for the play. Stop by if you change your mind and want to talk." He leaned his head forward, trying to get me to make eye contact. "Okay?"

"Maybe," I said.

"Okay," he said. He stood to go.

"Thanks," I said.

"You're welcome." He looked at me for a few seconds more as if making sure I *was* okay, then pushed the stroller in front of him and turned toward the road.

Lights, Action!

I finished up at Daddy's shop early, sometime around three. I could have found Evie and Mary Jordan or ridden my bike back to the house or gone over to the grocery store and bought one of the books I'd been reading, but instead I rode my bike to the high school. Maybe I wanted to talk to Mr. Banks, or maybe I just wanted that feeling again of someone older and wiser, someone who noticed when something was wrong. I couldn't remember the last time my parents had done that. They'd talk and maybe listen if I went to them and said I needed to talk, but this was different. This was someone noticing me, kind of like a soft mattress you can sink into when you're not feeling very good. And maybe it was more than that, too. Mr. Banks was probably the best-looking man who had ever spoken more than two words to me. It was thrilling, pure and simple.

As I rode up the driveway to the school, I saw his car out front. No one else was there. I left my bike in the rack at the edge of the parking lot and headed up the steps. The door was unlocked. The auditorium was through the commons area. The squeaking of my sneakers against the slick floor seemed to echo, the building was so quiet, and I thought how quickly that would change in a couple more months.

Inside the auditorium, the stage lights were on, but I didn't see Mr. Banks. I walked toward the front row and sat down, wondering for the first time if I should have come.

"Lucy." He'd been off to the side of the stage, his bare feet almost silent against the wood floor. "I've been sorting through some of the props," he told me.

He jumped off the edge of the stage, then walked over and sat beside me, planting his feet in front of him so that his knees squared off to the sides, lightly touching mine. I didn't pull away.

"I wasn't sure you'd stop by," he said. "Decided to talk after all?"

I remained quiet, not sure what to say.

"You know, I was a teenager once."

He was trying to be funny. I laughed a little.

"Really," he said, bumping his knee against mine.

I laughed a little more.

He sat up straighter.

"So I was wondering, you think I'll fit in here?" he asked.

I was surprised by his question. "Sure. Why wouldn't you?"

"I don't know. Small town and all."

"Do you like it here?" I asked.

He nodded his head slowly, as if he was thinking. "I especially like some of the people."

His face turned toward mine. I was staring forward at the stage. For a moment I thought he was flirting, but I told myself he couldn't be flirting. He was a teacher. He was just being nice.

"So what was on your mind today?" he asked.

"Nothing."

"Hasty recovery?" he said.

"I guess so."

He reached for my hand and stood. "Come here. I want to show you something."

I felt honored and devious all at the same time, a sensation of warmth and curiosity as his fingers held mine.

We climbed onto the stage, him still holding my hand.

"Over here," he said.

I followed him offstage to a large room where the high school kept its costumes and props.

"Looks like they performed *Cleopatra* at one time," he said, lifting our hands toward a black wig with thickly cropped bangs on a Styrofoam head. "Or *The Princess Bride*," he said. He let go of my hand and reached for a headdress with a long silk veil the color of icy pink. He placed the headdress on my head and lifted the veil away from my face.

"You'll make a beautiful Hermia," he said.

Hermia was the biggest part in the play, and he thought I'd be right for the role? I hadn't even wanted to try out for the play. Part of me was happy. Part of me said I was somewhere I shouldn't be, and yet another part of me didn't want to leave, like when you know something is bad, but you want to see just how close to the bad thing you can get because you're not completely sure it's bad.

"I should probably go," I finally said. I removed the headdress and handed it to him.

"Hold on, I'll walk out with you." He set the headdress on

the shelf. "Why don't you get the stage lights. I'll close things up in here."

I left the prop room and went to find the light switches, guessing they must be somewhere behind the curtains. I was right. I flicked each one off, only to find myself standing in total darkness. My own house had never felt so dark. So dark, I didn't see him approach me, didn't notice his hand reaching for my chin, never even felt the air change. One second I was thinking how dark everything was, and in another second his fingers were touching my chin. I gasped, pulled back. "What are you doing?"

Just as I was about to say I had to get going, just as I was about to turn away, I felt the heat of his body move closer to mine. I knew I should step away or scream or something, but I didn't say anything. I didn't move, either. Instead, I let him move closer, my mind telling me one thing, and my southern region telling me another. No matter how much I tried to tell my body to stop feeling so good, it went right on feeling the way it wanted. And all the while my mind and body were conversing, Mr. Banks kept moving closer, pressing himself into me, touching my hips with his fingers, then sliding his fingers into the back pockets of my shorts. I couldn't see his face, but before I knew it, his lips were touching mine, as light as a feather at first. One kiss, then another. And the third kiss a little harder, more urgent, his tongue searching for mine. I knew if I didn't get out of there, I would surely collapse.

"I gotta go," I said, using every bit of strength I had to muster those words out of me.

He drew slowly away, reached for my hand, held my limp

fingers. I didn't resist. My body felt like a rag. I was aroused and horrified all at the same time, swimming around in one big mess in my head, swimming and swimming and needing to come up for air.

He led me onto the stage and toward the steps. By now my eyes had adjusted to the darkness. I pulled my hand away from his, descended the stairs, and walked up the aisle, running my fingers alongside the seats to steer me in the right direction, to keep my feet steady. He walked behind me.

As we entered the commons area, he said, "Do you need a ride?" his voice just as calm and casual as if nothing had happened.

I looked toward the front doors, stared through the glass. I didn't see a living soul. "No. I rode my bike."

We walked outside, the afternoon air thick. A mosquito instantly glued itself to my leg. I rubbed it off, smearing blood down my calf.

"I'm glad you decided to stop by," he said. "I'll see you later tonight." He started down the steps toward the parking lot.

At first I wasn't sure what he was talking about. Play rehearsals were on Tuesday and Thursday nights. This was a Friday. I had that feeling a person can get when staring at something until the eyes no longer focus and everything becomes a blur. My mind was a blur. My vision was a blur, and somewhere behind all that blur Mattie and Savannah began to appear. I was supposed to babysit that night. In less than three hours, I was supposed to be at his house, and I had no earthly idea what I was going to do.

Germany

As I rode my bike home I felt like a stranger in my own skin. There was this awful, thick feeling strapped across my heart that I couldn't get rid of. I didn't want to claim it. But there was also something else stirring around inside me. I had liked kissing Mr. Banks. And that sensation made me feel like a stranger even more.

When I walked into the house, Mama was teaching piano lessons. I knew Daddy was still at the shop and would be playing golf after work. I went straight to my room and lay on the bed. A giant movie reel seemed to be playing in my head from beginning to end and back again, and I was the third party watching the whole thing in slow motion, watching the way Mr. Banks's fingers had reached for me, watching the way he had pulled my body toward his. I shut my eyes, as if I shouldn't watch, like a bad part in a movie that you know your parents don't want you to see, but you look anyway. And then when it's over, you feel guilty, but you also feel grown up. That's when it hit me like a stab wound. Lying on my back, I drew my knees to my chest, wrapped my arms around my legs, and held myself, trying with all my might to keep a part of myself from slipping away, that lanky little girl perhaps, who had believed in flying reindeer and guardian angels. The part of me that didn't want to grow up.

I'm not sure how long I held myself like that. Maybe a half hour. When I looked at the clock, it was almost five-thirty. I thought about calling the Bankses to tell them I couldn't make it, and yet something inside me wouldn't let me. I *wanted* to see him. Then I tried calling Evie, but she wasn't home, so I left a message with her mom telling her where I'd be. I knew Mary Jordan was still in Beaufort at Doug's baseball tournament.

I picked out some clean clothes from my dresser and went down the hallway to the bathroom. I filled the tub almost full, eased my body into the hot water, and slid my spine down the porcelain till the warm suds touched my chin. I stayed there until the water turned cool. Mama was now moving around in the kitchen. I realized almost seven hours had passed without my thinking of her and Mr. Savoi once.

As I dried myself off, she called me for supper. I knew I had to hold myself together. I couldn't let her know what had happened, and hated the thought of what she would think of me.

Mama had cooked hamburgers with salsa. We ate at the small table in the kitchen. Daddy's plate was wrapped in cellophane on the counter.

"How was everything at the shop?" she asked.

"Good," I said. "Evie and Mary Jordan stopped by wearing costumes they'd picked out for the play. They performed practically an entire scene right there in front of everyone."

"I hope you joined in," Mama said.

"No, but Ms. Pitre did."

Mama smiled. "Maybe I should have tried out."

"Why didn't you?"

"I suppose I didn't want to stand in the way of your opportunity. I wanted you to have something that was your own."

I looked at the clock. "I have to get going. I'm babysitting for the Bankses." I was half finished with my supper, but knew I couldn't eat any more.

"I saw them in town yesterday," Mama said. "They make such a nice-looking couple."

I wasn't sure if I felt jealousy or remorse. Either way, just hearing her say Mr. Banks's name made my stomach feel like it had catapulted itself to the northernmost region of Canada, or maybe Iceland.

The Bankses lived a little over a mile from my house, which on that particular night seemed like a couple of states away. I don't know how it is a person's sweat can feel like the Arctic Ocean in the sultry heat of a Louisiana summer night, but mine did.

I leaned my bike against the house and walked up to the front door. Just as I raised my hand to knock, Mr. Banks called my name from behind. I turned around as he came jogging toward me from the driveway, wearing nothing more than his running shoes and nylon shorts. Before I knew it he was standing on the steps, his hot breath on my face. He reached around me and opened the door, then followed me inside.

"Savannah and Mattie will be home in a minute," he said.

He was still breathing heavily from his run. I glanced at him just long enough to see the beads of sweat covering his bare chest.

"You look nice," he said.

I was wearing a pair of white shorts and a red T-shirt. I looked down at myself as if I'd forgotten what I'd put on.

"Thanks."

"You okay?"

"Sure," I said.

His fingers reached up and brushed lightly against my arm. "Look, this afternoon . . . I don't know what came over me. One minute I was thinking about the play, and then . . ."

"It's okay." I felt an edge to my voice and was certain he had heard it.

"You're just so damn pretty," he said.

Suddenly, all the tenseness in my body softened, melted like warm butter.

"You want something to drink?" he asked. "I think there's some iced tea in the fridge."

"No, thanks."

He wiped the sweat from his brow with his arm. "I'm going to get a shower."

After he left the room, I sat on the sofa, wondering why he was always taking a shower every time I came over.

I heard the water turn on and wished more than anything that Savannah and Mattie would walk in. And for a split second, which I'm embarrassed to admit might have been a little longer, I thought about Mr. Banks's body in that shower, thought about the way his body had made mine feel. Then the water stopped, and I knew Mr. Banks was drying himself off, which got my blood swimming even more.

When he walked back into the living room, he was dressed

in a pair of jeans and a short-sleeved plaid shirt. He sat in the chair next to the sofa, his skin smelling strongly of Irish Spring soap.

"You sure you're okay?" he asked.

"I'm okay," I said.

He combed his fingers through his wet hair, tilting his head down and leaving his hand on the crown of his head.

"If you weren't my student, Lucy, and if you were just a little older. . . ." He shook his head back and forth.

"It wouldn't matter," I said.

He looked up at me, not understanding what it was I was saying. I wasn't sure I understood what I was saying, either.

Still looking at me, he moved over to the sofa, his legs no more than three inches away from my own. I didn't know what it was I'd said that made him move over next to me. While I was trying to figure it out, he took my hand in his and kissed me on the cheek. It wasn't one of those little kisses like Papa Walter always gave me. When Mr. Banks's lips touched my skin, they lingered there for a while, sending a quiet shudder through me, and for a moment I wanted him to kiss me again as he had earlier that day, even though everything in my head and my heart knew it was wrong.

"Lucy, you're okay."

Then he squeezed my hand.

I didn't know if what he said meant, "You're okay; I want to kiss you again," or "You're okay; I'm going to leave you alone from now on." And because I didn't know exactly what it was he meant, I also had no clue what I was supposed to say or do.

Fortunately, it didn't matter a whole lot at that particular moment, because no sooner had he kissed my cheek and squeezed my hand than the door opened and in walked Savannah with Mattie in one arm and a bag of groceries in the other.

By the time they rounded the door, Mr. Banks had already let go of my hand and was just sitting there like he didn't have a care in the world. With all the goods Savannah was carrying, I don't think she noticed us at all.

It wasn't until she'd put the groceries down on the kitchen counter, and Mr. Banks had walked over and taken Mattie from her arms, that she acknowledged me.

"Why, hey, Lucy," she said, looking at me through the doorway.

"Hey, Savannah," I said.

"I picked up a frozen pizza and some popcorn for you."

I didn't feel like eating, but I didn't tell her so.

"I'm just going to freshen up, and then we'll go," she told Mr. Banks.

A few minutes later they were out the door, Savannah giving me instructions over her shoulder. I sat on the floor with Mattie, entertaining her with some of her toys. After a while I gave her a bottle, changed her, and put her to bed.

I walked quietly around the house, picking up pictures of Mr. Banks, staring intently into his face. He kissed me, I kept thinking. He held my hand. Every part of my body was alive and yet frightened at the same time. Then I picked up a picture of him and Savannah. I thought about Mattie in the next room. All of a sudden, my mind might as well have been submerged in ice water. How could I have kissed him, knowing he had a family?

As I set the picture down, someone knocked on the door. When I opened it, Mary Jordan and Evie were standing side by side on the front stoop. They had grins on their faces and looked like they were up to no good.

"Hey," I said, surprised to see them.

They stepped apart, and Billy, who'd been crouched behind them, jumped out and grabbed me in his arms. He carried me over to the sofa, tossed me on the cushions, and plopped down next to me. Mary Jordan sat in the armchair. Evie stretched out on the floor.

"How's my Hippolyte?" he said.

"Where'd you come up with that nickname?" I asked him.

"She was Queen of the Amazons," he told me.

"I don't want to be called an Amazon," I said, shoving his leg with my foot. "Amazons are big."

"Amazons were strong women who came from the god of war. And the queen of the Amazons was so beautiful that Theseus traveled to the ends of the earth to kidnap her and bring her back to Athens."

"Oh," I said.

"And I suppose you're Theseus," Evie teased.

He tossed one of the throw pillows at her and said, "What I want to know is, how is our baby bird getting along?"

He read my face. "You *have* checked on her, haven't you?"

How could I tell him I'd been preoccupied with more important matters?

He stood. "Come on."

The four of us headed out to the tree. We craned our necks to see the bough stub where the nest was.

"I don't see anything," Evie said.

Mary Jordan said, "Me, either."

Billy took a running start toward the garage, jumped, grabbed hold of the roof ledge, and hoisted himself up. He walked to the peak of the roof. It was then that the mama robin dove toward the nest, an earthworm dangling from her beak.

"I do believe I see life," Billy said.

"It's a sign," Mary Jordan said.

"What kind of sign?" Evie said.

"A sign for hope," Mary Jordan said. "And love."

Evie scowled and gave Mary Jordan one of those penetrating stares. "Is Doug doing this to you, or are you doing this all on your own?"

"Doing what?" Mary Jordan asked, her voice as light as down.

Evie shook her head and walked over to the garage. "Give me a lift, Dreamy."

Mary Jordan clasped her hands together, creating a stirrup for Evie to step into, and raised her up.

I wished I could climb up, too, but I was worried about leaving Mattie in the house alone. Instead I observed Evie and Billy sitting together on the roof, looking out over the tree and watching the mother bird feed her young.

"So you think it's a sign?" I asked Mary Jordan.

She was still staring up at the tree. "Mm-hmm." She linked her arm in mine. "'Ah, happy, happy boughs! That cannot shed, your leaves, nor ever bid the Spring adieu; And happy melodist, unwearied, forever piping songs forever new.'"

I'm fairly certain the look I gave my friend was a close re-
semblance to the one Evie had given her only moments before.

"Keats," Mary Jordan said.

"Keats," I said, slightly annoyed.

"The bird, the one who made it, who refused to be shaken
from her happy bough. She's a sign. For us. For love."

Suddenly, I felt an aching in my belly. Was Mr. Banks shaking me like he had shaken the other birds out of their nest?
Questions were shooting through my mind like arrows.

I wanted to talk to Mary Jordan about Mr. Banks. I wanted
to tell her what I had done. I started to, tried to, but the words
wouldn't come. I felt as if I had been kidnapped and taken
somewhere far away, like Germany, and all I could do was
stand there at a loss, unable to speak the language or understand the words.

The Swing Set

Before my friends left, I pulled Evie aside and told her I needed to talk with her. She said to call her when I got home, that it didn't matter how late.

I was asleep on the sofa when the Bankses returned. With Savannah there, Mr. Banks didn't try to hold my hand or say he was sorry or in any way refer to his earlier actions. In fact, he acted so normal, it was almost as if I could pretend the whole thing had never happened.

It was sometime after eleven when I climbed on my bike to ride home. About a quarter of a mile from my house, I heard Evie call my name. She rode up beside me.

"What are you doing?" I asked.

"My mom's got a guest at the house. I was going to see if I could spend the night."

"Of course you can spend the night."

We kept riding.

"Want to stop by the park?" I asked.

She didn't say anything, but instead rode up ahead of me and took a right toward St. Vincent's. I followed.

We laid our bikes in the grass. "You okay?" I asked as we walked over to the swing set.

"Nothing I'm not used to," Evie said.

We took off our shoes and situated ourselves on the swings, then swayed just the slightest bit back and forth while we dragged our toes in the sand.

"So what did you want to talk about?" Evie asked.

I wanted to tell Evie everything that had happened, but suddenly I felt like the Wall of China had erected itself over my mouth, and not a single word was going to find its way out.

One thing about Evie, which no one would have guessed without knowing her, was she had a lot of patience when it came to conversation. She just waited, swinging back and forth and drawing swivel lines in the sand with her toes.

Finally, I said, "How old do you think Mr. Banks is?"

"I don't know. Somewhere in his twenties probably. Why?"

"What if I said I liked Mr. Banks?"

"Depends on how you mean?"

"Evie?"

"Hmm?"

"Mr. Banks kissed me."

Evie stopped swinging. I stopped swinging, too. We must have sat still like that for a good whole minute. Sometimes a minute can feel like eternity.

"When did he kiss you?" Evie wanted to know.

"I stopped by the school earlier today to talk to him. I was helping him get the lights. Once it was dark, he just kissed me."

"Did you kiss him back?"

"I think so," I said.

"How did you feel?"

"Well, my South Pole felt kind of good, but my North Pole felt really bad, and the longer I think about it, the worse I feel."

Evie hooked her ankle around mine and started swinging back and forth again, gently pulling me with her.

"It's not because he's older than you," she said. "I think a teacher kissing a student would kind of be like a priest kissing some girl at confession. You know what I'm saying?" Evie said.

"I think so."

"I mean, he's good-looking and all. And maybe it'd be fun to think about kissing him. But thinking and doing are two different things. Remember those kids we were teaching vacation Bible school to last year?"

"Mm-hmm."

"Remember how cute little Peter Jeansonne was?"

I smiled. "Mm-hmm."

"Well, how do you think it would have been if one day I'd gotten him in the broom closet and gave him mouth-to-mouth resuscitation, even though he was suscitating just fine?"

Every part of me cringed. "I would have thought you were a pervert."

"Mm-hmm."

"That's not the same thing," I said.

"And why isn't it?"

"It's just not. Mr. Banks isn't a pervert. I don't even like saying that word. You've seen him."

"Lucy, you don't even know him. You can only like someone once you get to know him. You think you like him because he's the best-looking thing that ever walked into

Sweetbay, and on account of the fact that he notices you. Everyone likes to be noticed."

I knew Evie was right, but I didn't want her to be right.

"Besides," Evie went on to say. "Think how you'd feel if last night we'd walked in on Dewey's dad kissing your mom. Or think how you'd feel if you saw your dad kissing somebody else. My parents are divorced, and I still don't like it when I see my mom kissing another man."

I stopped swinging. I felt the blood in my face sink clear to my toes.

"What is it?" Evie said.

"I'm a sinner." My voice was as dead as a crawfish that's been stewed and swallowed and digested.

Evie laughed.

"Evie, it's not funny! 'It is better for you to lose one part of your body than for your whole body to go into hell.' "

"What are you talking about?"

"I'm going to hell," I said.

Evie laughed some more.

"Evie!"

"You're not going to hell."

"That's not what the Bible says. You know how Mama is always quoting scripture. You remember when Ms. Pitre's husband died and everyone found out he'd been having an affair? Mama started quoting Matthew. Said that if a person so much as looks at someone else with lust in his heart, that person might as well gouge out his own eyes. That it's better to lose your eyes than burn in hell for eternity."

Evie's face got all serious, and I thought for sure she was

taking heed to my words, until she said, "Don't you know if those words were true there wouldn't be a person around with any proper hormones that had their two eyes left."

"You're saying that isn't in Matthew?"

"I'm not saying it isn't in Matthew. I just think some people go interpreting things any ole way they want to interpret them, that's all. Seems to me it suited your mom just fine to go quoting that scripture against Ms. Pitre's husband. But I can't help but wonder what scripture she got to quoting last night before she started in on those cooking lessons."

"I don't know that I like this conversation anymore," I said. "Of course, I don't know that I like my mom hanging around Mr. Savoi's house, either. And I sure don't like her taking her clothes off for him. The only two people my mama should go taking her clothes off for are my daddy and Doc Fredericks, and Lord knows I'm not going to worry about her and Doc Fredericks."

"You know, my mom says Doc Fredericks was quite the specimen in his time."

"I'm not talking about Doc Fredericks," I said.

"I know you're not talking about Doc Fredericks," Evie said.

"I'm talking about my mom," I said.

"Well, whoever you're talking about, I don't think either you or your mama are going to hell," Evie said.

The air poured forth from my mouth in a giant gust. "What should I do?"

Somewhere in our discourse, Evie had stopped swinging. So had I.

"You're going to act like nothing ever happened," Evie told

me. "And just to be sure your South Pole doesn't go getting it-self confused again, you're going to abstain from any more private encounters."

"Should I speak to him?" I asked.

"You can go speaking to him. But try and be like one of those Orange Dream Bars that's been sitting in the freezer too long. Gets that freezer burn all over it."

I started laughing and gave Evie a push to the side. Her swing slid directly back into me, bumping my hip. Then the two of us locked an arm around each other's swings and began gliding back and forth.

"What do you bet Mary Jordan's up to right now?" I said.

"I bet she doesn't have any more Tabasco sauce on her lips."

I laughed. Evie did, too.

Maple Syrup

Life seemed a little better after talking with Evie, but early the next morning, all my bad feelings returned. From the looks of the light filtering through the window, I guessed it to be around six. Evie was lying next to me.

"Are you awake?" I asked, Mr. Banks's kiss completely fresh on my mind.

She didn't answer.

I knew I wasn't going to hell for what had happened. Instead, what I felt was an understanding that I would never be the same. I felt the guilt of growing up.

I crawled out of bed and dressed, then closed the door behind me and walked downstairs, the house quiet, letting me know Mama and Daddy were still in bed. In the kitchen, I made coffee, poured myself a cup, adding cream and a little sugar. I carried the mug outside with me to the front stoop. The sky was already a clear blue. It would be a nice day for the wedding. Anita and Clyde had invited the whole town. Surely Mr. Banks wouldn't be there. Then I remembered the tryouts for the play and wondered if he had posted the results.

I finished my coffee, left the mug on the stoop, and rode my bike into town.

Daddy's shop wouldn't be open for a couple more hours. I stopped in front of the glass door, but didn't see the results. I was supposed to work that day, and hoped I wouldn't run into Mr. Banks. I wasn't just thinking about him kissing me at the school. I was also trying to understand what had happened the night before. He had held my hand. He had kissed my cheek. Had I said or done something to make him do that? I turned my bike around and headed home.

Evie was up when I got back to the house.

"You feeling better?" she asked.

"Not really," I told her.

"Try not to think about it," she said.

After breakfast, we rode into town. Ethel Lee had opened the shop early, and people were already gathered inside, no doubt waiting to see whom Mr. Banks had cast for the play. By ten-thirty, the place was packed, and the results still weren't up. Daddy sent me down to the Piggly Wiggly to buy more coffee. Shortly after I returned, Tante Pearl arrived.

"What are you doing here?" I asked.

"Is that any way to talk to your favorite aunt?"

"Tante Pearl, the last time I saw you in here was at the Christmas parade when it got rained out and you didn't want to get rained out, too."

"Maybe I wanted to find out how my favorite niece did in the tryouts." She strolled herself to the back of the shop and poured herself a cup of coffee. Then she walked back up to me and said, "Did you know the Queen of Sheba and King Solomon were soul mates?"

For the life of me I couldn't understand where this popular fixation on the Queen of Sheba had come from lately.

"Mm-hmm, they sure were," she said.

"Since when did you start reading the Bible so much? Next thing I know you'll be turning into Mama."

Tante Pearl went right on with her reverie. "King Solomon gave the Queen of Sheba all she desired and asked for, besides what he had given her out of his royal bounty. Isn't that just beautiful?"

"Tante Pearl, what are you talking about?"

Tante Pearl looked at me as if she had just noticed I existed, even though I'd been standing right in front of her the whole time.

"It's called *love*," she said, and the way she rolled that word off her tongue, I thought for sure she'd died and been reincarnated into someone as sappy as maple syrup.

Ms. Pitre ambled her way over to us. "What do you think is taking him so long?"

But I didn't get a chance to answer, and neither did anyone else, because just then Miss Balfa flung the door open like a train going a thousand miles an hour. "He's coming!"

I thought I'd die right there on the spot. Mr. Banks came strolling up to the window with a piece of paper held in his hand. Everything inside the shop got so quiet, a person could have heard a piece of dust drop. He pulled out a roll of tape from his back pocket, tore off four pieces, and taped each corner of the paper to the shop's front door. I swear not a one of us moved or blinked.

Mr. Banks never even looked our way, never once noticed that I was there. He finished taping up the results, turned around, and jogged off. He was wearing running shorts and his Adidas running shoes and one of those mesh tank tops, with big gaping holes revealing the muscles on his chest. I knew right there, he had the most beautiful body I'd ever seen. For just a moment I got to reasoning that maybe it wasn't such a bad thing kissing him after all, since officially he wouldn't be my teacher for another two months. But then I remembered Savannah and Mattie, and all that guilt that had sunk into my skin throughout the night took on a startling thickness, making it difficult for me to breathe.

Everyone remained as still and quiet as could be. But once Mr. Banks disappeared around the corner of First National Bank of New Orleans, I thought for sure someone was going to get trampled to death as folks squeezed through the doorway to glimpse the names on that piece of paper.

Ethel Lee was the first one to see the list, and as soon as she saw it, she let out a squeal. "Lucy, you did it! You got the lead!"

I was sandwiched between Tante Pearl's rear end and Ms. Pitre's bosom. Ethel Lee stretched her arm out over Tante Pearl and patted me on the head. Daddy hooted and waved at me from the back of the shop. I thought Evie should have gotten the lead. Maybe if she had been the one kissing Mr. Banks, things would have turned out differently.

I didn't care if I saw the list or not. I inched my body away from everyone and made my way to the back of the store. Just as the back door was in reach, Daddy grabbed me up in his arms and swung me off the ground, which with my height isn't an easy thing to do.

"Way to go, Lucy!" he cheered, as proud as could be. I knew he wouldn't have been so proud of me if he had been in the auditorium the afternoon before, which made me want to get out of the shop even more.

My bike was parked in the alley. I rode around town for at least a half hour, not knowing exactly where to go, and somehow thinking that the more I sweated, the better I'd feel, as if I'd cleanse all the guilt out of my body. But sweating wasn't working, so I finally rode up to St. Marc's Catholic Church, perspiration dripping off of me like a downpour. Luckily, there wasn't a soul around.

I couldn't remember ever having walked into the church when it was empty. It felt entirely different than it did on a Sunday morning. The big wooden doors creaked behind me as they shut me in, and the air smelled musty.

I walked up the red velvet carpet to a pew toward the front and knelt on the predieu. No sooner had I genuflected and begun to ask the Lord's forgiveness than the organ started playing "Avé Maria." I froze and just listened. Mama once said listening was the best kind of praying anyway. Of course, I can't say she practiced her theory a whole lot. Seemed to me she always had a lot to tell the Lord.

I hadn't inherited Mama's musical talent, but I knew beautiful music when I heard it, the kind that burns somewhere deep inside you, making you aware of yourself in an entirely new way, as if each note is God himself tiptoeing across your heart.

As the music rang through the church, I got to thinking of all those paintings I'd seen in Mr. Savoi's gallery, and the same kind of yearning I'd felt that day started up slow inside me, then began to surge through my body like an electrical current. I closed my eyes and let my body sway slightly from side to side, as if I were in some sort of trance. I hardly even noticed when the music stopped. Didn't even hear Dewey when he walked up to my pew. It wasn't until he knelt beside me that I was aware of anyone else's presence at all.

It was the sleeve of his shirt brushing lightly against my arm that broke my reverie. I think I must have startled a good four inches away from him.

He laughed just a little. "Sorry," he said.

"What are you doing here?" I asked.

"I was just going over the songs for this afternoon."

"You're playing at Clyde and Anita's wedding?"

"Yeah. Your mom set it up. The regular organist couldn't make it." Then he smiled that bashful smile of his, the kind where he kept his lips together and tucked his chin down.

"You okay?" he asked me.

"Sure," I said. "Don't I look okay?"

"You look beautiful."

I heard myself swallow. I didn't feel beautiful. The more I thought about kissing Mr. Banks, the more *un*beautiful I felt.

Dewey laid his hand over mine. At first I wanted to pull away, as if the weight of his hand was trapping me, but the longer he held it there, the more that panic floated away.

"You coming this afternoon?" he asked.

I wasn't sure what he was talking about.

"To the wedding," he said.

I'd already forgotten. "I'll be there."

He stood to leave.

"Dewey?"

"Yeah?"

"Thanks." I didn't know how he had done it, but he had made me feel better.

Dewey looked puzzled for a moment. Neither of us said anything. We just looked at each other, and as that long moment slipped by, an ocean of understanding seemed to pass between us, only I had no earthly idea how it had happened.

The Wedding March

A Catholic wedding is no brief affair. A woman can shave her legs before the wedding starts, and by the time it's over, she may need to shave them again.

I rode to the church with Mama and Daddy. St. Marc's is only a few blocks from our house, but in the summer, *no one* walks to church in Sweetbay. It's one thing to sweat in a pair of shorts and a tank top. It's another thing to sweat when you're dressed to your finest. The three of us sat about halfway down on the left. Technically, there wasn't a bride and groom side. Everyone just sat where they wanted. The staff from the Walbridge Wing served as the ushers. They'd brought over a busload of residents from the facility. A covey of wheelchairs was lined up at the back of the church. From the looks of it, nearly half of Sweetbay's population was crammed inside the sanctuary. I had no idea that watching a couple of old people getting married would draw such a crowd, but it did.

Mama leaned toward my ear. "Isn't this just something?" She was sitting along the aisle. I was sitting next to her. Daddy was on my other side.

I said, "Mm-hmm."

She opened her purse and pulled out a couple of tissues. Mama always cries at weddings.

"You need one?" she said.

I said, "No, thanks."

She lowered her head and gave me one of those under-the-eyebrow looks. "Every lady should have a tissue at a time like this."

Mama also believed there were certain ways a lady should use a tissue. From the time I was little, I was thoughtfully instructed on the virtue of dabbing, not blowing, one's nose. "A lady never blows her nose in public," Mama would tell me. "She dabs it, like this." Mama would then proceed to demonstrate. "And, should her eyes begin to tear, she wipes them gently, moving toward her nose, to prevent premature aging. You never want to stretch the skin underneath your eyes," Mama would advise. "It's delicate."

"I don't need a tissue," I told her.

She placed one in my lap anyway. "You never know."

The organ began playing "Whither Thou Goest." Try as I might, I couldn't see Dewey, on account of the whole Neuville family of five sitting in front of us. The Neuvilles have big heads.

Mama recognized my dilemma. "Makes every child-bearing woman south of the Mason-Dixon pity that woman," she said real quiet in my ear.

I concentrated on Dewey's playing, and as I did, every square centimeter of me began to relax. Mama let out one of her long, dramatic sighs. When I looked at her, she was holding a hand to that flat area just above her breasts, and kept it there for the duration of the song. Daddy was adjusting his tie. He didn't like to wear ties, but decided it was in his best interest to oblige Mama every once in a while.

Next, Dewey began playing "The Wedding March." Everybody stood and strained their necks toward the back door, where Mrs. Forez stood arm in arm with her grandson, Johnny. Mrs. Forez's dress looked like a cream-colored nightgown. A wreath of baby's breath was woven into her white hair. I thought she looked like an angel.

Mama held her tissue to her face and dabbed her eyes. My tissue was already wadded up in my hand and had turned to sticky lint.

I knew Father Ivan and Clyde were standing at the front of the church, but because of the Neuvilles' heads, I couldn't see them. After Johnny and Mrs. Forez walked past us, I couldn't see them anymore, either. Mama had an aisle seat, so all she had to do was lean out over the edge of the pew to get a better view, which she did.

I didn't know why an old couple would want to have a Catholic wedding. Seemed to me their legs would give out from all that standing, and I hoped Father Ivan would talk fast or else cut out part of the service.

"Oh, good," Mama said.

I said, "What?"

"Someone brought them chairs."

Daddy started to laugh. After a time, Mama started to laugh, too.

"What?" I said.

"Mrs. Forez is asleep," Mama said.

Before Holy Communion, Mary Jordan's grandfather, Pappy Jacques, was wheeled to the front. He stood and nodded to Dewey, who began to play "Grow Old Along with Me." Pappy Jacques sang his heart out.

Mama told me Mrs. Forez wasn't asleep anymore. "Oh, Lucy, she's crying," Mama said. By now my mama was crying, too.

It was then that Daddy reached his arm over my lap and took Mama's hand. I looked at his face. He wasn't adjusting his tie anymore. He was listening to Pappy Jacques sing. I looked at Mama. She was still crying, and I couldn't help but wonder if her tears were solely for the wedding or had something to do with her and Daddy, as well.

Shortly after the song finished, we took our place in line for Communion, stepping out right behind Doug and Mary Jordan, who had just entered the aisle from the right side of the church, though neither of them saw us. Doug's hand traveled around Mary Jordan's waist and dropped itself onto her behind. Mama had her eyes so fixed on Doug's hand, I felt sure she was going to burn a hole clear through his palm. She waited just long enough to see if Mary Jordan was going to do anything about it. Mary Jordan didn't. Mama then took it upon herself to correct the situation. She reached out, took Doug's hand in hers, and moved it up a good four inches so that it was across the middle of Mary Jordan's back. That got Doug's attention. He turned around. Mary Jordan turned around, too.

"Why, hey," Mary Jordan said.

I said "hey" back.

Mama didn't say anything.

Returning to our seats, I looked around the church for Evie. I didn't see her. Instead my eyes caught Mr. Banks sitting in the last row. He was staring right at me with those big brown eyes of his sending a nervous jitter clear down to my toes. I turned around and sat in the pew, all the while feeling his eyes watching me, and all the while thinking they shouldn't be.

A Different Symphony

After the wedding, Daddy drove us to the reception at the Mason Lodge, a three-story antebellum in the center of town. As soon as I opened the car door, I heard Gussie Guthrie and the Troubadours playing *"C'est Si Bon."* "C'est Si Bon" means "it's so good," and Gussie played it so good, too. I stepped across the front porch, filling my lungs with all that warm summer air and Bessie Faye's gumbo d'herbes and garlic. Bessie Faye was catering the whole affair, compliments of different businesses in town.

Mama said her how-d'ya-dos to a half dozen people. Then she and I stopped by the restroom, where I found Zina Thibodeaux, Evie's mom.

"Was Evie sitting with you at the wedding?" I asked.

"No, honey. Evie left the house early this morning."

"Where did she leave the house to?" I wanted to know.

"I was in the shower."

Getting answers out of Ms. Thibodeaux was like trying to pull a fly out of an ice cube. Evie accounted it to the fact that when her dad left home, part of her mama's good sense left with him.

Mama picked up her purse off the edge of the sink. It had been sitting in a puddle of water, and dripped a stream down the front side of her peach satin chiffon. Mama was fit to be tied.

"I just hate untidy women," she said.

"Mm-hmm. Such inconsideration," Ms. Thibodeaux said.

I took some toilet paper and tried to dab Mama's dress dry, but all that did was leave little pieces of white lint all over her bodice, so she shooed me away.

The bathroom didn't have paper towels. It had hot air dispensers. Mama situated herself underneath one of those dispensers, arching her back. While she was doing the hot air limbo, I decided I'd try to find Evie.

Past the parlor downstairs was the ballroom, encircled with tables draped in white linen. I'd helped Daddy with the decorations earlier that afternoon. We'd woven pink cellophane with white lights and ivy around the ceiling beams. In the center of each table were floating magnolia blossoms and heart-shaped votives. Gussie and the Troubadours were on a platform in front of the dance floor. Gussie has skin as black as a coffee bean, and long wild hair. She was wearing a tightly fitted dress with black-and-gold fabric that wrapped around her like a turban. Thick strands of colored beads hung clear down to her waist. Gussie was entertainment no matter what she wore. Mama had once said Gussie's face could have a hundred years of gravity on it, and it'd still be smiling.

I looked all over for Evie but couldn't find her. I couldn't find Doug or Mary Jordan, either. Then I felt a finger run lightly up my spine, sending a spray of shivers down my arms. As I turned around, I came face to face with Mr. Banks.

"You look stunning," he said.

I'd never had anyone tell me I looked stunning before.

"Where's Mattie?" I asked, because I didn't know what else to say, because I wasn't sure if saying "thank you" would imply more than I'd wanted to imply.

"Savannah's parents are in town," he said. "They're watching her."

I said, "Oh."

"They're down for the weekend."

I didn't say anything.

"They live in Jackson."

I said, "Oh."

"Mississippi."

I said, "Mm-hmm."

Someone whistled, and cheers went up around us. Clyde was leading his new bride onto the dance floor. Gussie tapped her foot on the wooden platform, snapped her fingers, and within seconds she and the Troubadours began playing Frank Sinatra's "You Make Me Feel So Young." Clyde held one of Anita's hands in his palm, his face one big, beaming grin. He pressed his cheek against hers as he slowly whirled her across the floor. I knew that very moment, I would remember the two of them dancing like they were for the rest of my life.

Other people began joining the newlyweds on the dance floor. Someone took my hand. At first I flinched, thinking it was Mr. Banks, but he'd gone over to the bar.

"May I have this dance?"

I looked at Dewey. He looked at me. He seemed different, older, handsome in a gentle kind of way. He was wearing a pair of khakis and a shirt the color of cobalt blue, opened at the neck, revealing just a glimpse of his tan chest. His shoulders looked broader, his height taller. It was like seeing him for the first time. No sooner did he have me out on the dance floor than he took my hand in his like he'd been dancing all his life. He pressed his other hand around the small of my back. No one had ever held me like that before.

I pressed my arm tentatively around Dewey's shoulders while he moved us across the dance floor. My feet felt like they were skating on ice, even though I'd never been ice-skating before.

Looking over Dewey's shoulder, I couldn't help but smile at all the smiling people around me. Then I saw Daddy. He wasn't dancing with Mama. He was dancing with Ima Jean Balfa. I could have sworn her face looked ten years younger. Every soul in that room looked younger. Mama says love will do that to you. Just getting a glimpse of it will take years off your face.

"Sing it again!" someone shouted as the song wrapped up, and sure enough Gussie and the Troubadours swung all their energy into another round, jazzing up that song with so much gusto, I could have sworn my heart was doing somersaults.

Daddy approached us, looking about as debonair as I'd ever seen him, and tapped Dewey on the shoulder. As Dewey stepped aside, Daddy took me in his arms.

"Lucy Marie, you're a knockout."

"You're not so bad yourself," I said, grinning from here to kingdom come.

I loved my daddy. I loved the whole wide world at that moment.

Someone bumped me from behind. It was Ernie from Steppin' Out Shoes, dancing with Evie's mom.

"Sorry, lovely lady," Ernie said, laughing with all the giddiness of the day.

"Where's your mother?" Daddy asked me.

I began searching the room. Then I saw Evie dancing with Billy. But they weren't dancing like everyone else. Billy had his arms wrapped completely around Evie's waist. Her whole body was curved against his. I was so surprised I barely moved.

"Hey, Lucy," Daddy said. "You okay?"

"Sorry," I said, picking up my steps a little, though still watching Evie. She and Billy shifted their weight from side to side, their feet never leaving the floor. Her face was pressed against his shirt and her eyes were closed. Billy's eyes were closed, too. It didn't matter how much gusto Gussie and the Troubadours invested in Mr. Sinatra's song; Evie and Billy kept right on swaying in their own little world. They weren't just dancing a separate descant—they were writing their very own symphony.

As the song ended, I saw Mama. Sure enough, Daddy saw her, too. She and Mr. Savoi were sitting at one of the tables, each of them sipping a glass of wine, their heads entirely too close together. I thought Daddy was going to ask her to dance. Maybe he was, but he never got the chance. As soon as he started to walk toward her, Mr. Savoi helped Mama out of her chair, and the two of them left the room. Daddy stopped mid-stride and watched them go. I wanted to tell him to go after her, but I didn't. I just stood there and watched him watching her, all the youth and liveliness I'd seen in his face only moments before vanishing like the moon when a storm blows in.

Bare Necessities

———

Gussie and the Troubadours started in on "Hellzapoppin'." Ethel Lee grabbed Daddy by the arm and pulled him onto the dance floor. He didn't look in the right frame of mind to dance. He looked more preoccupied with where Mama had gone. As I stood on the side of the dance floor watching them, Mr. Banks walked up to me with a drink in his hand.

"Do you want anything?" he asked.

"What do you mean?" I asked.

"Do you want me to buy you a drink?"

"You can't buy me a drink," I said.

"I can't?"

I didn't know what he was saying. Of course he couldn't buy me a drink.

"Vodka doesn't look any different than Sprite. Jim Beam doesn't look any different than cream soda." He took a sip from the plastic cup he was holding. "How old are you, anyway?"

"Seventeen," I said.

"Practically an adult," he said.

I liked someone thinking of me as an adult; I just wasn't sure I liked Mr. Banks's thinking of me as an adult.

"We could go for a walk," he said. "Get out of here."

I didn't know where it was we could go for a walk. It was still daylight outside. People would see. But then maybe he just wanted to go for a walk. Maybe it would look perfectly normal for a teacher and a student to go for a walk. I didn't know what to think anymore. I wanted him to speak clear English to me.

"I'd like a Sprite," I said.

He smiled with this tiny bit of glistening in his eyes. Then he finished his drink, turned around, and headed back to the bar.

Maybe I should have walked away, disappeared into a crowd of people, found Dewey and danced again, but I didn't. I stood there and waited for my Sprite.

Mr. Banks approached me and handed me the plastic cup. I'd never tasted vodka before, but the moment it hit my tongue, I knew that's what it was. And then I realized the mistake I'd made. He'd thought I was insinuating that I wanted alcohol, when actually I meant exactly what I'd said, that I wanted a Sprite. I stood there not knowing what to do, so I drank a little more.

"You finish that one, I can get you another," he said.

"I don't want another one," I said.

"You sure?"

"I'm sure."

All the while I sipped from the cup, he just kept standing there beside me. I didn't much care for the way the vodka tasted, but I liked the way my body was beginning to feel. All my bones and muscles seemed to experience a new sort of gravity, and I got to thinking maybe I could let Mr. Banks buy me one more drink. But I also got to thinking something was out of sorts. I'd never known an adult I couldn't trust before. The ground beneath me was feeling like entirely new territory the past couple of days, making me plenty uneasy.

I swallowed the last of the vodka, the ice cool as it fell against my lips. When I lowered the cup, Mr. Banks reached for it, walked away, and I knew he had gone to buy me another.

I looked for Daddy and Ethel Lee, but couldn't find them among the crowd. I looked for Evie and Billy, but couldn't find them, either, and I had no idea where Mary Jordan and Doug had taken off to. Then I got to thinking about my mom and Mr. Savoi. And the more I got to thinking about all the people whom I couldn't find, the more frightened and alone I felt. I didn't want my mom with Mr. Savoi. I didn't want to be away from my friends, and I didn't want to spend any more time with Mr. Banks.

I spotted him standing by the bar. I didn't want another vodka. I didn't want him running his hand up my spine or taking me for a walk or kissing me in the dark. All I could think about was getting away from everything that felt wrong, and that's exactly what I did. I eased my way through the crowd of people and walked to the back of the ballroom, where a door opened out into a courtyard. For a moment I thought maybe my mom and Mr. Savoi would be there, but they weren't.

The courtyard was shaded by magnolia trees and encircled by a white privacy fence. At the back of the fence was a gate. I unlatched the gate and turned down the alley, the sun feeling as hot as a frying pan sitting on top of my head.

The alley wound itself around the backside of Market Street, aligning itself with the delivery doors of the different shops and businesses in town. The door to Bessie Faye's Creole in the Mornin' Diner was wide open. Just walking past there, I could feel the air around me warm up a good twenty degrees from all her cooking. I'd been flat out starving by the time the wedding was over. Now I felt like my stomach had twisted itself into a tiny knot, squeezing out every bit of the appetite I'd had. I didn't know how anyone could smell Bessie Faye's talent incarnate and not be hungry.

It didn't take me long to come upon the back of Mr. Savoi's art gallery. For a second, I thought I'd just keep walking myself straight home. But then I thought about Mr. Savoi's painting my mama butt naked. I thought about the painting being displayed for the whole world of Sweetbay to see. Before I knew it, I had my fingers wrapped around the metal handset, and pushed my thumb down on its latch. I thought the door would be locked. It wasn't.

I slipped my feet out of my shoes so as not to make too much noise, pushed the door open, and stepped barefoot over the threshold. I was standing in a storage room that was mostly empty except for a couple of canvas crates. There was a hallway at the other end of the room.

I thought I heard something, though I wasn't exactly sure what. I moved toward the hallway—a narrow space about five feet long. At the end of it was another door. The sound came again, reminding me of someone with a bad cold trying to breathe. As I got closer to the door, I thought I heard *two* people with a bad cold.

I probably should have left right then and there, but instead, I just kept inching my way down the short hallway.

The noise in the other room grew louder. It didn't sound like a couple of bad colds anymore; it sounded like downright pneumonia. With the tips of my fingers, I nudged the door open enough for me to look in. In the far right corner of the room, on a couple of blue packing blankets, was the barest bottom I'd ever seen. I don't know why it looked any barer than my mama's had a couple of days before, but it did. From the angle of my view, I couldn't be sure whom it belonged to, much less be sure of the other person lying beneath it, but the fear that the other person might be my mama gave me such a shock, my breath seized up in my chest like a ball of wax.

I wheeled myself around as fast as I could and ran like there was no tomorrow. I slammed the back door behind me and kept on running till I was at the road, only then realizing I'd left my navy heels outside the gallery in the alley. I wasn't about to go back for them. As far as I was concerned, the world had become one big messed-up place, and I had no idea how to put it back together. I missed Evie. I missed Mary Jordan. I missed seeing my mama and daddy do more together than just occupy the house. And I missed how I'd felt before Mr. Banks had walked into my life, when right seemed right and wrong seemed wrong and there weren't so many feelings caught in between.

I was walking down the sidewalk toward home, thinking all these thoughts, when I heard Dewey hollering my name.

As I turned around, he came riding up beside me on his bike.

"I've been looking all over for you," he said. "Where'd you go?"

"Nowhere," I said.

He just smiled that grin of his that I was starting to like real well. "What's wrong?" he asked.

"Nothing's wrong," I said.

I was still walking. He was riding slowly beside me.

"Want to hop on?" he asked.

"My legs are too long."

"Your legs are perfect," he said.

I smiled despite myself.

"Hop on," he said.

I did.

Florence Nightingale

"Where to, Florence Nightingale?" Dewey asked as he pedaled us down the street.

"I thought I was the Queen of Sheba," I said, balancing myself on the seat.

"You're Florence Nightingale tonight."

"And may I ask why?" I said as Dewey pedaled us right past my house.

"I'll tell you later."

I was glad I was with Dewey, and yet I wanted to be angry at him, too, as if he were to blame for the attention between his dad and my mom.

"So where are you taking me?" I asked.

"Where do you want to go?"

"How long do you think you can ride like this?"

"Didn't I tell you I'm a triathlete? I can ride this way as long as you want," he said.

"You're not a triathlete," I said.

"It's that obvious, huh?"

Once again Dewey made me laugh, no matter how hard I tried not to. "This is pretty pathetic," I said.

"What's pathetic?"

"Us. Two seniors on a bicycle. I feel like we're a couple of little kids."

"Pathetic, or romantic?" he said. "I choose romantic."

We were almost out of town, riding beside moss-draped oaks and azalea bushes as lush as velvet. The heat from the day was relinquishing its punishing fist, the air becoming softer. I hadn't forgotten about what I saw at the gallery. I hadn't let go of my fear that the couple might be my mom and Mr. Savoi, yet I kept telling myself over and over it wasn't them. Mr. Savoi had gray hair that hung down to his collar. I didn't remember the person I saw as having gray hair.

Dewey took a right onto the county road that led south of town. I continued to hold my legs out to the sides, my short navy skirt riding clear up to the seat, the salt air touching my face and tossing my hair behind me. The world still weighed heavily on my shoulders, yet riding as I was with Dewey made my shoulders feel a little stronger.

"Nice night for the beach, don't you think?" Dewey said.

"You can't ride all the way out there like this. It's a good seven miles at least."

"Who says I can't ride like this?"

"I say," I told him.

"Well, that just goes to show you that you don't know me very well." His voice was lighthearted.

"Well maybe *I* can't ride that far like this."

"And why's that?" Dewey asked.

"Suppose a car goes whipping by us entirely too close. It might just take off my left leg."

"I'll make sure that doesn't happen," he said.

"How can you make sure?" I said.

"Don't you trust me?"

I closed my mouth for a good solid minute, contemplating his question. He didn't give me time to answer.

"Trust me," he said.

And I knew Dewey meant a whole lot more than not letting me get dismembered by an automobile. Those two little words of his dug down deep inside of me, as if wrapping a strong arm around all my troubles.

Neither one of us said another word until after we reached the parking area for Skinny Neck Beach. Dewey planted his feet on the ground while I climbed off. He laid the bike in the grass.

I took off running for the levee. He followed after me, both of us gasping for air before we were even halfway to the top.

"Told ya you weren't a triathlete," I said, the two of us laughing.

At the top, Dewey took my hand, making me stop. "Hold up," he said, catching his breath.

We stood together, looking out over the ocean. The sky was a perfect blue, as if God had ground chalk the color of cornflower and blown it evenly before us.

We didn't run down the hill. We walked slowly, still holding hands, my bare feet sinking into the sandy earth.

Down the right stretch of the beach were a couple of people walking away from us. Other than that, we had the whole place to ourselves. Dewey let go of my hand and knelt to untie his shoes. After he took off his shoes and socks, we sat beside each other, planting our hands behind us in the sand.

"So how come you called me Florence Nightingale?" I asked him.

"You know who Florence Nightingale was?"

"Sure. She was a nurse."

"She wasn't just a nurse," he said. "She was the pioneer of nursing."

"So why'd you call me that?"

"Seems to me you've had a lot of people to look after these days."

"What do you mean?"

"I just think you have a lot of people you care about," he told me.

"Everybody has a lot of people they care about," I said.

"I don't know. Maybe not everybody. Maybe not everyone cares as much as other people."

"What other people?" I said.

"Oh, let's see. She's about five ten with long black hair and big black eyes."

For some reason unbeknown to me, my throat tightened itself up into one big knot.

Dewey leaned forward, resting his arms on his knees. "Remember what I said back on the bike? Trust me."

I didn't say anything.

"Talk to me, Lucy."

I pulled my knees up slightly, wrapped my fingers around my toes. "Who says I have anything to talk about?"

"Didn't expect you to leave the reception so soon."

I shrugged my shoulders.

"Didn't expect to find your shoes outside my dad's gallery, either," he said.

With those words, my heart seemed to fling itself against my rib cage like a shot put. "You found my shoes?" I said.

"I saw them outside the door when I was looking for you."

"What did you do with them?" I asked.

"Didn't do anything with them. Thought maybe you'd come back for them."

"Did you go inside?" I was staring straight out over the ocean, afraid to meet Dewey's eyes.

"No, why?"

I continued to stare straight ahead. Before I could blink, my throat tightened itself up again, so much so that before I knew it, big tears squeezed out of my eyes. I tried to wipe them away, but as I raised my fingers, Dewey clasped them in his hand, letting my tears roll off my cheeks.

"I don't know why I'm crying," I told him.

He didn't say anything. He just kept holding my hand.

"I just don't understand what's happening to everyone," I said.

"Who?" Dewey asked.

"All of us. Evie, Mary Jordan. Mama and Daddy."

"What's happening to everyone?" he said.

"I feel like something's pulling us apart. Mary Jordan's with Doug, and Evie and . . ."

"And what?"

How could I tell Dewey about everything that was bothering me? How could I tell him I worried his daddy and my mama were having an affair? Or that part of me had liked Mr. Banks's kissing me? How could I tell him about my mom and dad when I didn't even understand what was going on between them? Or about Mary Jordan spending all her time with Doug? Or about Evie dancing with Billy, and that I wanted to be dancing like that, too? How could I tell him that life and everyone I loved suddenly felt all disjointed at the seams.

All of a sudden, I realized Dewey wasn't just holding my hand. His thumb was rubbing back and forth ever so gently over my knuckles. I'd been so busy thinking about everything, for the life of me I couldn't remember when he'd started doing that, but once my brain acknowledged it, I couldn't even remember exactly what it was I'd been thinking about.

"You still have everybody," Dewey said. "Just because people find someone they care about doesn't mean you've lost them. It just means your circle's gotten bigger."

"It's not the same," I said.

"What about you?" he said.

"What about me, what?"

"What if you find somebody you care about?"

I sat silent for a moment, letting Dewey rub my hand the way he was. "It's not the growing up part I mind," I said. "It's just that I want us to all grow up together."

"You are growing up together."

"Maybe," I said.

"Anyone who's been around the three of you would say the

same thing. I bet you can't go twenty-four hours away from each other without having withdrawal symptoms."

I smiled. "You're right."

We squeezed each other's hands.

"Hey, Dewey?"

"Hmm?"

"Thanks."

And then he did something I will never forget. He lifted my hand to his mouth, held it there for a moment, his breath warm against my skin, and kissed my fingers. At that moment, I felt so much, I hurt, and I wanted to tell it all to Dewey like a story. I wanted him to understand it and explain it back to me, but there weren't any words, there was just all this feeling.

"Do you understand me?" I finally said. I wasn't even sure where those words had come from.

He didn't answer right away. I felt my heart start to pull back from him, as if I had stepped somewhere I shouldn't go.

Then Dewey said, "I understand a part of you, but not all of you. I want to understand you better. I'm still coming toward you."

I pressed my body closer to his, leaned my weight against him. "That's good," I said, but it was better than good. Dewey's words made me feel different inside, as if I was becoming something wonderful, and I wasn't even sure how it was happening. I laid my face against his shoulder, breathed him in, the smell of his shirt, the ocean air. The sun was setting, and I was certain I could even smell the colors seeping into the sky around us, the muted gold of a mango, a sliver of tangerine and violet. I felt free. Free of my troubles, free of words. I let go of Dewey's hand, slipped both arms around his waist and locked my fingers together, because at that moment, I just wanted to hold on to everything good.

Warm Honey

The next morning after I showered, I rode my bike to St. Vincent's Park, wanting to sort my way through the previous day. Cirrus clouds stretched overhead and seemed to darken by the minute. I hoped it would rain. I loved the smell of rain on hot asphalt. I loved the way the rain made the grass smell, too, and the way it curled up my straight hair.

I was wearing my basketball shoes without any socks, and my bib overall shorts, and one of Billy's old T-shirts from a baseball clinic he'd attended in junior high. My hair hung down my back. I rode up to the park and laid my bike in the grass, then walked over to the swing set. I sat on one of the rubber swings and pushed myself slightly back and forth, creating rivulets in the dirt with the heels of my shoes.

"Hey, there."

I hadn't seen a soul when I rode up to the park, but I'd know Mary Jordan's voice anywhere. When I turned around, I saw her sitting on one of the corners of the sandbox at the bottom of the fort, a two-story gym set the Lions Club had donated to the park the year before.

"What are you doing?" I said.

"Just sitting."

"Want to come sit over here?"

Mary Jordan crawled out from underneath the fort. She brushed the sand from her legs and walked over to the swing next to me.

"How's Doug?" I asked.

"Good."

I kept swinging back and forth, dragging my shoes along the ground. Mary Jordan started swinging back and forth, too. She held her legs straight out in front of her.

"Hey, Lucy?"

"Hmm?"

"Do you ever wonder about love?"

"What do you mean?"

"It's such a big thing. I mean, how do you know if somebody loves you?"

"I can't say I'm the best person to be asking. It's not like I'm real seasoned on the matter."

Mary Jordan laughed. Not one of those deep, hearty laughs she was capable of, but rather one of those faraway kind of laughs that doesn't last very long, and when you get right down to it, you're not really sure if it was a laugh or a sigh.

The wind whipped my hair across my face, and the air felt damp.

"I'd like it to rain," Mary Jordan said.

"Me, too."

"It's been so hot."

"Mm-hmm."

"You didn't answer my question," Mary Jordan said.

"I know."

The swings whined. The wind blew some more, tossing Mary Jordan's curls in front of her face.

"'Head up, chin out, hair blowing in the wind,'" I said, quoting our favorite line from the movie *The African Queen*.

"Humphrey Bogart. He was the best," Mary Jordan said.

"I wonder what he was like out of the movies," I said.

"I think he loved Katharine Hepburn."

"Who wouldn't love Katharine Hepburn?" I said. Mary Jordan and Evie and I had watched old movies for as long as I could remember, *The African Queen* having been our favorite.

We swung some more.

"Do you love Doug?" I asked.

"I think so."

"You're not sure?"

"How does a person know?"

That's when Evie rode up, squeezing hard on her brakes and skidding her bike in the sand. "Nice to be included!" she said. "I already rode to both your houses. No one knew where you were."

She sat in the swing on the other side of me, her overalls rolled up to just below her knees. Her hair was pulled through an LSU cap. I knew it was Billy's.

"What are you two looking so serious for?" she said.

"We're having ourselves a philosophical discussion," I told her.

"Are we talking Plato or Socrates?" Evie asked.

"More like Freud," Mary Jordan said.

"Mary Jordan is wanting to know what love is," I said.

Evie took off the cap and tossed her head back, shaking out her long red strands. "It's the yin and the yang."

"What does that mean?" I asked.

"I don't know. I just thought it sounded good."

"Papa Walter once told me love is like the wilderness. It's easy to get lost in it. He said, forty-one years and he still hasn't found his way out," I told them.

"You think we'll ever feel that way?" Mary Jordan said.

"Hope so," I said.

The three of us locked arms as the swings carried us slowly hither and yon. I leaned my head back, my face to the sky, my hair blowing in the wind. Giant gray clouds hung over us as if they'd tangled themselves in the cypresses. Before long, warm spatters of rain began to fall.

Mary Jordan stopped her swing and let go of my arm. "I better get home. Mom's got her crawfish pie in the oven."

Mary Jordan's mom always fixed crawfish pie for afternoon dinner on Sundays. Raindrops beaded Mary Jordan's lashes and tightened her natural curls.

"Where's your bike?" Evie asked her.

"I walked."

Mary Jordan took a few steps away from us, then turned back around. "I think your grandfather's right. I think love *is* like a wilderness."

"Why do you say that?" I asked.

Mary Jordan had her hands tucked in her khaki shorts. Her T-shirt, wet with rain, clung to her skin. I could tell her mind was lingering in one of its reflective moods. "A wilderness can be beautiful," she said, "and exotic, and powerful. But it can also be scary."

"Like love," Evie said, her voice dead serious.

"Yeah, like love," Mary Jordan said.

I thought about Dewey, and Mama and Daddy, and the Bankses. I knew Evie and Mary Jordan were right.

"I'll see you all later," Mary Jordan said.

"Later," Evie told her.

Evie and I continued to swing, the rain washing over us as we watched our friend leave.

"You got anywhere to go?" I asked Evie.

"Nope." She tilted her head back, letting the rain slap down on her face, and opened her mouth wide.

"It's polluted," I said.

"I don't care."

The rain fell harder, soaking us clear through.

I made a run for it, heading for the shelter of the fort. Evie pumped her legs, swinging higher and higher, her head still tilted back.

I sat in the sandbox underneath the fort and watched her. I loved my friends. I loved everything about them. I loved them so much, sometimes my heart hurt, as if any moment it would burst itself wide open.

Lightning tore through the sky, followed by one great thundering *boom,* as if God had just looked down on the exact earthly spot Evie and I had occupied, and decided to speak. Evie shrieked, jumping off her swing, and ran for cover. We sat in the middle of the sandbox as the rain dripped onto our heads from the cracks in the wood above us. It was a warm rain, and it smelled wonderful.

"That was a nice wedding yesterday," Evie finally said.

"I wasn't sure you were there." I knew Evie had been at the reception, but I hadn't seen her at the wedding.

"I was sitting in the balcony."

"I guess you weren't sitting there alone," I said, thinking about the way she and Billy had been dancing.

Evie smiled and gave me a nudge. She was sitting cross-legged, and started drawing little diagrams in the sand with her fingers. "Hey, Lucy?"

"Hmm?"

"Remember when you were asking about love?"

"Yeah."

"I don't think love happens overnight."

"Go on," I said.

Evie drew more pictures in the sand. "I think it's buried in your heart. I think maybe it's been there all along. Maybe it's buried inside that other person's heart all along, too."

"You're talking about Billy, aren't you?"

"Yeah, I am."

The rain continued to fall. We continued to sit there while Evie drew pictures in the sand.

It's funny how you can completely forget a moment in your life, and then with one instant, one comment, you remember it, as if you've lived it all over again.

I thought back to our first year in high school. Evie and Mary Jordan and I were sitting in the cafeteria. We'd just finished eating the school's lunch. "I don't feel so good," Evie said. We decided it was probably her lunch not sitting right on her stomach. That night her mom took her to the hospital in New Orleans, where she had her appendix taken out. The doctors said we could have lost her.

Billy drove Mary Jordan and me to the hospital, none of us saying a word the whole way there. When Evie got out of the recovery room, the doctors still wouldn't let us see her. Billy walked right into the room anyway and pulled up a chair beside Evie's bed. He took her freckled hand in his. His shoulders slumped forward, his elbow on one of his knees, his forehead supported in his hand. He sat like that for the longest time, as if he was praying.

And so it wasn't Evie's appendicitis that I had forgotten, or the fear that we had almost lost our best friend. It was Billy sitting like he was, holding her hand.

"Suppose love is buried inside a person's heart," I said. "And suppose it has been there all along. What do you suppose wakes it up?"

"I'm not sure. Maybe sometimes it's just not love's time."

"And maybe sometimes it is," I said.

I remembered the catcher's mitt Billy had given Evie. "To catch you when you fall," Billy had said. I thought about seeing them dancing together at the wedding reception.

"Maybe it's your and Billy's time," I told her.

Evie stopped drawing pictures in the sand. "I don't know."

"What does Billy say?"

"He hasn't said anything. I don't think either of us knows what to say. When I got to the church yesterday, I was looking for you and Mary Jordan to sit with. Mama had been out late the night before. I didn't think she'd ever get herself ready. As soon as I stepped inside the church, I didn't see you or Mary Jordan. I saw Billy, standing off all by himself. I thought that was so sweet of him to come. He asked me if I had anyone to sit with. I said, 'Not really.' The church was pretty full, so we went up to the balcony."

Evie stopped and looked at me. "It was when Mary Jordan's grandfather sang. That's when it happened."

"What happened?" I asked.

Evie was still looking at me, as if somehow by looking at me, she'd find all the answers. "It was like something inside of me started to wake up. Something I'd known all along."

"Did Billy feel it, too?" I asked.

"I think so. About halfway through the song, he took my hand, holding on to just my fingertips. He held it like that for the rest of the service, even when everyone went forward to take Communion. We just kept sitting like that, as if someone had poured warm honey all over us, and we were too stuck in one place to move."

"That's why I didn't see you," I said.

Evie went on. "When the service was over, he asked me if I'd like a ride to the reception. I said that I would. I've always ridden around with Billy. All of us have. But it didn't feel like all those other times."

"How did it feel?" I asked.

"I was aware of everything," she said. "Kind of like if some-one had told you this was your last day to live and you'd want to remember every detail, how each person looked, how they made you feel, how your mama's food tasted on your tongue, how the air smelled. I can still see Billy's hands on the steering wheel. I can still see the way his thumbnail was nicked on the side."

I locked my arm with Evie's. I had felt the same way with Dewey at the beach, as if I could smell and taste every color around me.

"Do you think I'm weird?" Evie asked.

"No, I don't think you're weird at all."

We sat quiet for a couple more minutes.

"I saw you two dancing," I said.

She didn't say anything.

"It was really beautiful," I told her.

Evie sifted sand through her fingers. I could tell she was thinking. "After the reception was over we walked around town for a while. Then we sat on this bench and just talked. He wanted to know about school, and how I was getting along with my parents. I asked him if he'd found a job yet. Then he got to telling me about this big idea he has. He's planning on opening up a pet store at the old Conoco."

"A pet store?"

"That's what he said. He's going to turn the garage into boarding kennels. He says he's going to make it a real nice place for animals to stay."

"Mama always said we weren't ever going to get a dog because there wasn't anyone to look after it if we went on vacation."

"That's what everyone says. People have to drive clear over to Beaufort to drop their pets off if they want to go anywhere," Evie told me.

"And the closest PetsMart is an hour away," I recalled.

"Mm-hmm."

"Well, what do you know," I said.

"Billy said he'd give me a job. I could work with him after school."

"When's he planning on opening his pet store?"

"As soon as he can get the place ready. He's meeting with the bank next week. His parents have agreed to cosign on a loan."

Billy seemed awfully young to be opening up his own business, but I knew if anyone could do it, he could. Everyone liked Billy, and he'd always done whatever he made up his mind to do, whether it be winning a football game or deflating the tires on every teacher's car in the parking lot without getting caught.

Evie took a deep breath and let it out slowly. "Did you notice how blue the sky was yesterday?"

I smiled, thinking about Dewey, thinking about the beach. "Yeah, I did."

"It must have been ten o'clock before Billy finally drove me home. When we got to the house, he told me he'd like to talk to me again sometime. Then when I got out of the car, he leaned his head out the window and said, 'I'd like to dance with you again sometime, too.'"

"He said that?"

"Mm-hmm, he did."

"What did you say?"

"I just stood there thinking how I'd like to dance with him again sometime, too, but I was so busy thinking about it that I never got around to saying it. So he smiled and waved, and drove off."

"You should have kissed him," I said.

"He told me I was beautiful," Evie said. "He told me I'd grown into a beautiful lady."

The rain was passing over us, though the sky remained steamy and gray. I thought about what Billy had said to Evie. He was right. Evie had grown into a beautiful lady. She wasn't like the other kids in Sweetbay. When Evie's dad left home the summer after we were in fifth grade, part of her childhood left with him. People may not have seen it on the outside of her. You had to know the kinds of thoughts that went on inside her. You had to watch her pick her mom up and put her back together when her mom's life had fallen to pieces. I remembered the days after school, not long after Evie's dad had moved out, when we'd drop by Evie's house and find her mom still in bed. Evie didn't play with us on those days. By the next morning when we'd stop to pick up Evie for school, Ms. Thibodeaux would have clean clothes on and the house would be straight.

Ms. Thibodeaux didn't fix shrimp toast on Sunday mornings or crawfish pie on Sunday afternoons. But every morning before school, Evie brought her mom coffee in bed. And every Saturday morning, Evie rode out to her dad's to make sure he'd gotten in from his shrimp boat in one piece.

I was glad Billy had said what he did.

Garden of Eden

Evie said she was hungry. "Let's get some ice cream."

The Dairy Freeze was next to the Piggly Wiggly. We straddled our bikes and rode slow and easy beside each other.

"Hey, Evie, there was something I didn't tell you," I said. "Yesterday, after I left the reception, I stopped by Mr. Savoi's gallery."

"All by yourself?"

"Yeah. It was some time after I saw you and Billy dancing. I went in through the back door."

"Why'd you do that?"

"I'm not sure. I guess I was thinking about that painting of Mama."

"You took the painting?" Evie asked.

"No. I didn't get the chance. When I walked in, there was a couple, completely naked, making out on the floor."

Evie rode onto the sidewalk in front of the post office and stopped. I pulled up beside her and stopped, too.

"Completely naked?" Evie asked.

"Completely," I said.

"Who was it?"

"I don't know. I didn't see their faces."

We stood there a little longer.

"Do you think Mr. Savoi was one of those people?" Evie asked.

I knew what Evie was thinking. If Mr. Savoi was involved, perhaps my mama was involved, too.

"I don't think so," I said. "I don't remember the guy having gray hair. Of course I only saw them for a second. The next second I was on my way out the door."

Evie seemed to be registering what I had told her. "The back door wasn't locked?"

"Nope."

"So if the door wasn't locked, maybe it's not locked now."

"What are you thinking?" I said.

"Same thing as you."

"You suppose my mom's painting's in there?" I asked

"I suppose it might be."

"You suppose Mr. Savoi works on a Sunday?" I said.

"I don't suppose he does," Evie said.

Then she smiled and turned down the alley. I followed.

We leaned our bikes against the back wall of Mr. Savoi's gallery and approached the door.

It opened just as easily as it had the day before.

"He doesn't keep his door locked," Evie said.

"Mm-hmm, I know."

Evie and I set foot in there as if any second something big and ugly was going to jump out at us.

It didn't.

We asserted ourselves a little more. The door to the room

where I had seen the couple was wide open. Evie and I stood in the entranceway, looking around. There were a couple of easels up, and on the floor next to one of the easels was a mug.

"So this is where you found them?" Evie said.

I said, "Mm-hmm."

"Dang."

We stood there a couple of seconds longer, then Evie said, "I don't think Dewey's dad keeps his paintings back here."

"He probably has everything in the front room," I told her.

"There are windows in that front room," Evie recalled. "Someone might see us."

"What do you want to do?" I said.

"If we get on our hands and knees, maybe we could go unnoticed."

The two of us crawled to the front of the gallery. Every wall was covered with artwork. It appeared as though Mr. Savoi had everything in order for his open house, which was to take place the next night.

The gallery looked different from the first time we visited. Flowering white amaryllis and anthurium were situated on top of the Roman pedestals, and around the pedestals were peace lilies and bird of paradise.

"It looks like the Garden of Eden in here," Evie said.

Mr. Savoi's personal exhibit was still along the back wall. We searched the display of paintings for my mom. My eyes followed the contours of the women's bodies, their breasts, their thighs. In a number of the pieces, the women were either faceless, or else their features were shaded.

"I don't see your mom," Evie said.

Mr. Savoi must have had twenty paintings along that wall. "He's painted a lot of women," I said.

"Lucy?"

"Hmm?"

"I think it would be an honor to be painted. I think it would make me feel beautiful."

I wanted to tell Evie she *was* beautiful, but thoughts like that never seemed to find their way out of me, as if I were too afraid of how they might sound. Evie would have said those words to me. Evie always found the words to express her feelings. Like when we read *The Little Prince* in French class, and the prince had drawn a boa constrictor, but no one knew what it was. If he had shown it to Evie, she would have known what it was, and she would have had just the right words to tell him she understood.

"I think the women whose bodies are imperfect are the most beautiful," Evie said.

She was staring at a painting on the far left. I crept over beside her on my hands and knees. The painting looked like one from the eighteenth century. Rays of sunlight seemed to dance over the woman's large body. Her long brown hair cascaded over her breasts.

"Evie?"

"Hmm?"

"That's Tante Pearl."

"I know."

Jaybirds

Daddy and I had agreed to accompany Mama to Mr. Savoi's open house. She said we were to be ready by six o'clock. When I got home from work that day, I immediately knew she'd been in one of her benevolent moods.

"Lucy, help me bring these plates of food out to the van," she said.

Mama makes her turtle candy with semisweet chocolate chips, maple syrup, and pecan halves. She makes her Cajun mimosas with Asti and a touch of Tabasco sauce. I love Mama's turtle candy. I love her Cajun mimosas, too. But I wasn't the least bit fond of her making them for Mr. Savoi's open house. It seemed to me with all the cooking lessons she'd been giving him, he could make his own food.

"I don't see why you had to do all this cooking," I told her as I was carrying a couple of trays outside.

"It isn't often culture visits our town, and when it does we should give it our finest welcome," she said.

I decided it best not to push the subject any further.

When she got home from delivering her preparations, I was in the shower.

"Wear something nice tonight," she hollered through the door.

"Why?" I hollered back.

"A lady should always dress for the occasion."

I didn't have a clue what I was going to wear. It might not have mattered so much if Dewey wasn't going to be there.

I wrapped myself in a towel and walked back to my bedroom. Laid out across my bed was a black dress with spaghetti straps and sequins embroidered across the bodice. I thought it must be Mama's, but when I held it up I saw the tag. It was a size ten and marked "Tall." Mama didn't wear a size ten. She wore a size six. Mama didn't wear dresses marked "Tall," either.

I combed out my long black hair and dabbed a little of Ethel Lee's Amour Oil behind my ears. I fixed up my eyes with her waterproof eyeliner and mascara. For my birthday Ethel Lee had given me a tube of steamy red lip gloss. I never thought I'd want to wear red, but that night, I applied some of it, too. Standing in front of the full-length mirror attached to my closet door, I stepped into that black dress, pulled the straps up onto my shoulders, and ran the zipper up my back. The dress hugged my small breasts and waistline. I stared into the mirror, hardly recognizing myself. Am I beautiful? I wondered.

I still wasn't happy about Mama's helping Mr. Savoi, but seeing myself in the dress she'd picked out for me, somehow all that anger inside of me seemed to wane. I couldn't believe she'd bought me a black dress. Mama always said a woman shouldn't wear black until she was eighteen, unless she was dressing up for Halloween.

When I came down the stairs, Daddy was in the kitchen

making himself a sandwich since Mama wasn't fixing dinner that night. He turned around as my black heels tapped against the floor.

"Lucy Marie," he said, staring at me. "Aren't you a sight for sore eyes."

"You like it?" I asked, afraid he wouldn't approve.

"I wasn't sure I had the right size," he said.

"You bought this?"

"Doesn't a dad have a right to spoil his little girl?"

I was shocked. I walked over to him and put my arms around his neck. "Thank you."

He hugged me so tight, I didn't want to ever let go.

Daddy drove Mama and me over to the gallery. I couldn't remember the last time we'd all ridden together as a family. I knew Mama didn't approve of my black dress, but she didn't say anything. She wasn't wearing black. She was wearing a long apricot skirt with a cream-colored shell and pearls. I thought she looked beautiful. I wanted Daddy to tell her she looked beautiful, but he didn't.

Daddy wasn't wearing his jeans. He'd put on a pair of khakis and a black blazer, his dark hair brushing against the collar in the back. I thought I smelled a trace of cologne on him, but I wasn't sure.

Daddy didn't say anything on the drive over to the gallery. Mama didn't say anything, either. I'd never known my mama to ride anywhere without saying something. I hated all that silence. I wished Daddy would turn on the radio.

We pulled up in front of the post office. After Daddy parked, he walked around to Mama's side, but she'd already opened her door for herself.

"We don't want to be late," she said as she climbed out and shut the door behind her.

We followed Mama down the sidewalk to the exhibit hall. In front of the gallery's window, roses and ivy petunias surrounded a sign on an easel. THE EYE OF THE BEHOLDER, the sign read. I couldn't help but think of all the women Mr. Savoi's eyes had beheld.

Inside, a cellist and a flutist had arranged themselves in one of the corners. I didn't recognize the musicians, and knew they must be from out of town.

Mama seemed to have read my thoughts, because she leaned close to my ear and said, "They're from New Orleans. Victor hired them from the Chamber Symphony."

There were a lot of things I didn't care for lately, and one of them was my mama slipping in the mention of Mr. Savoi's first name.

Scattered around the room were small round tables draped in white linen with parfait chairs, and in the center of each table was an antique glass vase holding a single red rose. I didn't recall Daddy getting an order for a dozen red roses, and wondered if they'd come from New Orleans, too. No one was sitting at the tables. As I glanced around the room, I realized no one was looking at the paintings, either.

Daddy disappeared into a group of people near the food and drinks. Ethel Lee walked up to Mama. "Isn't this wonderful?"

A flash went off from somewhere behind me. As I turned

around, I saw Mitchell Priest, the editor of the *Sweetbay Times*. He was taking a picture of Mr. Savoi and Dewey in front of Mr. Savoi's display. That was the first time I'd seen Dewey since I'd arrived. He was wearing a long-sleeve white sweater with a pair of pleated gray slacks. I knew Mama would have thought he looked refined. His hair was blonder than when I'd first met him, bleached out by the sun. His skin was tan against the white of his sweater. He didn't resemble his dad, I realized. I thought of his mom and wondered what had happened to her. And as I stood there looking at him, I saw something in his eyes that made my heart ache. Mama had said Mr. Savoi was a widower. I wanted to tell Dewey I was sorry for what-ever had happened to his mom.

I glanced at the display behind him, instantly relieved that a replica of Mama's bare body wasn't there.

Daddy brought me a cup of punch and Mama one of her Cajun mimosas.

"J.C., isn't this wonderful?" Ethel Lee said.

Daddy smiled.

"And to think we have a genuine artist living right here," Mama said.

I turned to look at Daddy, but he wasn't there anymore. Then I saw Evie and Billy sitting at one of the tables, each with a plate of food in front of them. I walked over to join them. That's when Dewey broke away from his father and Mr. Priest.

He gently took me by the arm and leaned his face close to mine. "God, you look beautiful."

No one in Sweetbay talked like that. They didn't say "God" unless they were uttering a prayer.

Dewey told me to go ahead and sit down and he'd bring me some food. I sat next to Evie.

"You're a knockout," Billy told me.

No sooner had Billy said that than a loud voice rang out, "Mitchell, you're going to have to move. I can't see a thing with you and that camera in the way." Miss Balfa had arrived.

Mitchell begged her pardon and stepped aside. Mitchell was almost as big as Tante Pearl.

"Well, they're as butt naked as a jaybird, aren't they?" Miss Balfa said.

Billy started to laugh. Evie and I laughed, too.

"Hey, Pearl, that looks like you," Miss Balfa called out.

I hadn't seen my Tante Pearl, but sure enough she appeared from a group of people, not looking the least bit embarrassed.

"I studied some guy in college who painted up women like this," Miss Balfa said. "I had to take an art history class."

Mr. Savoi appeared behind Miss Balfa. "Heironymus Bosch?" he asked.

"Mm-hmm," Miss Balfa said. "Are you related?"

Mr. Savoi laughed. "Perhaps you would let me paint you sometime," he said.

Miss Balfa said, "Perhaps not," then headed over to Ms. Pitre's crab-stuffed mushrooms and crawfish dip. Ms. Pitre had been cooking all day, too.

Dewey handed me a plate of food and pulled up a chair beside me. As he sat down, his knee touched mine underneath the table, sending a wonderful warmth tingling through my skin. He didn't move it away. He just kept it right where it was, so I kept my knee right where it was, too.

He shook Billy's hand. "I'm Dewey," he said.

"Billy Jacques. So this is all your dad's doing?" Billy asked.

"Yeah. He always wanted to open a gallery."

"Nice," Billy said.

A hand pressed against my back. It wasn't Dewey's. Dewey's hands were on the table.

"We tried to call you."

It was Mr. Banks.

He pulled up a chair from the other table and sat between Evie and me. "We were going to ask you to watch Mattie. I should have known you'd be here." He lowered his voice, "You look incredible."

"Hey, Mr. Banks," Dewey said.

"How are you all doing?" he said back.

Then I felt his knee press against my other leg.

"This is Mary Jordan's brother, Billy," Evie said.

While they shook hands, Mr. Banks's left hand slipped underneath the table and onto my leg, startling me to no end.

"So, I hear you're directing a play," Billy said. "How's it going?"

"It's coming along," Mr. Banks said.

I thought I'd casually slip his hand off my leg, but as soon as my fingers reached under the table and touched his, he clasped hold of them so that I had no idea what to do.

That's when I saw Savannah. She was standing by the door, holding Mattie, who was squirming something fierce.

"I'll see you all tomorrow night at rehearsals," Mr. Banks said. "Billy, nice meeting you." He stood up, finally letting go of my fingers, the heat of his hand still on my leg, and walked over to a group of people by the food, never once paying any mind to Savannah or Mattie.

Billy and Evie and Dewey started talking about the play and who had gotten what part, but I was still so caught up in the discomfort of Mr. Banks's hand on my leg that I wasn't participating in their discourse.

Mr. Banks had now gotten himself a drink and was standing with Ms. Pitre, who seemed to be carrying on a one-way conversation. No sooner had I noticed them than he looked my way, catching my eye, and smiled, as if there was some sort of understanding between us, though I had no idea what that understanding was. I was sure he was going to join us at the table again now that he had his beverage, so when Mama walked up to me and said, "Lucy, maybe you could help Savannah with Mattie. That woman's not going to have a free minute to enjoy the paintings," I just knew God had intervened.

"I'll be right back," I told Dewey.

Savannah smiled when she saw me.

"Want a hand?" I asked, reaching out for Mattie.

"I just fed her. I don't think the milk agreed with her," Savannah said.

"I could take her outside," I said.

"You don't have to do that."

"I want to," I told her.

"You're sure?"

I bounced Mattie up and down in my arms. "I'm sure."

"Her stroller's out front," Savannah told me. "We walked."

I carried Mattie with me back to the table. "I'm going to take her for a walk. See if I can get her to calm down."

Mattie's fussing turned into a downright wail.

Dewey stood up beside me. "Want some help?"

I adjusted Mattie on my shoulder.

Dewey smiled. "Let's go."

Cold Fronts

By the time we got Mattie in her stroller, she was still crying up a storm. "You'd think she'd wear herself out," I said. We walked almost five blocks before she started to settle down.

Though it was still light outside, the temperature was pleasant, and with Mattie finally getting quiet, Dewey and I had a chance to talk.

"What did you think of the gallery?" he asked.

"I thought it was impressive."

"And the paintings?"

"They were beautiful."

"I hoped you would say that."

After a few more blocks, I decided to take off my heels, and stopped at a bench in front of a small garden by the church. Mattie was still being quiet.

"Should we chance it and sit down?" Dewey asked. "Maybe she'll sleep."

"We could try," I said.

I checked on Mattie. Her eyes were closed. I secured the brakes on the stroller and sat next to Dewey.

"A lot of people showed up tonight," he said. "I was glad for my dad. I wish my mom could have been there."

I had never known anyone our age who had lost a parent. "What happened to her?" I asked.

"She got cancer a couple of years ago. She went through chemotherapy and radiation. For a while we thought she might make it. But then the cancer came back. She died last fall."

"Dewey, I am so sorry." I laid my hand over his.

"It's been a tough year on Dad," he said.

"It's been tough on you, too," I told him.

He turned his palm over and glided his fingers between my own. Holding his hand like that made me feel as close to another person as I had ever felt. It wasn't my body responding this time. It was something in my heart. With the fingertips of my other hand, I traced the veins running from the crevice of Dewey's palm down the underside of his arm. Slowly traced them back and forth.

"Hey, Lucy?"

"Yeah?"

"I'm really glad we met."

"Me, too," I said.

Dewey let go of my hand and wrapped his arm over my shoulder. His fingers gently touched my arm. We sat like that a few more minutes, the night air smooth and balmy, the colors beginning to soften. Then Dewey's face turned toward mine. "Lucy?"

"Yeah?"

"May I kiss you?" he asked.

"I'd like that," I said.

His eyes settled upon my mouth. I reached up, holding my hand upon his warm neck. Dewey pressed his lips against mine, sending a honey-thick flush through my body. We kissed several times, our breathing lingering against each other, my fingers tangling themselves in his thick, blond curls. His tongue tasted sweet, his mouth sweet. I knew I had never enjoyed anything as much.

His hand reached up to mine and grasped my fingers in his. We kissed a few more times before I laid my head against his chest and let him hold me. I closed my eyes, feeling his chest rise and fall beneath my cheek. Everything was so peaceful, I didn't want to move.

Dewey was the first to speak. "Let's keep getting to know each other."

"I think that's a good idea," I said.

I wrapped my arms around his waist, squeezing him against me. "We should probably get going," I told him. "The Bankses may be ready to leave."

I carried my shoes to the side of me while Dewey pushed the stroller. Mattie was still asleep. "Thanks for telling me about your mom," I said.

"Thanks for caring."

Walking back to the gallery, I realized how differently I saw Dewey compared to that first day when he was playing the piano for Mama. I didn't mind that he was a couple of inches shorter than I was. I thought his nose was handsome. We turned down Park Street, which ran parallel to the square where small groups of people ambled along the sidewalks.

The gallery was still packed with people. I slipped my feet

back into my shoes. Dewey stayed outside with Mattie while I went in to find Savannah.

I spotted her right away, talking with Mama.

"She wore herself out," I told Savannah. "She's asleep in the stroller."

Mama's face looked aghast. "You didn't leave her out there by herself I hope."

"Of course not. Dewey's with her."

"Thank heavens," Mama said.

"I didn't bring my purse," Savannah told me. "I'll see if Ted has some money."

"All I did was take Mattie for a walk. You don't need to pay me," I said.

"I'll tack on some extra next time," Savannah offered.

She left to get Mattie. As I looked around the room, I didn't see Evie or Billy or any other young person that I knew. I didn't see my daddy, either.

Mama was still standing next to me. "Where's Daddy?" I asked.

She glanced around, her face appearing rather surprised. "I don't know. He *was* right here."

I checked the room again, but didn't see him. "Are you staying much longer?" I asked.

"Well, I don't know. I wouldn't want to be one of the first to leave the party."

"I'm going to go ahead and walk home, then," I told her.

"You sure?"

"I'm sure," I said.

Outside, Dewey was still with Mattie. "Where's Savannah?" I asked.

"She went to find Mr. Banks and see if he's ready to leave."

Dewey was holding on to the stroller, rolling it slightly back and forth. "Thanks for hanging out with Mattie," I said.

"No problem."

I scanned the sidewalks, thinking maybe Daddy had stepped out for some air. "Hey, Dewey, have you seen my dad?"

"Not since we got back," he told me.

It was then that I saw the light on in Daddy's shop, about a half a block down the street that ran almost perpendicular to the gallery.

"I think I'm going to go on," I said. "Do you mind?"

"I don't mind. Is everything okay?"

I reached for his hand. "Everything is fine." By now I was smiling and he was smiling in reply.

"I liked kissing you, Dewey."

"I liked kissing you, too," he said.

Before I got to Daddy's shop, I turned down the alley that led to the back of the store. The door was unlocked. As I stepped inside, I saw Daddy sitting at the table on the other side of the work area. In front of him was a bonsai tree.

"Daddy?"

He didn't look at me. He didn't say anything.

I walked around the counter to the table and pulled up a chair beside him.

"You okay?" I said.

He set down his scissors.

"Do you know how your mama and I met?"

"You were both at a crawfish fest over in Beaufort," I said.

Daddy laughed a little. "That's where it started. After the crawfish fest, there was a group of us that decided to head down to the beach. Your mother was climbing over a barbed-wire fence. She snagged the back pocket of her jeans. Ripped it clear off, tearing a hole through to her backside. I gave her my jacket to tie around her waist. She wore it home. I'd put my phone number in the pocket."

"Mama called you?" I asked.

"She needed to return my jacket," Daddy said.

"And it was love ever after," I said.

Daddy smiled. "Something like that." He picked up the scissors again.

"So why are you in here alone trimming a bonsai tree?"

Daddy snipped at a couple of branches. "Didn't like the way the first tree turned out, I suppose."

"That's not why," I said.

I reached for the scissors and set them aside. "You don't like Mr. Savoi, do you?"

Daddy propped his elbow on the table. He turned to face me, his knuckles against his temple. "I don't know him. He might be a nice enough man."

"Daddy?"

"Hmm?"

"How did you know you were in love with Mama?"

He took a deep breath, then let it out slowly. "I thought about her a lot," he said. "I wanted to be with her all the time."

"What about now? Do you still want to be with her?"

Daddy smiled. "Yes, I still want to be with her."

"Then why is she at the gallery while you're in here?"

Daddy looked away. "I don't know."

"Do you think maybe you should go back?" I said.

"You have a lot of questions stirring around in that head of yours, don't you?" He wrapped his arm around my shoulder, pulling me against him. "You know how once in a while we'll get us a cold front? The kind that comes along in January or February and brings all sorts of unexpected weather?"

"Are you and Mama having a cold front?" I asked.

Daddy still held his arm around my shoulder. "Cold fronts down here never last very long." He smiled, rubbing his hand over my hair and messing it up a little.

I tucked my head against him. "Maybe instead of sitting here cutting a bonsai tree, you and Mama ought to go home and build a fire."

The Chamber

The day after Mr. Savoi's open house, I left the shop around two to meet Evie and Mary Jordan at St. Vincent's park. I'd promised Tante Pearl I would give Moses his bath since I'd have to work late the next day. Evie and Mary Jordan said they'd help, then we could ride out to the beach.

Evie didn't smell like Coppertone that day. She smelled more like a piña colada.

"What's with the new perfume?" I asked.

"The store was out of Coppertone. I thought I'd try a different brand." Evie lifted her arm to her nose. "Personally, I think I smell rather nice."

"I'm sure all those gnats are going to think you smell rather nice, too," I told her.

We left the park and began our ride to Tante Pearl's, staying as close to each other as we could, except when a car drove by.

"What did you think about Mr. Savoi's open house?" Evie asked.

I felt myself smile. "I had myself a mighty fine time," I said.

"You had yourself a fine time at the reception, or a fine time after you and Dewey left the reception?" Evie asked, all too knowingly.

"Why do I feel like I'm missing something?" Mary Jordan said.

"Because you *are*," Evie said.

"Last night Dewey and I took the Bankses' daughter on a walk," I told her.

"I remember that part," Evie said.

"Once she settled down and fell asleep, we stopped by a bench over at St. Marc's."

"And?" Evie said.

"And Dewey asked me if he could kiss me."

"He asked you?" Mary Jordan said.

"Mm-hmm. And I'm here to tell you that was the finest kissing I've ever had in my life."

Evie about startled me off my bike with the loud *whoop* she released.

"I had no idea," Mary Jordan said. "I thought you two were just friends."

"We *are* friends," I said. "That's what's so cool."

"Girlfriend, I'm happy for you," Evie said.

"I'm happy for you, too," Mary Jordan said.

As we turned onto Tante Pearl's driveway, Moses ran to greet us, prancing up a storm. We laid our bikes in the grass and went around back to get the hose. Tante Pearl wasn't home. Seemed to me Tante Pearl wasn't home a lot these days. Next to the hose pipe was a bucket with a brush and a bottle of Palmolive. Evie and Mary Jordan and I soaked Moses down and lathered him good, getting a shower of suds all over us from time to time as he'd shake out his coat.

I went into the house to get a towel. Tante Pearl's linen closet was bare. I checked the dryer. It was bare, too, so I went back to her bedroom. Sure enough there was a laundry basket next to her nightstand, and stacks of clean laundry that she had yet to put away on top of a fluffy pink chenille spread. I didn't recall Tante Pearl ever having a fluffy pink chenille spread. For as long as I'd known her she'd had a tie quilt on top of her bed that smelled like mothballs. I sank into the mattress, running my hands over all that soft fluff. That's when I saw the piece of paper on the nightstand. "Soul's Desire," was written across the top in Tante Pearl's large, bold cursive.

The back door opened. "Where'd you disappear to?" Evie hollered.

"In here," I yelled back.

Evie and Mary Jordan appeared in the doorway.

"My aunt writes poetry," I said, hardly believing my own words.

Evie and Mary Jordan sat on either side of me, looking over my shoulders.

Evie read it out loud. Mary Jordan and I followed along silently.

> Yearnings into a quake of desire.
> Open my heart, the vessel is full,
> The chamber is empty.
> I will waste on nothing.

The night sings,
Like a white moon in a black sky.
Fill me, my love.

"Just what chamber do you suppose she's talking about?" Evie said once she'd finished reading.

"I'm not sure I want to know what chamber she's talking about," I said.

"I think it's beautiful," Mary Jordan said.

Evie looked at Mary Jordan. I looked at Mary Jordan, too.

"What?" Mary Jordan said.

"Nothing," Evie said.

I set the poem back on the table where I'd found it, and grabbed a large towel from one of the stacks on the bed.

We dried Moses, wrestling around with him in the grass for a long while. After a time, Evie said the grass was starting to make her itch, so we dragged the hose back around the house, then climbed on our bikes and headed off toward the beach, Evie scratching at herself the entire way.

By the time we pulled into the parking area, Evie looked fit to be tied.

"Do you suppose it was gnats or chiggers that got to me?" she asked us, scratching herself something awful.

"If they got to your privates, they're chiggers," Mary Jordan told her.

There wasn't a soul around. Evie stripped out of her clothes. Sure enough her southern region looked like it had a record outbreak of the measles.

"Chiggers," Mary Jordan said.

"Mm-hmm, chiggers," I said.

I thought Evie was going to cry.

"Maybe the salt water will make all that itching go away," I said.

Evie grabbed her clothes, and the three of us headed over the levee. There were a couple of people down the beach a ways. Evie didn't care. She ran for that water just as fast as her freckled legs could carry her.

Mary Jordan and I stripped down to our underwear and dove in after her. Evie had already swum out a good ways.

"How is it?" Mary Jordan hollered to her.

"I wonder if they use chiggers at torture camps," Evie yelled back.

"I've heard nail polish can help," Mary Jordan said.

"And where am I going to get nail polish all the way out here?" Evie inquired.

"I've got some in my bag," I told her.

We didn't swim long. Evie said she was itching too bad.

Instead, we hiked back over the levee, Evie's polka-dotted derriere leading the way.

I dug the nail polish out of my backpack.

"Do you need any help?" Mary Jordan asked her, laughing.

"I think I can manage by myself," Evie said, disappearing behind a tree with the bottle of polish and her clothes.

Evie's disposition had settled quite a bit by the time she re-emerged.

"Did you give it time to dry?" I asked her.

"I did," she said.

"That's good," Mary Jordan said.

We climbed on our bikes and started back to town.

"I think maybe you ought to stick to Coppertone," I told Evie.

"I think maybe you're right," Evie said.

Improper Advances

When I got home, I took a quick shower and changed clothes. I told Mama I'd grab some supper after rehearsals. By the time I got to the school, most everyone was there. I smeared my long, damp hair away from my face with both hands and took my place next to Evie and Dewey.

"You made it," Evie said.

Mary Jordan was sitting behind us with Doug. Then Billy walked in, wearing a threadbare white T-shirt and a baggy pair of jeans.

"What are you doing here?" Mary Jordan said.

"Your director told me he was short a part. I thought I'd help you all out." He took a seat on the other side of Evie.

"Since when did you talk to Mr. Banks?" I asked.

"I didn't talk to Mr. Banks."

"Who'd you talk to, then?" Evie said.

Billy looked up and pointed to Mr. La Roche, who had just stepped onto the stage.

"Mr. Banks isn't going to be here," Mr. La Roche told us.

"He has some personal things going on. I've been asked to

take over." He paused before continuing. "I'm going to be directing the play."

The auditorium fell so quiet we could have heard a mouse breathe.

"What personal things?" Evie asked in my ear.

I shook my head, all the while my stomach feeling terribly uneasy.

Mr. La Roche went on. "Billy Jacques has agreed to play Mr. Banks's part as Puck."

The auditorium remained silent. Mr. La Roche took a deep breath. "So . . ."

Again Evie leaned into my ear. "Does anyone else know about—"

"Shhh." I immediately cut her off.

Evie pulled back, giving me one of her sorry expressions, her mouth all puckered up and her eyes big.

"So let's get started," Dewey said.

Several people stood up and approached Mr. La Roche, no doubt asking for more information. The rest of us walked backstage to get ready to rehearse. People in Sweetbay are as curious as a tomcat with a feline in heat, but when something needs to get done, they get right down to business, and that's exactly what we did.

Doug had been cast as Demetrius, upon whom Helena's affections passionately fell. Mary Jordan had been cast as Helena. Evie had been cast as the Fairy Queen.

Mr. La Roche called me to the stage and gently steered me to where he wanted me to stand.

"Do you understand the scene?" he asked me.

"I think so," I said.

He looked out at the rest of the cast and explained that I was in love with Lysander, who would be played by Dewey. However, my father, Theseus, had ordered me to marry Demetrius. If I refused to marry Demetrius, my only option would be to become a nun.

Mr. La Roche then motioned Dewey and Doug to come forward, and situated them on the stage, as well. I enjoyed playing Hermia. I enjoyed being onstage. I wasn't as shy as I had thought. When Mr. La Roche and I had finished our discourse, Doug immediately took his cue. " 'Relent, Sweet Hermia, and Lysander, yield thy crazed title to my certain right.' "

" 'You have her father's love, Demetrius; let me have Hermia's,' " recited Dewey.

I loved having Dewey beside me. The further into the play we rehearsed, the more immersed into the character I became. I forgot about Mr. Banks. I forgot about my parents and Mr. Savoi. All I saw were my friends around me. We had entered another world. I was as high as a kite. If Hermia loved Lysander, then I would love him, too.

It was when we took our places onstage for Act II, Scene 2, where Oberon anoints the Fairy Queen's eyes, and Puck squeezes love juice on Hermia and Lysander, that I noticed Evie's polka-dotted derriere from her nail-polish job, clear through her white shorts. Before I had a chance to say anything to her, Billy walked up behind her. He placed his hands on her waist and steered her off the stage. He wasn't laughing at her or making fun of her or anything. A few minutes later she appeared with a long-sleeve shirt tied around her waist, which they had no doubt retrieved from the costume room. I was glad Evie had Billy. I was glad Billy had Evie, too.

Billy was a natural onstage. Just having his easy way about us seemed to bring out the best in everyone. I decided Mr. Banks's leave of absence might not be such a bad thing for the play. It was as if we'd been singing in the shower with an audience, and now the audience was gone and with it all our inhibitions.

"We can do this," Dewey said to me as we were waiting for our next scene.

"Of course we can," I said.

He put his arm around me lightly. "Wait for me after practice."

As I looked at him, his eyes held mine for a split second. He didn't smile.

"What's wrong?" I asked.

"I'll tell you later."

After rehearsal, I stayed behind with Dewey, waiting for the auditorium to empty. We sat together on the edge of the stage. Dewey's hands were spread out on his thighs. He was staring straight ahead.

"What's up?" I asked.

He continued staring straight ahead.

"Dewey?"

He took a deep breath and let it out slowly. "Mr. Banks is in trouble."

"What kind of trouble?"

"I don't think he's going to be teaching this year."

I waited for him to go on.

"Today while I was at the gallery, Savannah came in to see if Dad might want to show some of her photographs. She'd brought her portfolio. She said she was looking to pick up more work."

"What does that have to do with Mr. Banks?"

"Dad gave her his list of fees for wall space. They were talking back and forth when Mr. Banks walked in. He said he'd been looking all over for her. Things got a little heated. Dad and I disappeared into the back, but we could still hear them. Mr. Banks was telling her to believe him, and how could she take their side."

"Whose side?" I asked.

"Dad talked with Ms. Pitre later in the day. She heard your principal got a call from the school Mr. Banks used to work at in Atlanta. Seems like one of their students came forward, making accusations against him."

"What kind of accusations?" I asked.

"From the sounds of it, he got involved with some student up in Atlanta. She didn't come forward until after he was gone."

As Dewey talked, I felt a well of heat rise to my neck and face, as if I were suffocating from the inside out.

"How do you mean 'involved'?" I said.

"Involved enough for his old school to be looking into it, and maybe enough to make Trudeau not want him teaching this year."

"You're sure?"

"Pretty sure. Ms. Pitre said there was going to be a board meeting next Tuesday to make a decision."

Dewey reached for my hand. My face and neck were

aflame, my palms were clammy, and queasiness curdled in my stomach.

"Will you tell me what happened between you and Mr. Banks?" Dewey's voice was so tentative and quiet, I wasn't sure I'd heard him right.

I tried to pull my hand away, but Dewey wouldn't let go. He turned his body slightly toward mine and searched my face. I kept my eyes pinned to the blue-speckled carpet in front of me till each of those blue speckles became a blur. I wasn't crying. I was just trying to make the whole moment disappear.

"Something happened," Dewey went on.

"Did Evie say something to you?" I asked, trying for the life of me to understand how Dewey could have known.

"No. She didn't have to."

"How do you know something happened, then?"

"Just the way he's been acting toward you, always coming around wherever you are, and the way you've been acting toward him."

"What do you mean, the way *I've* been acting?" I could hear the edge in my voice.

"You hardly say a word to him, and when he walks up to you, your whole body seems to shrink back, like last night, or at the wedding reception before you and I danced."

I didn't know Dewey had noticed. I didn't know anyone had. I wanted to be angry. I wanted to feel like he was accusing me of something, but I knew he wasn't accusing me.

"It wasn't any big deal," I finally said.

Dewey just kept sitting there like he was, searching my face with those blue eyes of his.

"He kissed me," I said. "That was it."

Then Dewey's thumb did that thing he'd done at the beach. He started stroking my hand ever so gently, making all that queasiness in my stomach go away.

"Hey, Lucy?"

I didn't say anything.

"You didn't do anything wrong."

I still didn't say anything.

"He shouldn't have been kissing you."

"That's what Evie says."

I sat quiet for a moment, my mind wandering. "You think that's all he did with that other student?"

"I don't think so."

"Why do you say that?"

"You know how people are always talking about a woman's intuition? Well, guys have a certain intuition, too. I think Mr. Banks goes just about as far as a person will let him, student or no student. He couldn't take advantage of you because you wouldn't let him."

Dewey was still looking at me. I was still staring at the carpet, my eyes watering bad. I think guilt is about as bad a feeling as anyone can have toward oneself. I didn't tell Dewey that part of me had enjoyed Mr. Banks's lips on mine. Ever since Mr. Banks had kissed me, I'd tried to disown the memory of my own physical pleasure, no matter how subtle it was, but it was still there.

"What if Mr. Banks convinces the school otherwise?" I said.

"What do you mean?"

"It would be his word against that student's. What if they believe him?"

Dewey finally looked away. "I've been thinking about that."

"And just what, exactly, have you been thinking?" I said.

"I was thinking that if anything happened between you and Mr. Banks, maybe you ought to go talk to the principal."

"I can't," I said, maybe too quickly.

A few solid minutes passed between us. "Just think about it," Dewey said.

He let go of my hand and pushed himself off the stage.

"Where are you going?" I asked.

"I didn't think you wanted to talk anymore."

"I don't." I walked with Dewey up the aisle. "You think there's a chance he won't get fired?" I asked.

"I don't know."

"You really don't like him, do you?"

"No, I don't."

"Why did you try out for the play, then?"

Dewey stopped walking. He tilted his head back and raised his eyes to the ceiling. "I like Shakespeare," he said.

"Oh."

Slowly Dewey lowered his head and looked straight at me. "And I like you."

My eyes looked off at nothing in particular. "When did you decide you liked me?" I asked.

"When you sang 'Happy Birthday' to Mrs. Forez at the Walbridge Wing."

"That was the first time you saw me."

"Not the first," Dewey said.

"Oh?" I looked at him inquisitively.

"I'd seen you on your bike riding around town."

"So you'd had your eye on me, huh?"

"I guess you could say that." Dewey stepped closer to me. "You don't have to mention anything to the school if you don't want to."

"I know I don't have to."

"Okay, then," he said, his face moving toward mine, his voice softening.

"Okay," I said, our words mingling together as our lips touched.

Car Doors and French Quarters

By that Friday, I still hadn't talked to the principal, Mrs. Leigh. I hadn't seen Mr. Banks or Savannah, either. The school board was to meet on Tuesday. I had less than four days to decide what to do.

While I was deliberating things over in my head, Papa and Sissy arrived at their forty-first wedding anniversary. That night Mama and Daddy and Tante Pearl and I met them for dinner at Tujague's in New Orleans' French Quarter. After we were all seated, Daddy ordered the wine. Everyone's glasses were filled, except for mine.

Papa said, "I want to make a toast." He reached for Sissy's hand and held it against his cheek. "For the love of my life," he said. "For my heart and soul and body. For the one who rescued me and taught me to love. I am yours." With her hand still held to his face, he kissed her, long and slow and meaningfully. Tante Pearl and I cheered, then we all clinked glasses and drank, even me with my water goblet.

Somewhere toward the end of the dinner, Mama excused herself from the table. By the time the bill was brought and paid for, she still hadn't returned. We decided we'd wait for her outside.

"Oh, what a beautiful evening," Sissy said as we stepped out onto the sidewalk. Thick striations of muddy rose and deep lavender colored the sky. Suddenly I felt as if I were in a sort of vacuum, and everything else around me, other than the beautiful sky, was many light-years away. For a few seconds, maybe more, I was on my own planet in this peaceful space of silence. And then it crashed, loud and hard, like a glass ball dropping to earth as I heard Mama's voice from just around the building. "Okay, Victor. That will be perfect. I'll see you tomorrow night."

I could feel Daddy's body stiffen as if it were my own. Mama turned the corner, her cell phone in her hand. She stopped abruptly when she saw us. "Oh," she said. She slid her phone into her purse.

Papa said he was feeling mighty ready for his bed and hoped we would understand if he and Sissy made for an early departure. Mama gave them each a hug before they left. Daddy started off down the sidewalk toward Mama's van, not saying a word to anyone.

He wasn't any more of a conversationalist once we got to the car, and the way he slammed his door shut, you would have thought we were climbing into an eighteen-wheeler instead of Mama's Dodge minivan.

"It's not good to slam the door so hard," Mama said.

Daddy didn't say anything.

"It puts extra strain and wear on the bumpers," Mama told him.

Tante Pearl and I looked at each other, both of us raising

our eyebrows to the heavens, with a big "uh-oh" written all over our faces.

"You know, Papa always said slamming a door can break the window brackets, too," Mama said.

I hoped there wasn't a policeman around, because I was certain Daddy's driving didn't fall within the legal speed limit. From where I was sitting I couldn't see the speedometer, and with my daddy's emotional state, I didn't think it such a good idea to make an obvious effort to look.

"I've always liked to look at the houses when I go for a drive," Tante Pearl said, her knees squared out in front of her as if bracing herself for the ride.

The way Daddy was driving, we might have missed entire towns.

Daddy stayed as quiet as a stone. We dropped off Tante Pearl at her house first. "Have a pleasant evening," she said before getting out.

"Don't leave me," I mouthed to her.

"Sorry," she mouthed back. Mama and Daddy didn't say anything.

It wasn't until Daddy parked the van in the driveway that he spoke. "I'm going down to the shop." After he got out of the van, he slammed the door again.

Mama pinned her chin to her collarbone and gave him a long, slow look, which didn't do a bit of good, because he was already halfway to the garage, where he parked his motorcycle.

I didn't want my daddy riding anywhere on his motorcycle in that particular frame of mind, even if it was only five blocks away. I wanted to throw an all-out temper tantrum right then and there. I wanted to tell Mama I was tired of Mr. Savoi and all their cooking lessons and painting sessions. I wanted to tell Daddy to stop slamming his door and hiding all his thoughts. I wanted him and Mama to go take a walk or a trip to Hawaii, or make love on the back porch under a full moon. But I didn't throw a temper tantrum. I didn't say a word. Instead I watched my mama walk into the house and my daddy drive away, leaving me fairly certain they hadn't built any fires lately. I wondered how it was my granddaddy and grandmama could make it forty-one years, and as of lately my parents couldn't go a day with twenty-four good hours between them.

Faraway Places

As far as Mama and Daddy's relations were concerned, the rest of the weekend didn't fare any better. They avoided each other like the plague. Mr. Savoi's art classes were scheduled to begin that Monday afternoon, which I was fairly certain wouldn't help the state of my parents' affairs.

From all the commotion around town, it seemed to me every woman in Sweetbay considered herself an artist, or at least a potential one. I'd just returned to Daddy's shop after making a delivery when Miss Balfa walked in.

"I don't know why everyone wants to pay their good money to take some class so they can draw naked people. Seems to me it'd be a whole lot cheaper just to strip down in front of a mirror."

"It's the instruction," Ethel Lee told her.

"Lord be with us. You've signed up, too, haven't you?"

"I'm not even going to answer that," Ethel Lee said.

"You don't have to. It's written all over your face."

I was watering Daddy's potted plants. Daddy was processing a new shipment of day lilies and chrysanthemums. I knew Mama was going to Mr. Savoi's class. I had a feeling Daddy knew she was going, too.

"What time does it start?" Miss Balfa asked.

"Why? Are you interested in participating?" Ethel Lee said.

"No, I'm not interested in participating. I just thought I might go over there and see who it is he's got modeling for him."

"Ima Jean, he isn't going to let you in," Ethel Lee informed her.

"Well then I'll hang out on the sidewalk bench and see who comes out."

Ethel Lee rolled her eyes.

Daddy still hadn't said a word.

"What's with you today?" Miss Balfa asked him.

Daddy looked at her like he didn't know what she was talking about.

"You haven't even asked me how my day is going, much less said hello."

"Ima Jean, how are you?" Daddy said.

"I'm hot, and thank you very much for asking."

"So why aren't you taking Mr. Savoi's class?" he asked her.

Miss Balfa said, "If I was to spend two whole hours of my time painting, it'd be with a roller and a gallon of Sherwin-Williams. That garage of mine's been needing painting for two years now."

Daddy laughed. It was the first time I'd heard him laugh in days.

Dewey picked me up from work that afternoon in his father's Karman Gia. We drove out to the Dairy Freeze. On the way over we talked about rehearsals and how everyone was doing. The performance was scheduled for the night of Sweet-bay's Founders' Day, which was a little over three weeks away.

"Do you think we can pull it off?" I asked.

"We'll pull it off," he said.

He didn't ask me if I had talked to the principal or if I was going to. I knew sooner or later the subject would come up, but at the moment, I was grateful he hadn't mentioned it.

When we got to the Dairy Freeze I ordered a vanilla cone dipped in chocolate. Dewey didn't order anything.

"Aren't you hungry?"

"No." He stood behind me and rubbed his hands along my bare arms.

A song came on the radio. I'm not even sure what the song was, but for some reason it made me think of Dewey and his music.

I leaned back against his chest. "When did you learn to play the piano?" I asked.

He thought a minute before answering. "I think I was in kindergarten. I could play the Minuet in G before I could write a complete sentence."

"I don't know a lot about music, but I love the way you play. I love how it makes me feel."

"How does it make you feel?" he asked.

"It makes me feel high," I said. "Like I'm flying. And it makes me feel like crying, because . . ."

"Because . . ."

"When I listen to you play, it's as if all the things I'm feeling overwhelm me. Everything good and beautiful and sad all comes together. I feel like I can't breathe."

"And that's a good thing?"

A big smile settled onto my face. "Yes, silly. That's a very good thing."

I looked at his hands, his palms square, his fingers long, and I wondered if his mother had had hands like his. "Did she play?" I asked.

"My mother?"

"Yeah."

"A little."

"Did she want you to be a pianist?"

"She wanted me to be happy."

"Are you happy?" I asked.

"I think so."

He reached for my free hand. "Let's go for a walk," he said.

The heat was draining slowly out of the day. Dewey led us down a side street behind the Dairy Freeze.

No matter how quickly I ate my cone, the ice cream continued to melt into little rivulets beneath the chocolate. As I was licking the side of the cone, Dewey leaned over and took a bite off the top.

"Hey," I said. "I thought you weren't hungry."

"I'm not. I just want you to hurry up and finish so I can kiss you."

I laughed. Dewey laughed, too. Then we both began eating, our heads bumping into each other and our noses touching.

After we finished, I wiped our faces with the napkin and slipped it into my back pocket. Dewey reached for my hands. Slowly, he traced the length of my arms, up to my shoulders, until his hands glided over the contour of my neck and along my jaw line.

"You are very beautiful," he said.

I didn't wait for Dewey to kiss me. Instead, I slid my arms around his waist and pressed my mouth against his. As we released each other, he kissed my face, my forehead, my neck. Then he hugged me so tight.

"I need to talk to you about something," he said.

We were still holding each other as I waited for him to go on.

"Before we moved here, I applied at a music camp up in Montreal. It's a type of conservatory for young musicians."

"And you got in," I said, understanding what he was about to tell me.

"Yeah. It's competitive, so that's a good thing. It runs for four weeks. I'll have to leave after the play."

I felt myself already missing him. "Why didn't you mention it before?" I asked.

"I don't know. It never seemed like the right time. And I wasn't sure about us, I mean . . ."

I rubbed his back, drawing circles with my fingers. "You weren't sure we'd like each other," I said. "Or that we'd be standing here like this."

"Yeah, something like that."

I thought about all the distant and exciting places I'd read about, places I'd only dreamed of visiting. Dewey was living his dreams. Part of me was jealous. He had done something with his life. He was getting to go to one of those faraway places and do what he loved.

"But you'll be coming back?" I said.

"I'm coming back." He nuzzled his chin into my hair.

"Dewey, you should feel honored, getting accepted into a place like that."

It was then that he loosened his grip. His face stared straight back at me. "I'm honored to be standing here with you."

We stood there for a few more seconds, just looking at each other. He sees me, I thought. He really sees who I am.

"Dewey?"

"Hmm?"

"Have you ever loved anyone before? I mean, I know you loved your mom, but . . ."

"No," he said. "Not before . . ."

"I think I'm falling in love," I said.

He traced my mouth with his fingertip, then lightly kissed me. "I think we're falling in love with each other."

As we held on to each other, I wondered if it was his music that had made me fall in love with him, and yet I knew there was more to Dewey than just his music. He was kind and funny and thoughtful in bigger ways than any boy I'd ever known. And he was honored to be with me. That meant more to me than anything.

"Dewey?"

"Yeah?"

"Be real?" I said.

"I'm real," he said, and he kissed me again.

One Breath

As soon as I walked into the house, I smelled Mama's shrimp and okra gumbo simmering in the Crock-Pot on the counter. A loaf of herbed bread was wrapped up in one of her dish linens. Mama still wasn't home. I set the table and put one of her Diana Krall CDs in the stereo. Then I stirred the gumbo and waited. Mr. Savoi's art class was supposed to be over at five. At quarter till six, Mama's van finally pulled into the driveway. When she entered the house, she was carrying one of Bessie Faye's pecan cream pies. A canvas bag with her art supplies was slung over her shoulder.

"I thought I'd pick up dessert," she said, as if explaining why she was late.

I was sitting in one of the oven chairs reading a book.

Mama dropped her things on the counter, poured herself a glass of chardonnay, and joined me, sitting in the chair beside me. She slipped off her sandals and pulled her legs up underneath her.

"How did it go?" I asked.

She looked tired. Something was different.

"Fine," she said.

I'd never known Mama to be so monosyllabic. "What's wrong?"

"Nothing." She leaned her head back against the chair, ran her fingers through her hair, and slowly closed her eyes.

"Savannah was there," she said.

"She was?"

"Mm-hmm. And Ms. Pitre and Ethel Lee."

I was glad Savannah had signed up for the art class, and yet I felt sad for her, too. I couldn't imagine having a husband like Mr. Banks, and I hated myself for ever having betrayed her.

"Mrs. Hazelbaker down at the bank was there, too," Mama went on to tell me. "She said Billy came by to see her this morning. He got his business loan. Looks like he'll start working on the old Conoco place soon."

"He's opening up a kennel," I told her.

"That's what I hear."

"Maybe we could get a dog," I said.

"We'll see."

Mama's eyes were still closed.

"You sure nothing's wrong?" I asked her.

Her head nodded the slightest bit.

Sitting there like we were, I got to thinking about Dewey losing his mama. I thought about her getting sick, and as I did, my stomach seemed to twist itself up into a painful knot. No one I'd loved had ever died.

"Mama?"

"Hmm?"

"Have you ever had anyone close to you die?"

Mama's body seemed to soften all over. "Yes."

I set my book on the table between us. "Who?"

"His name was Russell."

I pulled my knees up into the chair. Mama had never told me this story before. "Who was he?"

"We met at Camp Winnataska, where I worked as a counselor. All the girls in my cabin thought he looked like Magnum P.I., so that's what we called him." Mama lowered her head and looked at me. "You ever hear of Magnum P.I.?"

"Evie and I used to watch the reruns."

"Well, that's what we called him. Magnum. He had a mustache just like Magnum, too. We would sneak out of our cabins once everyone was asleep and hike up the hill at the back of the camp. We'd build a fire and sit up talking for hours. Then we'd kiss and we'd talk some more. There was a river just below the hill, and a bridge. Sometimes we'd hide ourselves under the bridge, wrapped up in each other's arms."

I had no idea. "I can't believe you never told me this before."

Mama took a deep breath, long and slow. "Sometimes it's hard for me to talk about it."

"Even after all these years?"

Again, she nodded. "Even after all these years."

"Did you love him?" I asked.

"Oh yes."

I held on to Mama's every word. I tried to picture her working at the camp, tried to picture the boy she'd described. "Was he your first love?"

"Mm-hmm."

I hugged my knees to my chest, still wanting to know more. "What did it feel like?" I asked.

Mama's eyes weren't closed anymore, but she wasn't look-ing at me, either. "It felt like one breath."

I wasn't sure I understood.

"When you love someone that much," Mama continued, "and that person is away from you, sometimes it literally feels like you can't breathe, as if your body is aching for air."

Mama pressed her palm over her chest, slowly inhaling, as if she were re-experiencing all the love and pain she had known so many years before. "And then that person walks into the room, and all that ache inside of you, all that longing, dis-solves, and you feel yourself breathe again. But it's as if he takes the same breath with you. You're both one."

I had never heard my mother speak in such a way. Her whole body was relaxed. Her eyes continued to stare off.

"What happened to Russell?" I asked her.

"He was driving his car one night . . . He must have fallen asleep."

"That is so sad," I said.

She finally looked at me. "Yes, it is."

"Dewey lost someone he loved," I said.

"I know."

Silence settled upon us like a fog. Thousands of emotions seemed to tangle themselves up inside me so that I would never be able to find the words to sort them out or make sense of them all.

I didn't have to.

"Mr. Savoi lost someone he loved, too," Mama said.

I hadn't thought about Mr. Savoi having lost someone. I'd

only thought about his messing up my parents' lives. I didn't want the conversation to stop. I had to know more.

"That one breath you were talking about. Do you feel that way with Daddy?"

Mama paused so long I thought I would die. I stared away, tears fighting their way to the surface.

Mama reached for my hand. I couldn't remember the last time Mama had held my hand. "Lucy, what's wrong?" she said.

Those tears burned themselves right out of my eyes. "It's you and Daddy," I said.

Mama got out of her chair and knelt beside me. She wrapped her arms around my shoulders. "Oh, Lucy."

"People shouldn't hurt each other," I said. "Daddy slammed his door because he didn't want you taking one breath with anyone else. He wants you taking it with him, only he doesn't know how to tell you."

Mama rubbed my back. "I'm not taking it with anyone else," she said.

"Are you sure?"

"I'm sure."

"What about Mr. Savoi?"

Mama still held me. "No. Not Mr. Savoi."

I took the collar of Mama's shirt and rubbed my eyes. My breathing slowed. "Why is it you and Mr. Savoi have been spending so much time together, then?"

Mama held me out in front of her. She wiped the remaining tears from my face with her fingers and smiled. "Come here. Let me show you something."

She took my hand and led me upstairs. Just off her and Daddy's bedroom were the pull-down steps to the attic. She unfolded them and began climbing up. I followed her.

At the top of the steps, Mama pulled the little chain on the lightbulb. She ducked below the slanting rafters and walked toward the other side of the attic. "Close your eyes," she said.

I did as she told me and waited, heard boxes scoot along the floor, then paper crinkle.

"Okay," she said. "You can look."

Propped against Mama's legs was a painting, at least three feet tall, of a beautiful woman with smooth olive skin and black hair sweeping over her left eye. Her small breasts were round and full. She stood completely exposed, her body aglow, with a deep midnight blue all around her. One knee was crossed slightly over the other, as if attempting modesty. However, even to the eyes of a seventeen-year-old, everything about the woman's body was alluring, as if daring the man who had slipped inside her heart to make love to her body and soul as well. I knew the painting was of my mother, and yet it wasn't my mother I saw. Instead, Mr. Savoi had captured a beautiful woman, thirsty for love.

As I looked at the woman in the painting in front of me, I recognized the burning ache Mama had described earlier of a woman waiting for her lover to walk into the room. Mama wanted to feel what it was like to share one breath. I just hoped with all my heart my daddy would be the one with whom she'd learn to breathe again.

Women in Love

―――――

"The painting is for your father," Mama told me as we went downstairs. "It's his anniversary gift."

Mama and Daddy's anniversary was more than a month away.

Back in the kitchen Mama poured herself another glass of wine. I sat in one of the oven chairs, pulling my feet up underneath me, my knees hanging over the arms. Mama stood next to the kitchen counter. She looked at her watch as if she was wondering where Daddy was.

"I think he's working late, on account of your and Mr. Savoi's art class," I told her.

She took a sip of her wine and swallowed it slowly.

"You said you aren't taking that one breath with Mr. Savoi, but do you think he's been falling in love with you?" I asked.

"When did you start asking so many questions?" Again she drank her wine.

"Do you?"

"I think Mr. Savoi is lonely. I think he fell in love with the painting, not me." She set her glass down. "Lucy, I'm not in love with Mr. Savoi. He knows that. I just . . ."

She turned her back to me and walked over to the Crock-Pot to check on the gumbo. "This isn't going to be a bit of good if your dad doesn't come home soon."

"You just what?" I asked her.

She continued to stir the gumbo, scraping the thick sediment from the bottom. "He made me feel beautiful."

I remembered Evie's words so clearly. *I think it would be an honor to be painted. I think it would make me feel beautiful.*

Then I got an idea. "Maybe you shouldn't wait until your anniversary."

Mama turned around with her hand in a fist on her hip. "Just what are you concocting in that head of yours?"

"Maybe you ought to take that gumbo and that loaf of bread and that painting down to Daddy's shop tonight. Maybe you ought to take a couple of candles and a bottle of wine, too. Maybe you ought to show him you'd rather be with him than at some art class painting naked people."

Mama swooped her eyes off to the side and smiled, her lips pressed together. After a second or two she started downright laughing.

"What?" I said.

"Lucy, I don't know that I can go back to Mr. Savoi's art class."

"Why?"

"You know who he's got sitting right up in front of us?"

I said, "Who?"

"He doesn't have us painting a woman. He has us painting Noel La Plume. For the life of me I couldn't get myself to look past his umbilical separation."

"Noel!" I said.

"Mm-hmm." Mama giggled some more. "Now how in the world am I supposed to get my hair done next week?"

All I could think about were the boys at Rummy River whom I'd had to face in geometry.

"You avoid eye contact," I said.

"Oh?"

"Mm-hmm. You look at a magazine or something."

"Well, maybe I will," Mama said.

I helped Mama bring the painting down from the attic and out to the car. Then we carried the food and wine and candles out to her car, too.

After she left, I made myself a peanut-butter-and-jelly sandwich and took my plate up to bed. Sitting on top of the covers, I laid out my lines to the play and tried as I might to memorize them. Before long, the phone rang. It was Evie.

"What are you doing?" she asked.

"I'm eating a sandwich and studying my lines so hard my eyes are about to go crooked. How's Billy?" I asked her.

"He's coming by later. We're going out for ice cream."

"I saw the painting," I told her.

"What painting?"

"Mr. Savoi's painting of Mama."

"Where?"

"She showed it to me. It was in the attic. She was saving it to give Daddy for their anniversary. She's down at the shop right now. She's going to go ahead and give it to him."

"So she wasn't doing it for Mr. Savoi?" Evie said.

"No. Hey, Evie?"

"Yeah?"

"It was really beautiful. And when I saw it, it made me think of my mom differently."

"What do you mean?"

"It made me think of her as one of us. Not just a mom."

Then Evie said, "A woman who wants to be loved."

And I knew Evie was right. "Yes," I said.

Blue Shoes

———

I awoke the next morning to the gentle patter of rain. The pages from the play were scattered around me. A few had drifted onto the floor. I hadn't heard Mama and Daddy come home, but I knew one of them had checked in on me, as the lamp beside my bed was no longer on. The house was quiet. I looked at my clock. It was a little before seven. I wondered what Daddy had thought of the painting. I wondered if Mama and Daddy had made up. I hoped they had.

I gathered up the pages and set them on my nightstand. I knew the school would be meeting sometime that day about Mr. Banks. I wasn't sure what time. Dewey told me I didn't have to talk to the principal, but I knew he wanted me to. A week ago, there was no way I would have even considered it. And yet, as I sat up in bed and listened to the rain, I knew exactly what I had to do. Maybe it was seeing the painting the night before. Maybe it was the story of Mama's first love. Maybe it was my feelings for Dewey. I'm not sure. All I knew was, something felt different. Mama might have said I was growing up. Maybe I was. Part of me was glad for it, and part of me wanted to turn back into that little girl who could still fit on Papa's lap, or who could sit cross-legged in a chair without her knees hanging over the sides like the wings of a 747.

After I showered and dressed, I went down to the kitchen. Mama and Daddy were still in bed. I made their coffee and left them a note on the counter: "Practicing my lines with Evie and Mary Jordan. See you later." Then I took off on my bike for the school.

The parking lot was empty. I circled around and rode back by the square, pulling up in front of a pay phone by the movie store, and looked up the number for Mrs. Leigh, the principal.

Holding on to the phone, every inch of my body trembled. I can't do this, I thought. I dialed the number anyway.

Mrs. Leigh answered.

"This is Lucy Beauregard," I told her.

"Hi, Lucy."

For a second, I thought someone would have to take a shovel to dislodge the rest of the conversation buried inside of me.

"Lucy?"

I watched a couple of cars drive by. "I need to talk to you about something," I said.

Mrs. Leigh waited. I didn't say anything.

"I'm getting ready to leave for the school," she told me. "Why don't you meet me there."

"Will anyone else be around?" I asked.

"Not until ten."

I said, "Okay."

That was it. I had an appointment with Mrs. Leigh. I was scared to death. Suddenly I wished I had told Evie or Dewey what I was doing. I wished they could go with me.

I rode up to the school, parked my bike, and climbed the stairs. The doors were locked. I sat outside the building on the concrete, leaning my back against the warm brick.

After about twenty minutes, Mrs. Leigh's Jeep pulled into the parking lot. I waited as she ascended the steps toward the school.

"Hi," I said.

She had just pulled her keys out of her purse to unlock the door. She hadn't seen me. Her free hand flew up to her chest. "Good heavens, Lucy. You sure know how to startle a person."

"Sorry," I said, standing up.

She went ahead and unlocked the door, then put her arm around my shoulders and led me inside. I followed her to her office. On the other side of her desk was a sofa and a chair. She sat in the chair; I sat on the sofa.

I liked Mrs. Leigh. All the kids did. She was a small woman, somewhere in her thirties, with short brown hair. And she played the electric guitar. I'd never known a woman who played the electric guitar. She and her husband lived about fifteen miles outside of town on a farm. They didn't grow anything or raise any animals. They just liked living off by themselves.

"So what's this about?" Mrs. Leigh got right to the point.

As I sat there, I had no idea how I was going to get the words I came to say out of the depths of my body, much less my mouth.

"It must be something serious," Mrs. Leigh said.

"I think so." I tucked my hands underneath my legs and stared forward. "It's about Mr. Banks."

She gave me about a whole minute, then asked, "What about Mr. Banks?"

I didn't say anything.

She was leaning forward, her knees pressed together, her arms on her legs. She was dressed up, wearing a short skirt and a silk pullover, no doubt for the meeting. "Okay, let's start over," she said. "I know you're playing the part of Hermia in the play."

"Yes, ma'am."

"So you've gotten to know him."

"I babysit for him, too," I told her.

"And he's gotten to know you," she said tentatively.

"I guess so."

"Should I ask how well he's gotten to know you?" Her voice still had a bit of a tentative edge.

"Maybe you shouldn't," I said.

"I see."

I wasn't sure what it was she saw, which got me to worrying. I'd kissed Mr. Banks. I hadn't experienced Holy Communion with him, Mama's definition for physical consummation.

"Mrs. Leigh, he kissed me. That was all," I blurted out.

"Was this at the school?" she asked.

I looked at the floor and nodded my head, feeling about as sheepish as a dog that's just been shaved.

"Have you told anyone, gone to any other adults?"

I wasn't sure which question to answer first. "I told Evie," I said. "That was it." I decided not to tell her about Dewey. With him being new, she probably wouldn't have known who he was anyway.

"Has Mr. Banks made any other advances toward you?"

"No, not really." I thought about his hand on my leg, but guessed that didn't need any special mention.

"You don't have anything to worry about," Mrs. Leigh told me.

I wasn't sure what she meant. "Will anyone know I talked to you?"

"No, absolutely not."

I was glad she threw in the "absolutely."

I stood to go.

"What's going to happen?" I asked.

"Let's just say I don't think he's the kind of teacher I want to have around my students."

Before I left, I said, "What will happen to *him*?"

Mrs. Leigh pressed her lips together and made a small smacking sound with her mouth. "My dad used to tell us, whatever jam we got ourselves into, he wasn't going to be spreading it on his toast come the next morning. In other words, Mr. Banks is going to have to figure things out for himself, but he isn't going to be solving his problems at our school."

After I left, I can't say I was real happy with myself. I felt like I had betrayed Mr. Banks. Yet, that person who'd been doing a lot of growing up knew Mr. Banks had betrayed me. Nonetheless, I didn't care for the way I felt.

I looked at my watch. It wasn't even nine o'clock. I didn't have to be at work until ten. I decided I'd round up my friends, thinking maybe if we had breakfast at Bessie Faye's, I'd start feeling better.

I stopped by Mary Jordan's first. Her mother told me to go on up, that Mary Jordan was still in bed.

I ran into her room and pounced on her bed. "Wake up!" I shouted in her ear.

She rolled over, pulling the sheet with her.

"Come on," I said. I got up and walked over to her closet to find something for her to put on.

I crouched on the floor and pushed Mary Jordan's dresses aside to grab a pair of shoes. Suddenly the air going into my lungs felt as heavy as cement. Next to a pair of Nikes were my navy blue heels.

Mary Jordan was still pretending to sleep.

I wasn't hungry anymore. I didn't want breakfast. I picked up my shoes. I stood. I walked out of the room. I didn't say anything.

Yellow Petals

Never in my wildest dreams had I thought Mary Jordan and Doug were the couple I'd seen in the gallery. We had vowed to wait until we were married. We were young when we made that promise. I knew that. But I thought it had meant something, especially because the three of us had made the promise together. We'd always talked about everything. Mary Jordan had made this decision without us.

I climbed on my bike, wanting more than ever to have a car of my own, to drive for miles and miles with the windows rolled down and the wind in my hair, and turn down roads I'd never explored before and just drive wherever they took me. But I didn't have a car, so I rode my bike, all the while wanting to disappear from the town and the houses and the people passing by.

I rode to St. Marc's, leaned my bike against the side of the church, and entered through the large arched doors. I wanted to be alone, but I didn't want to be alone. I just didn't want to be with people. I wanted to be with God. Strange, I thought. I couldn't remember ever having desired to be alone with God. I hadn't even thought of God in that way, as someone, something, that I could be close to. He'd always just been an ear off in the distance. That morning, after talking with Mrs. Leigh, after finding my blue shoes, I didn't want just an ear. I wanted a voice. I wanted life explained to me, and for the first time, I didn't feel like any human could tell me what I needed to hear.

And so I entered the church, as I had done after being cast as Hermia. Only this time Dewey wasn't playing music. The silence was so thick, it echoed in my ears. I didn't kneel. Instead, I sat in one of the pews midway, as if saying, "Here I am." That was all. Just, "Here I am," as if I had been all emptied out and I didn't know what to feel anymore.

I don't know how long I sat there, but long enough to get sleepy, so sleepy I wanted to curl up in the pew and close my eyes, maybe stay there all day. And then it hit me. I'd been doing so much deliberating in my head, I hadn't been listening. Mary Jordan *had* been talking to us, only we had chosen not to hear what she had to say. She'd always been the quiet one out of the three of us, and sometimes the quiet one never gets heard.

I left the church and rode back to Mary Jordan's house.

"She's not here, Lucy. She just left to go for a walk," Mrs. Jacques said after she greeted me at the door.

For a minute I thought about riding around the streets till I found her, or going over to Evie's house, but then I remembered the three of us as kids playing at St. Vincent's Park, and something inside me told me she'd be there. All along the edge of the playground, hibiscus was in bloom in deep shades of pink. Mary Jordan wasn't on the swing set. She was in the sandbox underneath the fort, where I'd found her the morning after Clyde and Anita's wedding.

"Hey," I said, walking up to her.

Her head was lowered over her chest, her knees pulled up to herself.

I crawled underneath the fort and knelt in the sand beside her. "Hey," I said again.

She still wasn't looking at me, so I reached for her chin, trying to lift it up, but she just rolled her head back and forth against her knees, as if telling me not to.

I sat next to her. "Do you want to talk?" I asked.

"I can't," she said.

"Since when did you forget how to talk?" I teased her.

On the other side of the playground was a small garden with three rosebushes. Mary Jordan and Evie and I used to say those rosebushes were planted just for us. They'd been there for as long as we could remember. Mama says roses can outlive people by decades, saying her own rosebushes are over a hundred years old. One of the shrubs was full of tangerine-colored blossoms, one bloomed red roses, and the other yellow. The red rosebush was the tallest. Evie had dedicated it to me. She dedicated the tangerine one to herself on account of her orange hair. Mary Jordan had always liked the yellow one best.

I climbed out from beneath the fort and strode over to the small garden. Pressing my fingers on one of the yellow rose stems, I broke off a flower, then brought it back to the sandbox and handed it to Mary Jordan. Her head was still lowered, so she didn't see it.

I slid it underneath her arms, which were snug around her legs, and held it up to her nose. She leaned her weight into me. I wrapped my arm around her, and held the rose out in front of me.

"Are you mad at me because I found my shoes?" I asked.

"I'm not mad at you," she said.

It was then that Mary Jordan lifted her head. She pressed her fingertips to her eyes, which were swollen and red. "He told me he loved me," she said, her voice raspy and weak.

I couldn't help but remember what Mama had said. *Sometimes boys tell you they love you, because their bodies get confused.* I wondered if Mary Jordan's body had gotten confused, too.

Mary Jordan buried her face into my shoulder. "He doesn't love me," she said.

I wrapped both my arms around her, feeling her tears leak through my shirt.

"He says he doesn't want to be serious; get that. We made love, and yet he doesn't want to be serious. What's wrong with me?" She continued to cry.

"Nothing's wrong with you," I told her. I held her tighter, rocking slightly back and forth. "Nothing's wrong with you," I said again.

Out of the three of us, Mary Jordan had been the last one to get her period. She'd been the last one to wear a bra. She was the first one to have sex. I wondered when things had changed.

I was still holding on to the rose. I leaned forward and pushed its stem into the sand so that it stood straight like a

tree. One by one I tore off the petals, rubbing each one between my fingers, feeling their silky texture, their gentle
residue coating my skin in a fine, fragrant wax. I held the petals
in the palm of my hand. Then I took Mary Jordan's hand and
pressed them into hers, folding her fingers over them.

"It's crazy," she said. "I thought Doug and I could be one of
those great loves. I felt important. I had the whole thing
planned out in my head. But now I feel so empty, like it never
meant anything to him at all."

"When did he tell you he didn't want to be serious?" I
asked her.

"We were supposed to get together last night. But then a
bunch of the guys wanted him to go out. He'd been acting different. I called him later. That's when he told me."

He'd told her on the phone. What kind of person would do
that? But then I thought maybe he'd just been afraid. Maybe
he hadn't been ready, either.

Mary Jordan was crying. I wiped the tears from her chin.
"When did you decide to go through with it?" I asked.

"It was after we made up at the play. We talked about it. At
first I wasn't sure. But then one night things just seemed to
happen. It's supposed to feel good, right?" she said.

I just listened.

"The first time it hurt. I thought it was going to be so incredible. I'd felt so much when we were kissing. But when it
was over, I didn't feel anything. It all happened so fast. I
thought the next time it would be better."

"Was it?" I asked.

"I wanted it to feel beautiful," she said. "It never felt beautiful. I wanted to talk to him about it, tell him how I felt, but I didn't know what to say."

Mary Jordan reached for my hand. She squeezed my fingers, held them against her face. "You know what's weird? For so long he told me he loved me. All those months. Then we had sex, and afterwards he'd lie there not saying anything, as if he were somewhere else. I'd tell him I loved him. He'd tell me he loved me, too, but it wasn't the same. He didn't look at me. He'd lie on his back and say it, but it was different."

Mary Jordan continued to cry, but they were slow tears now. "Maybe I wasn't any good," she finally said. "I know that sounds crazy, but that's what I keep thinking."

"Don't say that." I let go of her hand and took hold of both her shoulders, making her look at me. "You are so beautiful," I told her. "Don't you know that? When it's right, that's how you'll feel. Beautiful. And the whole thing will be wonderful."

"How will I know when it's right?" she asked me. "I thought this was right."

I knew I could tell her what the Church had always told us. I could tell her the same things we'd heard from our parents. But instead, I said, "I don't know," because that was the truth.

"Do you think I'm bad?" Mary Jordan asked.

I shook my head. "You're not bad."

She opened her hand and looked at the petals, then clutched them tightly in her palm. "Will you get Evie? I'll wait here," she said.

I climbed out from under the fort and began to walk away.

"Lucy?"

"Yeah?"

"Thanks."

"I love you," I told her.

"I love you, too."

Fais-Dodo

———

Over the next three weeks, the only time Mary Jordan saw hide or tail of Doug was at rehearsals, and the only discourse that existed between them was their dialogue in the play. For the most part, she kept to herself. Sometimes I'd find her at the library, or I'd come upon her sitting at the park. Evie said to just give her time.

Dewey and I continued getting to know each other, slow and easy, as did Billy and Evie. I was certain I'd never seen Evie as happy. Daddy stopped playing golf so much, and every once in a while I'd catch a glimpse of him and Mama holding hands out on the porch.

Ever since the night she gave Daddy the painting, she hadn't taken any more art classes with Mr. Savoi. She hadn't taught him how to cook, either. I guessed the portions of her pie were no longer lopsided. I'd hoped to goodness she wouldn't hang that painting of hers in the living room. She didn't. Daddy hung it in their bedroom next to his dresser.

One morning while Daddy and I were having our coffee, I asked him what he thought of the painting Mama had given him.

"I guess you can say that painting told me a lot," he said.

"What did it tell you?" I asked him.

"It told me what your mama needed."

I thought about the first time I met Savannah at Daddy's shop. She had needs, too, but Mr. Banks never paid any heed to them.

I saw him only one other time after Mr. Savoi's open house. I was riding my bike home from rehearsals and had just approached the Piggly Wiggly. Mr. Banks was walking out to the parking lot. He paused when he saw me. Maybe he knew I had talked to Mrs. Leigh. Maybe he blamed me for the school's canceling his contract. I would never know. I didn't look away, though. I slowed my bike and stared back at him for a couple of seconds before riding on.

About a week later, I heard some of the women at the shop saying he had left town. One day I asked Daddy if it was true. He said he guessed it was.

Savannah's parents had come to help with Mattie, so Savannah didn't ask me to babysit again. From what I gathered from Ethel Lee and the other ladies in the shop, Savannah was putting down roots. She was showing up at Mr. Savoi's art class on a regular basis and had been seen taking pictures for the *Sweetbay Times*.

Largely to the credit of Mr. La Roche, the play came together without Mr. Banks. By Founders' Day, I suppose we were as ready as we ever would be.

Founders' Day is Sweetbay's biggest celebration. The town is one enormous playground from sunup to sundown. But that morning, it wasn't the sun staring at me through my bedroom window that woke me up. It wasn't the smell of Mama's rum raisin French toast, either. It was the Acadia national anthem playing over Mama's stereo speakers. Before I had a chance to sit up and rub the sleep out of my eyes, Daddy flung my bedroom door open, his voice belting out, "Acadia, my homeland, to your name I draw myself."

My daddy didn't sing much. He either had to be drinking or in a very good mood. I knew Daddy hadn't been drinking. It was too early, which meant his mood was exceedingly jubilant that particular day.

I followed Daddy down the stairs and joined him at the table while the music continued to play. Mama set a plate of rum raisin French toast and bacon in front of me. Then she brought me one of her parfaits. Mama always made her patriotic parfaits on Founders' Day, bearing all the colors of the Acadian flag: raspberries, whipped cream, blueberries, and slices of mango, topped with amaretto sauce. She brought Daddy and me each a cup of coffee and joined us at the table. Her hair was tied back with a navy blue bandanna. Her face glowed. I wasn't so sure the condition of her complexion was on account of the blush she was wearing. In fact, I wasn't even sure she'd put on any makeup that morning. Sissy says cooking is good for a woman's complexion. She once said conjugation is good for a woman's complexion, too. As I sat there eating my breakfast, I couldn't help but wonder if Mama and Daddy had been doing their share of conjugating.

"Are you going to be seeing Dewey today?" Mama asked.

I didn't know Mama had a clue as to what was going on with Dewey and me. "Why do you ask?" I said.

"It's called a mother's intuition."

"We might be going to see each other," I said.

"That's good," Daddy said.

"Mm-hmm," Mama said.

Founders' Day begins with eating and ends with eating. I guess you could say the eating never really stops. The Lions Club throws an all-you-can-eat pig roast starting at ten o'clock in the elementary school parking lot. By the time Mama and Daddy and I got there, a line of people had already wrapped itself around the building. In front of the tables were two large speakers playing music from The Hoolie Brothers. The Hoolie Brothers were from Beaufort. One played the fiddle, the other the guitar. Good 'ole stomping music. The town was waking up, people tapping their feet to the Cajun rhythm, a couple of people clapping their hands.

By the time I got my plate of food, Mama and Daddy had a swarm of adults around them talking and laughing. Hearty laughter was considered Cajun etiquette in Sweetbay, and all over that parking lot, people were being socially correct.

I spotted the Jacques family about four tables over, so I joined them, sitting next to Mary Jordan. Except for church, I rarely saw Mr. and Mrs. Jacques out in public. They were both retired and stayed inside most of the day because they didn't like the heat.

"Lucy, did you ever hear how Forrest Gump got into heaven?" Mr. Jacques asked just as soon as I sat down.

"No, sir, I can't say I did."

"Well, now, I'm going to tell you, then. Forrest Gump got himself up to those pearly gates, and there, standing before him, was St. Peter. 'Forrest,' St. Peter said, 'in order for you to go through these gates, you have to answer three questions.' 'Okay,' Forrest said. 'The first question,' St. Peter said, 'is: What two days of the week begin with a T? The second question is: How many seconds are there in a year? The third question is: What's God's first name?' Now Forrest thought long and hard about those questions, and after a while he told St. Peter he was ready. 'The two days of the week that begin with a T are Today and Tomorrow,' he said. St. Peter looked a little surprised. 'Well, now, Forrest, that wasn't the answer I was looking for, but I guess I can't argue with it. What about how many seconds in a year?' Forrest said, 'That would be twelve.' St. Peter wanted to know how he figured that. Forrest said, 'There's January second, February second, March second, and so on.' St. Peter decided he couldn't argue with that answer, either. 'What about God's first name?' St. Peter asked. 'That would be Andy,' Forrest said. 'Andy walks with me. Andy talks with me. Andy tells me I am His own.'"

Mr. Jacques laughed so hard at his own joke, I thought for sure he might give himself a heart attack. Mrs. Jacques laughed hard right along with him.

"That's good, Dad," Billy said, and he and Mary Jordan and I laughed, too.

Mr. Jacques always wore khaki pants and a solid-colored Izod shirt. Mrs. Jacques always wore a dress or a skirt. For as long as I'd known her, I'd never seen her in a pair of pants. They weren't the type to ever tell a dirty joke, either. There weren't many clean jokes told around Sweetbay, so I think Billy and Mary Jordan and I were rather impressed.

"Has anyone seen Evie?" I asked.

"She said she'll meet us later," Billy told me. "Says she's got a surprise up her sleeve."

"What kind of surprise?" I wanted to know.

"She wouldn't say."

Mr. Jacques had finished eating. He stood and stretched. "It's getting mighty warm out here," he said. "You ready, Mama?"

"I'm ready," Mrs. Jacques said.

Billy and Mary Jordan and I threw our plates away and headed over to the courthouse lawn. At least fifty yards of Main Street had been roped off for the games, which would begin at noon. Scattered around us were all kinds of vendor booths selling everything from boudin to funnel cakes to pralines to homemade beer to T-shirts and bumper stickers that read CAJUNS DO IT BETTER to pickled alligator toes.

We hung out at the different booths, spending our money and eating more food. About fifteen minutes before the games, we saw Evie pushing a large blue wheelbarrow down Main Street toward the starting line. Walking beside her was her mama, wearing a hot pink tube top and a pair of white cutoff shorts.

Billy laughed. "They're going to enter the wheelbarrow race."

The wheelbarrow race was everybody's favorite. You needed two people to enter. One pushed the wheelbarrow, the other rode as the passenger, and the passenger had to be sixteen or older. Sure enough, as we watched, Ms. Thibodeaux climbed right into that wheelbarrow.

"Hey, Evie!" Billy hollered.

We all waved at her big, showing our support.

Before we knew it, Dewey showed up right beside her, pushing his dad.

We made our way toward the finish line to cheer them on.

Even Miss Balfa and Ms. Pitre had entered, Miss Balfa riding the bow.

As I was standing with Billy and Mary Jordan, waiting for the race to begin, I felt something nudge the back of my knees, sending my feet out from under me and landing my derriere in Tante Pearl's yellow wheelbarrow that had definitely seen its better days.

"Come on, honey!" Tante Pearl hollered from behind me as she pushed that wheelbarrow and ran for the starting line.

Mary Jordan and Billy hooted and whistled.

"Get ready to eat wind!" Miss Balfa hollered at Tante Pearl.

"In your dreams!" Tante Pearl hollered back.

Everybody around me was laughing, and the race hadn't even begun.

Father Ivan stood about fifty feet in front of us with an arm extended in the air. "Contestants get ready," he yelled. "On your mark, get set, GO!"

His arm dropped down, and he ran out of our way. Every part of me bobbed up and down while Tante Pearl puffed and grunted behind me.

Miss Balfa and I were neck and neck. Actually, Miss Balfa's

neck may have been a little out in front of mine. She was hold-ing on to the sides of her wheelbarrow and leaning her body forward, as if she thought it would get her there faster.

"Go! Go! Go!" Miss Balfa called out.

"I'm going!" Ms. Pitre yelled back.

Tante Pearl and I began to inch our way out in front of them.

"Oh no you don't!" I heard Dewey's voice call out from be-hind me.

Sure enough, he and his dad were coming up on our left.

Tante Pearl pushed that much harder.

No sooner did they start to pass us than their wheelbarrow took an extra bump and Mr. Savoi toppled out its side, stirring up the crowd's laughter even more.

Billy was whistling his head off. Mary Jordan was holler-ing, "Go, Lucy!" Then I saw Mama off to the right of the finish line, jumping up and down with her arms waving in the air.

"Out of my way!" Tante Pearl yelled as we crossed the finish line with a whole hoopla of cheers. Gussie Guthrie and Bessie Faye came in behind us for second. Evie and her mom were racing neck and neck with Miss Balfa and Ms. Pitre for third.

"Go, Evie!" I hollered.

I could tell Evie was using every bit of her strength. Ms. Pitre was using every bit of her strength, too.

Just as all four of them were nearing the finish line, Ms. Pitre tripped, and in rolled Zina Thibodeaux with Evie *whoop-*ing it up behind her.

Miss Balfa was yelling at Ms. Pitre. Ms. Pitre was yelling at Miss Balfa. Tante Pearl was laughing her head off at both of them.

That's when it happened. Tante Pearl was holding on to her sides she was laughing so hard, when Mr. La Roche walked up to her from behind and grabbed one of her hands. He pulled her toward him, and right there in broad daylight, smothered her mouth with a kiss.

"Why, I'll be," Miss Balfa said.

"Who would've thought?" Evie said to me.

I watched my Tante Pearl walk off with Mr. La Roche, the two of them holding hands, and I felt myself smile. "Who would've thought?" I said.

We didn't stay around for the gunnysack race. Billy and Mary Jordan and Evie and Dewey and I made our way to the booths and bought ourselves a funnel cake and a six-pack of Mountain Dew.

We sat underneath the Tallow tree on the courthouse lawn. The races would go on for a couple more hours. Then the street dancing would begin. The Hoolie Brothers were setting up stage a little ways from us. Billy used to play ball with the youngest Hoolie brother, so he got up and went over to be social. The rest of us ate handfuls of funnel cake and drank Mountain Dew.

"I've never seen anything like this," Dewey said.

"Anything like what?" I said.

"Like this. Everybody having a good time."

"Didn't you have a good time in Michigan?" Evie asked.

"Not like this," Dewey said. "I don't even know when Detroit was founded. And here all of you are, almost two hundred years later, celebrating the lives of your ancestors."

"I guess I never really thought about it before," Evie said.

"Me, either," I said.

"What did your ancestors do?" Dewey asked.

"Whatever they wanted," Evie said.

Dewey said, "I'm serious."

Evie said, "I am, too. Mama's great-great-grandmother grew cotton. She had an uncle somewhere down the line who raised sheep. Somebody off in my dad's family made boats. Daddy learned to fish."

"Sissy's grandmother built fiddles," I said. "Mama says that's where all her musical talent comes from."

"So you don't think we're so backwoods after all," Evie said.

Dewy laughed. "I wouldn't go that far."

Evie kicked Dewey in the arm, making him spill his Mountain Dew.

A little later, Billy joined us with a couple of his leftover buddies from high school. They tried to get Billy to go off with them.

"I'll pass," Billy said. He sat down next to Evie just as proud as could be.

At that moment, I realized love wasn't just one breath. Billy had all the respect in the world for Evie. And I knew she had all the respect in the world for him, too.

Dewey took my hand and lay back in the grass. I lay back beside him. The Hoolie Brothers started to warm up with "Bozo Two-Step." Already people were gathering in the streets for the dance, and once the dancing started, it would go on until evening. It didn't matter that it was over ninety-four degrees outside, or that the humidity was just as high as the day's Fahrenheit.

The play was supposed to start at seven. Mr. La Roche had invited the cast, and anyone else who wanted to come, to a crab boil afterward at the beach. As I lay in the grass next to Dewey, I realized I wasn't nervous anymore about performing. I was still angry whenever I had to be onstage with Doug, but that was a different emotion entirely.

We continued to lie beneath the Tallow tree as the music kicked up around us. Then Billy jumped to his feet and pulled Evie with him. "Let's dance," he said. With his other hand, he reached for Mary Jordan and pulled her up, too.

Dewey and I followed them out to the street, where half the community was already gathered and chanky-chank stepping to "Hot Chili Mama!" You don't have to have a partner to *fais-dodo* in the streets of Louisiana. You don't even have to be from Louisiana to fais-dodo, as Dewey soon found out. You just need an independent spirit and a lot of rhythm in your soul. And on that particular Founders' Day as I danced in the street with all my friends, I realized we had all the right ingredients.

A Midsummer Madness

Miss Balfa and the St. Marc's Altar Guild hadn't been able to find a dress long enough to fit me, so they'd just cut off the bottom half of one dress and sewed it to the hem of another. The top half of the dress was celery green. The bottom half looked like a huge tuft of pink cotton candy. All in all, Miss Balfa and the Guild did a fine job with the costumes. Ethel Lee arrived at the play early and made up everybody's faces. She wove baby's breath in my hair. Despite the strange colors and the proportions of my dress, all my friends said I made a pretty Hermia.

Evie was definitely the beautiful one that night. She looked like an angel. Mrs. Jacques had made her dress out of a sheer curtain, telling Evie to be sure she wore a white leotard and tights underneath. Miss Balfa had made Evie's crown out of clover blossoms. The way Billy kept looking at her, I knew he thought she was a sight for sore eyes.

The 4-H had created two stage sets. One was made to look like an Athenian palace, which the group had constructed out of corrugated cardboard and plywood. The second stage set was the forest that included ten trees made out of chicken wire and papier-mâché.

After Ethel Lee had finished fixing my hair, I poked my head out from the side of the curtain to see how many people had shown up. The auditorium was already full, and the play wasn't even supposed to start for another twenty minutes. I thought I'd made myself inconspicuous, but that theory was completely shot when I saw Mama in the third row smiling at me and waving big. I didn't wave back. I didn't poke my head out from the side of the curtain anymore, either.

By the time the play started, people were seated on the floor in the aisles and in front of the stage, as well. Mr. La Roche was afraid the fire marshal would say something, but he didn't.

Seeing all those people made my breath shorten itself a good couple of yards, but as soon as Mr. La Roche, playing Theseus, Duke of Athens, spoke the opening lines, my body began to relax. Tante Pearl was sitting in the front row and must have flashed her camera half a dozen times.

After I declared my desire to become a nun if I could not be with Lysander, my scene with Dewey began. Talking with him onstage felt just as natural as could be. All I had to do was look into those blue eyes of his. I didn't have to pretend I loved Lysander. I didn't have to feign my affection. I could have kissed him right there on the stage if Tante Pearl hadn't been sitting with her camera on the front row.

It was during Act II, where Mary Jordan as Helena was supposed to follow Demetrius into the woods, that the play began to take on grand proportions. Although Mary Jordan and Doug had been just fine at rehearsals, outside of rehearsals she

was as cool as a freezer whenever his name even arose, so Evie
and I had no earthly idea what she was up to. As soon as Doug
finished his line, " 'You do impeach your modesty too much, to
leave the city and commit yourself into the hands of one that
loves you not,' " Mary Jordan was supposed to leave the stage.
She didn't. Instead, she grabbed Doug by the arm, took two
giant steps forward so that their bodies blocked the curtain
from being drawn. She then thrust her free arm out to the side.

"What is she doing?" Dewey whispered in my ear as we
waited offstage.

"I have no idea."

"Oh Demetrius, my love. Who are you to talk about modesty when you have none?" Mary Jordan cried out, her grasp
still tight around Doug's arm.

"And is it not so that I have betrayed myself in casting my
affections upon thee? Respect, you have not shown me any, to
use the word 'love' as if it were a piece of gold to buy my fa-
vors. I am no whore, Demetrius, I will have thee know. And so
upon thee do I cast a curse that no woman shall henceforth
fawn upon you. You abuse her heart. You strike her with
ridicule. A woman's affection, you shall have none, oh my
Demetrius, thou hideous one."

And with that, Mary Jordan took a bow. Then, still holding
on to Doug's arm, she stepped backward. Evie and I didn't
miss a cue. Both of us pulled the rope, closing the curtains. By
then, the entire cast had gathered around us to see what had
prompted the change in the scene.

Doug flung his arm free of Mary Jordan and stormed off
the stage, failing eye contact with every living soul.

Mary Jordan turned to face us, looking a little sheepish at first.

Evie started clapping, holding her hands high in the air. I joined in. Billy whistled. With all our ruckus backstage, I guess the entire audience thought they were supposed to be making a ruckus, too, so they did, clapping and whistling and calling for more.

Dewey just shook his head. I knew he didn't have a clue as to what was going on.

"I think we lost Demetrius," he finally said.

"I think you're right," I said.

Mr. La Roche was starting to stress.

I had an idea. "I'll be right back."

There was a side door off the stage that led into the auditorium. As I opened the door, I spotted Daddy in the third row, sitting next to Mama. I crouched in the aisle and motioned him toward me. He gave Mama his video camera and followed me through the door to the room off the side of the stage.

"What is it?" he asked.

"We need a new Demetrius," I told him. "Doug quit."

"I don't know the lines," Daddy said.

"We'll give you a script to read."

Daddy laughed. "Why not?"

Miss Balfa found a very tight shirt for Daddy to squeeze into, and tied a gold scarf around his head. He looked more like a rock star than a young nobleman.

And so the show went on. With a little prompting from Mr. La Roche and the rest of the cast, Daddy read his part just fine. I was proud. And the audience loved every minute of it, chuckling each time he finished a line. Of course, our audience was in a particularly good mood; nothing like performing for a group that's already consumed half the county's fermented beverages. Someone could have sneezed and they would have thought it was the funniest thing in the whole world.

I guess you could say that's what happened when Ms. Pitre threw up. She didn't have a big part. Fact was, she only had one line, and that one line only had four words: " 'Over here, over dale.' " It was the first scene of Act IV, when Titania, played by Evie, appeared with her fairy attendants. " 'Over here, over,' " were the only words that came out of Ms. Pitre's mouth before she hurled.

Nothing makes me more woozy than the smell of someone's stomach contents. Her physical state didn't seem to bother the audience one bit. They laughed their heads off. Mary Jordan and Daddy and Dewey and I were supposed to be the four lovers asleep. I decided I'd sleep with my scarf over my nose.

It was Evie who came to the rescue. "Oh my, my lovely attendants. Someone has become sick. It must be Puck's potion. Quick, my lady servant. Fetch us some rags and some Mr. Clean."

And so Bessie Faye, being the only other attendant, headed off the stage for the janitor's closet.

"Shall I assist?" Noel inquired of the fairy queen.

"If you be so brave, my king," Evie said. And so Noel took leave as well.

Of course, with Evie's and Noel's ad-libbing, the audience was laughing so hard, they might as well have rolled themselves onto the floor.

Even Mary Jordan and I couldn't help but snicker. Daddy told us to "shh," which only got us to laughing more.

When Bessie Faye and Noel returned to the stage, they'd solicited the help of another fairy attendant, Miss Balfa. All Miss Balfa had to do was show her face, and the audience was ripping their sides. I'd never heard such a ruckus. Of course she didn't just show her face. After she'd walked onto the stage in her rolled-up army pants and white air-conditioned sneakers, she flashed all those people the coyest smile I ever did see, fanning their flames even more. I know I was supposed to be asleep, but with all the commotion, I couldn't help myself.

Once order was re-established, Billy blew a horn from the side of the stage to awaken the four lovers. We jumped to our feet. Daddy held his arm around Mary Jordan. Dewey placed his arm around me. Mr. La Roche appeared, ready to be wed with Hyppolyta, played by Linda Hazelbaker, who worked at the bank. The fairy king and queen had amended their quarrels and were happy again. Tante Pearl started flashing her camera once more.

Billy then leaped onto the stage, casting his arms out toward the audience. "'If we shadows have offended think but this and all is mended: that you have but slumbered here while these visions did appear. And this weak and idle theme, no more yielding but a dream, gentles, do not reprehend. If you pardon, we will mend. So, goodnight unto you all. Give me your hands, if we be friends, and Robin shall restore amends.'"

At that point, we all took our bows. The audience hooted and hollered and gave us a standing ovation. Mary Jordan and

I pushed Mr. La Roche forward for his bow. The audience cheered even louder. Mr. La Roche held out his arm to the rest of us. Tante Pearl's camera must have flashed a million times. I thought I would cry at the sheer joy of it all. I took Mary Jordan's hand. She reached her other hand back for Evie's. I couldn't have loved her or Evie or anyone else on that stage any more than I did at that particular moment. I know I cried then.

What a Wonderful World

Mary Jordan, Evie, Dewey, and I all rode with Billy out to the beach, the windows of his Bronco down, the wind blowing our hair. Green Day was playing over the radio. Our heads were up, our chins out. We were happy. By the time we got there, the parking area was full and cars were lined up alongside the sand-packed road. Somebody was playing the guitar, somebody else the harmonica.

Billy carried a blanket around his neck. He and Evie each held flashlights, lighting our path over the levee. Stars were scattered across the sky, as if God had held silver glitter in the palm of his hand and blown it before us, just for our pleasure. The breeze was sweet and salty, a mixture of honeysuckle and the sea. The tide churned and furled and unfurled and swished itself into a long sigh on the beach. All around us voices rose and waned and broke into laughter as the instruments continued their harmony of folk melodies.

We made our way to the fire, encircled by bodies, some standing, some sitting, others lying on blankets. In the center of the fire was an enormous pot, boiling with crabs. Everywhere there were coolers and beer and the sweet smell of soft drinks. Billy spread the blanket out. All five of us crowded on it together.

Dewey would be leaving for Montreal the next day. I couldn't believe he would be gone the rest of the summer. I couldn't believe he would be as far away as Canada. The farthest north I'd been was Memphis, Tennessee, and that was when I was three years old. I knew I would miss him. Fact was I'd started missing him as soon as he'd told me he was leaving.

Mary Jordan stretched her legs out and laid her head in Evie's lap. The sounds of the water and the music and the wind lapped over us. The sea rolling in and out, the voices bursting forth and ebbing, as if the very rhythm of the night was God's one pulse beating inside us.

My body was tucked into Dewey's, his arm wrapped around my waist. After a while, he said, "Let's go for a walk."

We took off down the beach, clasping each other's hands.

"I'll miss you," he said.

"I'll miss you, too."

"I'll call. Every day if I can."

And then, out of nowhere, I felt this terrible fear crawl under my skin.

We stopped walking and Dewey wrapped his arms around me. "What's wrong?"

"I'm scared," I said.

He rubbed my back, stroked my hair. "Don't be scared."

Tommy Pierre had said he'd call. He never did. Doug had told Mary Jordan he loved her. I wanted to believe Dewey would call. I wanted to believe that things between us wouldn't change. I wanted him to come home after his month in Montreal and hold me just as tightly as he was right then. Evie once told me to believe only in the things you want to come true. She said fear is believing in the things you don't want to happen.

Standing there with Dewey, I knew nothing was certain. I couldn't be certain that things between us would stay the same. I couldn't be certain he would come home. I realized a broken heart isn't so much the loss of the person as it is the loss of your dreams with that person. I decided Evie was right, and I knew I would rather believe and hold on.

Dewey held my face in front of his. "Don't fade on me," he said.

We stood there for a long time, as if memorizing each other, the sense of each other's presence, the smell of each other's skin. He took hold of my hands again, clasped his fingers between mine, lifted them slowly so that our palms were pressed together just beside our shoulders, and then he kissed me, as tenderly as possible, his lips as smooth as the moist ocean air, our mouths loosening into a long, deep kiss as each of us breathed the other one in.

Acknowledgments

Writing a novel isn't just a process, it's life—everything good and bad and in between. It's the joy and grief and comedy and love. And it's the people, without whom there would be no story. My deepest gratitude to Mom and Pete, for their love and faith and the sanctuary of their lives; for Dad and Jane and their stalwart encouragement, for sticking with me through tough times and keeping me on the forward road; for my brothers and all those friends and families from Nashville, who stay close wherever I go; for my grandparents, those still living (Grandma in Michigan and Marie in Tennessee), and those who have passed on (Mamaw and Papa Joe, Southern born and bred); for Taylor Littleton, whose love for Shakespeare and literature set my heart aflame; for Judy, Sue Ann, Michelle, Kathryn, and Laurie, spiritual compatriots and prayer warriors; for Michael White, Clint McCown, Suzanne Strempek Shea, and Ann Hood, for their mentorship and friendship and the books they have given the world; for the community where I live, the fellowship and the vistas; for Zippy and her hearth and home and soulful laughter; for Libby's wisdom and love for the written word; and Dolly Viscardi, author and confidante; for my benevolent comrade, Susan (doctor), who came through time and time again; for generous Lew, ally and sage; and Jim and Sue and Jim, as good and loyal as they come; for Scott and his sense of humor and sense of place; for big-hearted Brad and his passion for the wilderness; and Ran and his wealth of musical knowledge; for Melanie and grad school and that first walk on the beach; for the University of Southern Maine and all my fellow Stonecoasters; for Evie and the Brickhouse where the story first began; for Rita and Mary Frances, and the inspiration of their lives; for Kathy and Jim and Bill, and all my other archery advocates and competitors; for Tim and Margot and their support; and Dan and Karen for their intelligence and insight; always to Eveline for the vision and my first taste of Cajun; for the Conrados and Easter and birthdays and days of good cheer; for Cindy and her encouragement when I needed it most; for Glade, Johanna, Jessie, and Katie and all my archaeology mates; for my students who gave me an audience and knew when I could use a hug; for Jeannine and her bed and breakfast and her incredible faith and love; for Melanie Cecka, amazing editor and friend; and Steven Chudney, agent superb; for Nate, Seth, and Jake— I love you with all my heart; for Moab, in his memory, a woman's true best friend. As my student, Aaron Webster, captured with his words: *Love is like a heart beating strong. Love is like the sun always shining. Love is like a horse, wild and free. Love is like the grass, graceful and quiet. Love is like ice, strong but sometimes thin. Love is like a spirit, or the whisper of the wind.* My heartfelt thanks to all.

DIANE LES BECQUETS was hailed by *Publishers Weekly* as "a writer to watch" after the publication of her first novel, *The Stones of Mourning Creek*. She is an assistant professor of creative writing at Southern New Hampshire University, and she also enjoys archaeology, snowmobiling, bicycling, and archery. Diane lives in New Hampshire, where she is working on her next novel.

Let the good times roll, and learn even more about how to develop your own "Cajun style" with these fun extras!

Music, Cajun Style

CREATE YOUR OWN SOUNDTRACK WITH THESE MUSICAL VOICES FROM THE BOOK

SPICY SUGGESTIONS FOR MORE MUSIC TO READ BY

♥ ♥ ♥

Food for Thought, Cajun Style

FOOD FROM THE BOOK

♥ ♥ ♥

Conversation, Cajun Style

A READING GROUP GUIDE

Music, Cajun Style

CREATE YOUR OWN SOUNDTRACK WITH THESE
MUSICAL VOICES FROM THE BOOK

John Coltrane

Linda Ronstadt

Barbara Mandrell

Crystal Gayle

Patsy Cline

Billie Holiday

Fats Waller

The Doors

Green Day

Diana Krall

Nirvana

Vivaldi

Bach

Beethoven

Chopin

SPICY SUGGESTIONS FOR MORE MUSIC
TO READ BY

Buckwheat Zydeco

Clifton Chenier

Beau Jocque and the Zydeco Hi-Rollers

Waylon Thibodeaux

Michael Doucet and BeauSoleil

The Balfa Brothers

Lynn August and the Hot August Knights

Percy Mayfield

Charles Sheffield

Rockin' Dopsie, Jr. and the Zydeco Twisters

Food for Thought, Cajun Style
FOOD FROM THE BOOK

APPETIZERS
Creole Vegetable Soup

Shrimp Beignets

Herbed Bread

Oysters Iberville

Crab-Stuffed Mushrooms

Crawfish Dip

ENTREES
Étouffée

Crawfish Pie

Crabcakes Lisette

Seafood Consommé

Shrimp and Okra Gumbo

SWEETS
Bourbon Pecan Pie

Buttermilk Pie

Pecan Yam Muffins

Turtle Shell Cookies

Parfait

Rum Raisin French Toast

REFRESHMENTS
Creole Coffee

Iced Tea

Virgin Hurricane Punch

1 *Love, Cajun Style* is told from Lucy's perspective. How do you think events would differ if told through Evie's or Mary Jordon's eyes?

2 Lucy looks at the relationship between Ms. Pitre and Miss Balfa and wonders where she, Evie, and Mary Jordon will be in forty years. Where do you see yourself and your best friends forty years from now? What makes a good friendship withstand the test of time?

3 What do you imagine happens to Lucy, Evie, and Mary Jordon after they graduate high school?

4 "Once in church, Father Ivan read from the Bible that a cord of three strands is not easily broken. I'm sure that had something to do with God, but all I could think about was Mary Jordon and Evie and me" (page 54). What do you think it is about these three young women that keeps their cord entwined—and strong?

5 In the novel, Dewey comments on how slowly time passes in Louisiana compared to in the North: "'If you took an hourglass in Detroit and one from here, the sand from Detroit would move a lot faster'" (page 99). How would you describe the pace of your own life? Do you ever wish it was more (or less) like Lucy's small-town, Southern experience?

6 Southern turns of phrase are sprinkled throughout the novel, such as: "Tante Pearl once said that listening to Mama tell a story was like milking a cow with a bad teat. By the time she finished, you weren't sure whether to cry or get drunk" (page 33); and "'I swear you can crawl under a person's skin like a june bug'" (page 120). In what ways do you think these sayings enhance the story? What comparable phrases are native to your region?

7 One reviewer commented: "Here's a novel dealing with sexuality that can appeal to both conservative and liberal readers. Not all characters make good decisions, but the love of the three friends for each other heals wounds" (*Kirkus Reviews*). Do you agree or disagree with these comments? Why?

8 More than half the town attends the wedding of Mrs. Forez and Clyde. Why do you think this late-blooming love inspires hope in so many people of all ages? What was your reaction to their union?

9 Lucy's mother describes her own life as a pie made up of equal parts music, sex, art, and cooking. If you were to divide your life in similar portions, what would your main ingredients be?

10 This novel taps into a pivotal point in these young women's lives. They're dealing with emotional and physical changes that they both eagerly await and reluctantly delay. "Lying on my back, I drew my knees to my chest, wrapped

my arms around my legs, and held myself, trying with all my might to keep a part of myself from slipping away. . . . The part of me that didn't want to grow up" (pages 137–138). Have you ever felt this way? If so, what brought on those feelings?

⑪ Do you agree or disagree with Lucy's, and subsequently her friends', responses and reactions to Mr. Banks's behavior?

⑫ In the novel, Lucy wrote down a wish to throw into the ocean, much like Tante Pearl did at her family's wishing well when she was Lucy's age. Do you have any wishing traditions or superstitions? What do you wish for?

⑬ Lucy's aunt and mother are very different from each other. How do you think these differences play a role in Lucy's development?

⑭ If you and your friends had your clothes stolen while skinny-dipping, what type of revenge, if any, would you carry out?

⑮ "He told me that a kite string was like people's lives. In one way you could look at the string as holding a person back, but he said you could also say it kept the person grounded, like family, or having a place where you belong, or friends. That without it, a person can get lost'" (page 100). Which way best describes your life? Would you prefer it to be the opposite?

16 Lucy easily locates beauty in her friends, but she is self-conscious about her own height, resenting nicknames like "Queen of Sheba" and "Statue of Liberty." Why do you think people judge themselves with harsher standards than they do their friends? Have you ever come to terms with a personal trait or nickname you didn't like? How did you turn something you thought was a negative into a positive?

17 Lucy misconstrues her mother's behavior when it comes to her interaction with Mr. Savoi. Do you think she was overreacting? What would you do if you suspected (or knew) the boyfriend or girlfriend of one of your friends was cheating on him or her?

18 Lucy eventually realizes she misunderstood her mother's behavior. In what ways does the outcome of the situation between her mother and Mr. Savoi, and subsequently her mother and father, change Lucy's understanding of herself? Of her mother?

19 Religion plays an integral role in Lucy's life. Do you relate to her spirituality and beliefs? If so, how? If not, how do you differ?

20 If you were to produce the movie *Love, Cajun Style*, who would you cast in each role?

May - 2008